5-STAR REVIEWS FOR *Mahlon Blaine ~ One-Eyed Visionary*:

"[BLAINE'S] FRIENDSHIP WITH Steinbeck, his drawings for Jake Brussel and Sam Roth, his connection with Dunninger and Legman are all written to add texture and prospective to the art and industry of bookmaking in the last century." – A.S.

"BLAINE WAS A strange and contradictory man, whose life, like his artwork, was shrouded in ambiguity." – DoubleW

"AN AMAZING ACCOMPLISHMENT, considering that Blaine himself was very inventive about his past!" – C.B.

"[TRENARY] HAS GATHERED the visual evidence for the true story, in an amazing presentation of personal letters and photos few would have thought would have survived, and he gives a social insight into little known aspects of early Hollywood behind the scenes." – C.S.

"AS WELL AS including illustrations from rare publications, there are unpublished drawings and photos and documents relating to the artist." – G.O.

"AN ODD CHARACTER indeed! His art work was as varied as it was prolific. ... a splendid overview of Blaine's brilliant, unforgettable work. Blaine could illustrate anything from erotica to social satire to science fiction." – Richard A. Lupoff

"THINK ONE PART Aubrey Beardsley, one part Gustave Doré, and one part Egon Schiele, add a dash each of Art Deco and German Expressionism, then follow up with a few hits of BC Bud. You might come close." – AmeriCollector

"CERTAINLY BLAINE HAD a dark side which rivaled any monsters created by Maurice Sendak or the bizarre surrealism of Salvador Dali! The book is filled with many of Blaine's two thousand drawings. I find myself reading and rereading it trying to solve the enigma of just who this lonely and talented man was." – S.F.

"...INSIGHT INTO NOT only the artist's mind and literary style, and his work methods, but also to the ambience of the period in which he worked. A must for the literary historian as well as the book illustrator and general reader." – J.A.G.

"I HAD NO idea that such an incredible illustrator like MB was buried in a potter's field, or how vast his life's work really was. Trenary's handling of both his art and life are engaging and artfully done." – L.M.

"BLAINE'S WORK IS extremely detailed. Each viewing of his illustrations evokes new thoughts." – K.H.

"COUPLE THIS WITH pieces of [the author's] almost 40-year collection of Blaine, many of which are seeing publication for the first time (signs from bookstores no longer in existence, sketches and prelims for pieces some finished some not, and pieces from Blaine's own mother's scrapbook)." – B.H.

"...A TREASURE TROVE of revealing and oftentimes hilarious info about Blaine, his life, his ways, his attitudes..." – Trollbeard

Born in 1894,
Mahlon Blaine became
an American pen-and-
ink artist and painter
who devoted over fifty
years to his public
craft and his private,
personal creations.

He illustrated two
hundred books and
magazines during his
lifetime, accounting
for two thousand
published drawings.

A flourishing career
between 1926 and 1931
was followed by
thirty-eight years of
obscurity.

He died in 1969.
Four decades later he
remains an enigma.

This
blooming bally
bloody book
is his story.

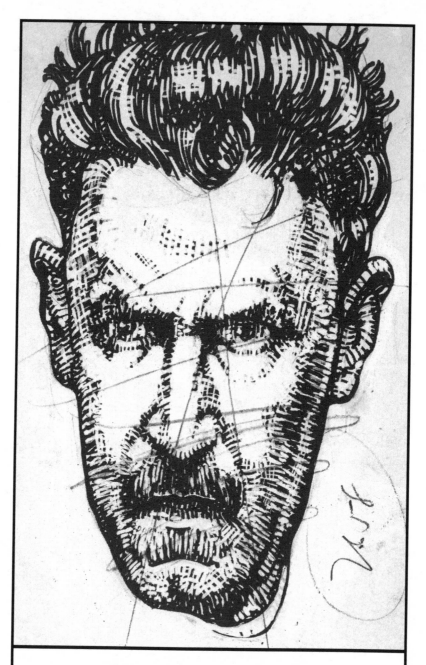

The abandoned self portrait, 1928.

MAHLON BLAINE's

Blooming Bally Bloody Book

An Illustrator's Novel

Including Over 100 Pictures by Mahlon Blaine

ROLAND TRENARY

Grounded Outlet
Kingston
2015

It has been suggested that I say:
This is a work of fiction. All characters and incidents are
imaginary and any resemblance to persons living or dead is
merely coincidental.
I am not certain what Mahlon Blaine would have said.

I shall commit my thoughts to paper, it is true; but that is a poor medium for the communication of telling. I desire the company of a man who could sympathize with me, whose eyes would reply to mine.

for Norma

The Pieces

Prelude

Drawing an Unsatisfactory Conclusion

AS A PUBLISHED illustrator, Mahlon Blaine's drawings were always right there to be seen on the pages. But the nagging question kept surfacing: *who, exactly, was the man behind the images?*

The frustrated researcher was a truth-seeker and Mahlon Blaine had been a liar. That didn't help either.

Maybe that's too harsh, he thought. *Maybe Mahlon had merely been a tale-spinner or an inventive self-advertiser. Maybe even a pathological bio-embellisher. Maybe...maybe-schmaybe.*

The truth about Mahlon Blaine? It really looked like he would never succeed in ferreting out the reality, for after four painstaking decades of being researched, old Mahlon had become an ill-defined and ever-fading smudge whose authentic aroma had all but evaporated. Bent twigs and footprints had led nowhere. Every scuffed trail had grown over, filaments flickered until light-bulbs were barely lit and all the crumbly compost was ready for spreading.

If it's ashes to ashes, then that's just how it is. So be it.

Prologue

The Occurrence of the Manuscript

BUT WHAT SHOULD turn up, out of the blue? It's the kind of thing that can convert unbelievers or cure the blind.

Evidently sometime near the end of his life, Mahlon Blaine had assembled a journal of sorts: a multi-part crazy patchwork of memories, accounts, opinions, hopes, laments – written on page after page of cheap yellowing paper. There was no strict chronological order to the content, although the pieces had been pretty obviously written down one right after the other.

Had he felt Death's breath on his neck and reconsidered his life-long secretive stance regarding his personal record? By letting his mind bounce back like a Mexican jumping bean, was he hoping to parse out his career, his achievement, his place in his profession? He hadn't bothered to really explain the 'why' of the writing, although an array of hints and intimations were strewn about.

AND THE PROVENANCE of the manuscript?

The researcher did not feel at liberty to discuss this, and his reticence is perhaps understandable. After all, he had put in those decades of work, making connections, digging deep, laying out tendrils of a detective-like network, establishing friendships, and remaining ever hopeful of anything that might be unearthed – dying to get into the history and the head of the long-dead artist. Something must have clicked, or a lock broke loose, or a memory was liberated, from somewhere. That is another story.

Let's just say that eventually the document had found its way to him.

Being able to add these personal reflections to his previous research, like the shimmer of a knowing light from beyond the grave, providing illumination into Mahlonesque shadows – no one had truly expected this, not even him, the increasingly discouraged optimist.

He resolved to share this bonanza, to publish what he could of these autobiographical renderings. At last, he need no longer be limited to the handful of public documents, the meager *official* record.

The manuscript didn't answer everything, but he realized that it was his skeleton key: a newly revealed means of opening up for the public a bigger picture and context, to help understand Mahlon Blaine, the man, his world and his work.

Mahlon deserved this chance, at least.

– the publisher

Posteriority
1968

I WILL SURELY die in my damn dinky room in this blasted biggest city of the stupid stinking hemisphere. That's what I predict. And probably sooner than later.

So they'll come and heft me onto a gurney and strap me down. Jesus, am I gonna run off or something? Did I mention that first they'll wrestle me into a body bag? That won't be any fun for anybody, including me, even though I'll already be dead, you see. Then these two or three gentlemen from the New York City morgue – looking and smelling damn official in bleach-white uniforms – will grab the sewn-in handles at each end of my bag, and groan, and lift. This will sort of squash my shoulders and feet together (much as my bed does now, come to think of it) but by then I will be beyond such discomfort. So no big deal.

Once I'm on the rig they'll glide me out the door and down the hall, around a few corners, and back to the freight elevator. What a pathetic dilapidated bucket of crap that thing is, and rank smelling, even *before* we get in. The way it works around here, I'll have been dead for fourteen hours, twenty-seven minutes and twenty-three seconds before Robert, the wispily coifed, dainty desk guy reluctantly uses his passkey to check out this pernicious odor that a concerned room-renter will have reported. Robert's call for the ambulance, a slow crank of bureaucracy, and I'll finally get all packaged up and wheeled around. My final tour.

Down and out to the Cadillac Bodywagon and we'll be on our way. A last ride in a truly first-class vehicle – at least on this planet. That's how it's done around here, NYC to the rescue!

Unbelievably, I've lasted more than seventy-four years! Bye-bye Ol' Life, been good to know ya!

BACK IN MY room is all my stuff. It won't be much. How much stuff might a fellow haul around with him when he's always moving from rented room, to borrowed bunk, to crappy cot in some god-forsaken hole in somebody's basement or attic? Not a lot.

As I sit here on my bed and look around me now, I spy my sketchbook with a half-dozen watercolor impressions of sleepy-eyed *femmes fatales du jour* caught as each made her own little slouch towards her workday. I dashed off a couple yesterday, a handful the day before that. I mostly appreciated the smoothly sashaying hips and alternating skirt-foldings as these Young Sweet Patooties matter-of-factly ignored me in their mad dashes for reliable paychecks. I'll probably see them in my dreams, forever, the unattainable hips…

What was I talking about? Well…

What else is here? There's my ancient beat-up portfolio, featuring my last two big drawings that I saved from 1927's *Vathek*. Not the best of the hundred published, but two that have had a certain *personal* appeal to me. Not a pornographic appeal. My. How times change. Except for when they don't. You can compare assholes and opinions: only one of two's worth a shit. Still, I say pornography has always been more in the eye of the beholder and less in the work itself.

In any event, those *Vathek* illuminations never crossed any "decency line" that I could ever see, glass eye or other. Not like some of my commissioned pieces might have. Never mind those, though. I was talking about the classics of my life, and these two *Vathek* are all that's left of that Golden Age of mine, in that portfolio.

I guess, now that I think about it, somewhere around here there remaineth also a few miscellaneous twinkie doodles and dripping-member portraits with their silly little expressions of embarrassment and defiance and pride. All them poor little Parts. You gotta feel sorry for 'em. They gots dirty little jobs, but somebody gots to do 'em! Let's face it, because it is true.

Will somebody eventually find these silly drawings, oh my, and be offended? Oh dear!

Fuck 'em.

Nah, let's not kill time talking about fools.

For once I'm dead, I'll still be dead, no fooling. And I can't really say I'll be liking that. I won't be grooving on it, or digging it. Not yet and I would guess not ever... but perhaps we'll see. Perhaps even *I'll* see...

So, that's how it will end? Yeah, maybe, and maybe real damn soon.

Am I ready?

Not yet.

First, a few thoughts.

Such a Good Boy

1899

I REMEMBER MOTHER saying these four most wonderful of words. Not infrequently, but not overdoing it either. At least in my young opinion. I have very few recollections of what I was specifically engaged in when those comments sprung forth from her, but maybe any specificity doesn't matter. I've heard mothers are often like that, everywhere.

Many years later, my wife Dusky said the same words to me: Such a good boy. I *do* remember several particular activities that solicited that particular response from her and, if I were a more genteel fella, I would blush – I most certainly would – at those memories. But instead they make me smile, even now. I can't help that.

Two opinions: Such a good boy.

Whether I was or wasn't, I don't want to add up the years since either. That's too double-damn depressing.

I believed myself destined for
some great enterprise.

Great Big Drawing
1903

I WAS IMPATIENT. "Mother. Mother look. Please? Pleeeeee-ase..." pulling on the frilly edge of her apron and holding out a rather large, roughly square piece of paper, a torn edge or two, slightly stained.

It was most of a brown paper bag I had pulled out of the wastebasket at the schoolhouse and used my fanny one whole afternoon to carefully flatten it for a very important purpose. I knew, or rather I'd been carefully taught, about the Angels helping the Israelites in their ancient conflict, and I had been pretty sure I could draw a really swell battle scene if I only had a piece of paper of a large-ish dimension. Big enough to allow every wing's flutter, and each mighty sword's swing – all the room each action required to defeat the Enemy.

It wasn't as easy as I'd thought, drawing the soldiers lined up properly, so that I could still see them well, each one that is, and yet sense the tide of battle shift toward the victors. And the Angel wings could be either large or small, depending on the amount of sky allotted. It had taken me four evenings and too much precious ink smeared by an accidental finger or wrist, to get to the point where I thought I could no longer hold my excitement from erupting. A nine-year-old knows what a nine-year-old knows – time for show and tell.

I knew I loved my mother. How could anyone not love Mother? She was round and soft and smelled of gooey cookies and warm bread; her voice so mellifluous in speech and song; her touch brought the stars to earth. She was perfectly perfect. But only *I* could love her as much as she deserved. Oh, I guess Poppa could love her too, in some Poppa-like scowling way. (Why did he scowl so much? I haven't really figured that out – even now.) But *my* love for her was very complete and utterly overwhelming and now I wanted her to look at my drawing and see in the faces and swords and wings and heat of battle, just how much I loved her.

She finished paring the last potato, rested the knife on the stained cutting board, dried her hands on her flowery-figured apron and slowly turned to me.

"And what's this big hurry, my little man? Where is the fire? Oh, my beautiful boy, what have we here?" as I thrust the drawing into her hands. "How wonderful! How intricate! How powerful!" She crouched to hug me. "You must show your Poppa. Or... maybe not."

She hesitated. She frowned. Had she been frowning more the last few days? I thought so.

"I've changed my mind, but about only one of the things that I just said. Your picture is wonderful, yes. Perhaps best not to show Poppa tonight though. Nor probably tomorrow." She almost smiled again, just a little bit, slowly. "But I suggest that you keep this big little scene of yours tucked away, just for a short while, and you and I will talk more about it."

I only knew some of what she meant in a very vague way, the part that she was hinting around at. But I wasn't looking to get myself into trouble, and I knew Poppa had been especially quick to swat, lately. Scowl and swat. So I hid the drawing in my crate at the foot of my bed, beneath the second pair of trousers that only were worn on Sundays or special occasions. Yet I couldn't help but wonder exactly what the real danger was she was worried about, and wouldn't spell out.

I never did find out, for sure.

POPPA DIED SUDDENLY, unexpectedly, two days later...

I think it was two days later. It's all greyed over in my memory. Foggy, almost. I try to see it in my head, yet a couple days might really have been a couple weeks. Why did he do that, anyway? Scowling so much, then dying? I hardly remember the good parts, back before that, either. There must have been good parts, right?

I do remember one thing though: he never saw my Great Big Drawing.

I wore my best pair of pants to his funeral. Mother wept, a little, and so did I. Part of me was already missing his scowls.

Soon we moved. That was, as they say, that.

Poppa was gone, we were gone, and a big *So What?* if the Angels had won that old paper bag battle. Great big deal!

Employability
1912

MY NEW STEPFATHER, Mister C.D. Jack, became a refrigeration salesman. But he liked to think of himself as an artist. A
purveyor of still lifes. We weren't rivals – much. I guess he was
artistic in his own way, maybe, but refrigeration held the promise
of putting *edible* fruit on our table.

He had started as an *Everyman's Ice Box* salesman a few years
earlier, but ice was on the way out, he'd said, and so he moved to
the cutting edge of electricity. He didn't sell the boxes in stores.
He sold them to individual residents, which was tough work as
not everyone had wires in their houses yet, even us, and he was
on commission. He optimistically would say, "the money is in
the melt, and I look to the future." It may have originally been
Mother's prodding for him to pursue that career move, as she
did have a practical view. Who doesn't need a better cold box for
flotsam, jetsam, or dead stuff?

Mother herself did sewing for neighbors. She was widely admired for her tiny French stitches. Everything needed mending,
eventually.

As for me, practicality arose again with Mother's idea of 1912. Of course, I had been doing drawings of one sort or another all my life, it seemed. All sixteen years of it. That's probably an exaggeration, as I doubt I came out of the womb with a double-ought nib in one hand and an inkwell in the other. Then again, maybe I did, as I admit I don't remember the moment clearly.

Mother was my biggest fan and she had foresight where I had doubt. We were all living in Dilley, renting an old farmstead. Mother had acquired a sow, four chickens and three cows to keep in a rather small barn (a shed, really) not too far from our back door. Within smelling distance for damn sure. I did most of the chores having to do with the livestock: milking, slopping, feeding, grooming, cleaning, swabbing, milking, milking, milking. Sometimes it was difficult to guide my pen steadily because the muscles in my hand would shake or spasm from, guess what, the milking. Yet in the long run, it may have been my salvation, as again and again through my life strong hands and fingers proved an asset in so many various ways. Yes, hands… and fingers… I digress.

Feeble cold-box sales meant C.D. was eating at home and not on the road, and believe me, he ate a lot when he got discouraged. With our paucity of household funds, Mother decided it was time for me to try a real career: newspaperman. As usual, Mother saw the necessity of invention.

She directed me to polish up several of my better drawings. Some were in pencil, but most were finished pen and ink works. I had some portraits, some local landscapes, a C.D.-type still life or two. She thought that me bringing a variety of pictures would be advantageous to my job hunt.

True, apparently, for soon I was going into town several days a week. Portland. *The Oregonian* had hired an office boy, and I was constantly on the go. "Copy! Copy!" was my signal to rush a piece of writing from a reporter or columnist, to an editor, to a linotype operator. But, of course, they also let me hang around in the Art Department whenever I could, to learn the ropes. Like I just hinted at: they'd thought my drawings had been okay.

Among the paper's artists, the best teachers were *the grizzlies.* Through clouds of heavy, oily cigar smoke I watched these experienced compositors fashion designs that could be used to frame photos and artwork on the printed pages. How efficient they were, and how their results blended with the overall layouts on the pages!

Every time he spotted me, one particularly grumpy fellow commenced barking out names of objects like "banana slug," "sea schooner," "locomotive," "Douglas Fir cone," and then he'd look at the drawings I did in response, to coach me, offer corrections. He kept me hopping.

Just being in that inky-stinky office every day grounded me in the printing trade, and taught me what it took to put together a finished product on a deadline. Funny how the stench lessened the longer I was there, and the grumpiness too. Luckily, with my teat-trained hands I could draw all day and never complain. So that's what I eventually did, basically. Of course.

True, it might have been more convenient if the family had lived a little closer to Portland, but actually I didn't mind commuting. Usually. Except for the occasional rainy day.

Finally, my weekly pay envelope helped us keep a Still Life on the table and Mister Woofy-wolf from the door. Both Mother and I could appreciate that, and C.D. too, certainly.

*Do I not deserve to accomplish
some great purpose?*

Bohemia, Bigin, Bosom Buddies
1916

"BIGIN! WE REQUEST your presence!, *s'il vous plais.*" Robo's chair squealed against the tile floor as he raised himself up and beckoned to the large-boned Italian restaurant owner. Several heads turned. Bigin (as everyone descriptively called him) ambled over from where he'd been lolling by the kitchen door. No hurrying for him!

"I am now here. What do troublemakers want?" His eyebrows, great multi-antennae caterpillars, scrambled around as his ruddy forehead furrowed. He crossed his arms. He tapped his foot.

Myself, Tina Modotti (a beautiful local actress), her boyfriend Robaix de l'Abrie Richey (my old friend Robo, of course), Betty de Jong, Clark Ashton Smith and the other writers and artists at our table, all enthusiasts of Bohemian culture and repartee, quieted. Robo rose, and pronounced:

"Want? Sir, your indubitably fine food, of course. But… could not you put an extra exquisite sausage or two to swim swimmingly across your luxuriant sauce for your best customers? For your most regular, reliable and redoubtable customers? We, the talking sandwich-boards who spread the word far and wide of the incredible edibles here in 'Bigins'? We are, I am reasonably certain, personally responsible for fully fifty percent of the crowd here this very evening for example?" Robo brandished a sweeping arm to encompass the whole room.

Everyone was now silent, carefully watching Bigin's gargantuan brow-insects dance, first to the right, then the left, then back to finish with a dual lift to the absolute middle. It was his standard response when thinking. "Ha. Ha. And ha again! But perhaps you underestimate selves, no? No fifty percent! One-hundred-fifty? Bah! I give you one-half extra sausage each, out of the kindness only of the heart. And I am supposing I thank you." He swiveled with an extra flourish of his ample shoulders and strode back into the kitchen.

We all saluted Robo, our hero!

There wasn't an undilated nostril nor unsalivated mouth in the place as olive oil, fennel and oregano permeated everywhere, reinforced by the steam of boiling pasta. When the huge platters were brought to our table we oooh-ed and aaaah-ed perhaps theatrically, but we truly did mean every satisfied sound. We'd gathered here twice a week (or three times, if out-of-town guests visited) every week for the last three months. And who wouldn't do as we had done? Even without the extra sausages, Bigin's meals were... big.

Our frenzy lasted until every last dollop of sauce was wiped clean by either slices of garlic-laden buttered bread or errant sleeves. My eyes leaked little extra-salty tears of satisfaction. We remained to talk, and drink more of the sweet house wine, and swing our arms about in emphatic punctuation – cigarettes from loose grips sometimes flying across the room – until all the other patrons had eventually filtered away. Bigin was surprisingly light on his late-night feet, ushering us human sponges on our way. We left what tip we could, too, for this had been a deliciously swell evening indeed, and exited our separate ways.

A damn chilly breeze snuck around from the San Francisco bay and charged along the street, flapping my scarf ahead of me. I made my long sobering walk to the room in the house on Van Ness where I had come to hang my hat and my shingle. I was, I admit, rather proud of the listing in the City Directory:

Mahlon Blaine – painter.

True.

A painter, a pasta eater – at twenty-two, what more would one wish to be in this world?

A Portland Spectator
1919

THERE WAS A lot of political stuff going on in Portland, which I observed from the sidelines. One day I reckoned I'd do some cartoons, just to pass the time. It would be quite a change from my daily detailing the Wonderment of Beauty, especially the nude variety. I kind of surprised myself.

So I drew a few rather recognizable characters sluicing about the local landscape, sticking their noses into stuff, throwing their fat-cat weight around, stinking up the place. You know, the usual thing for politicians and capitalists who maybe weren't getting laid (or paid) as much as they imagined they deserved. And I didn't forget to depict the poor little guys, victims *en mass* that suffered being systematically shit upon. You know: the day-by-day. I showed these sketches to columnist Dean Collins at *The Morning Oregonian*, and a few other people, and was encouraged to take said sketches to *The Spectator*.

The Spectator wasn't a hardcore politic rag. I didn't expect much reaction from them, but they loved my stuff! I guess at least mine was an artistic style that would reproduce well (which

I already knew) and maybe wasn't too obviously hard on the Boys Downtown. It was just subtle enough.

First off they asked me for something about a current political situation. I inquired of them what kind of commentary they wanted, and they just said "It's up to you, Mahlon. You're the artist, the citizen, the observer, the commentator: *The Spectator.*" They said that they even were willing to pay me in dollars. Can't beat that, my friend.

I went home and poured out a cheap glass of wine and broke open a new wire-bound sketchbook packed with cheap paper. I put a fresh load of tobacco in my pipe, grabbed a fresh pencil with a nice sharp lead, and started in. Two hours later I had illuminated what I thought were four pretty good ideas. Then I went to bed. I dreamed of women, naked, as is customary with me. Normal, you might say.

I only had to get up once in the night, also for the usual reason, having nothing to do with the wine…

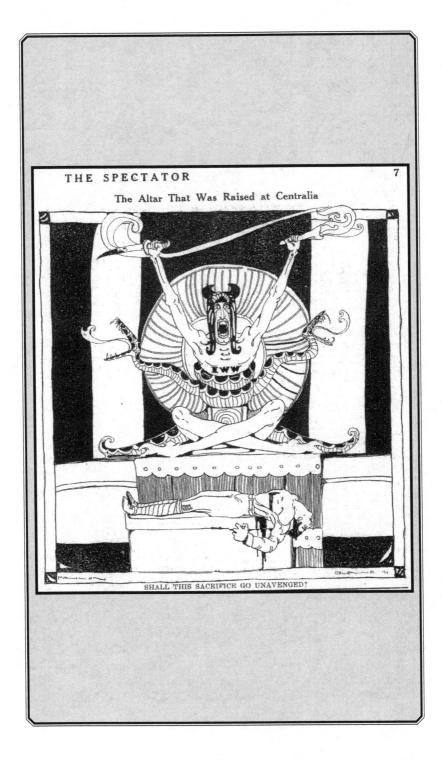

THE SPECTATOR   7

The Altar That Was Raised at Centralia

SHALL THIS SACRIFICE GO UNAVENGED?

The tranquility which I now
enjoyed did not endure.

Mr. Lampman
1934

IN MARCH OF 1954 I buried my good friend and co-conspirator, Ben Hur Lampman.

Of course, I didn't actually bury him myself, lower him down or dig the hole or anything of the sort. But I was there at the funeral, and getting there wasn't easy. I don't drive much, I don't own an automobile even. I had to catch a *Coastal Carriers* bus from Los Angeles, which took me two transfers and two days to barely get to Portland in time. But I needed to say goodbye, in person, at Lincoln Memorial Park.

I had originally run into Ben about the time of the dinosaurs, as we both were at *The Morning Oregonian* in 1916. He had come in as a reporter, having had some experience at a paper in the fly-speck of Gold Hill, Oregon. About five years older than me, he was a pretty serious guy, but we hit it off anyway. I kept in touch, kinda irregular. That's because I became kinda irregular back and forth to the Portland area.

But in 1934 we'd partnered up on a project and it turned out to be one of my best experiences as an illustrator, bar none.

See, Ben had written this amazing story, *Here Comes Somebody*, full of imagination and heart. He asked me to read the thing. Darned if I didn't get a few goose bumps. More than a few. I told him as much, which, I think, pleased the heck out of him. Then he asked if I'd consider doing some drawings that could maybe be used in the book version. He'd already gotten a local publisher interested (any publisher would have been a fool to *not* be interested in it, if you ask me) just for the unadorned story.

Talk about perfect timing! I'd recently left New York because of some Decency League stuff, gone back to Hollywood for a while, and gotten married to Dusky. In fact, it was when I was taking a visit up to Mother's with Dusky and Bernita, that this meeting with Ben took place.

By that time the legit New York publishers had left me going broke, basically, with barely any illustration work at all, and the bookleggers were sometimes using my stuff but paying practically nothing. I hadn't scared up anything worthwhile in a plethora of months.

With a family under my wing, my whole mood had changed. I was responsible. Wife and kid. And I could always use a job. These were far and few between.

It was summer so school was out. Dusky was let go at Universal Studios (I knew she could get that position back, though, whenever she really wanted – she was great at her job), so we moved in with Mother for a while. There was a spot on the screened porch where I set up the drawing table (Mother still had my old one in the little cow barn). D. and I got the bedroom at the head of the stairs, tucked up in the rafters, almost like a honeymoon suite. Bernita got to make a little pallet behind the sofa - a camp out, with the extra blanket stretched across to make a tent. Everyone was set for fun.

Ben and his publisher, Metropolitan, noted that 1929's *Little Spotted Seal* was a particular favorite of theirs, of all my work that they were aware of anyway. Well, I thought so too. And I was even more excited about going all out with Ben's story, if they were interested. Boy! Were they!

I wanted to make the drawings extra large. They had to confirm with the photo-litho people that there was a camera set-up that could handle such a big format. There was, just. So I had the go-ahead to put as much detail in each illustration as I wanted. Hot dog!

I used Dusky as my model for The Dark Lady as that seemed to fit so well both visually and psychologically. Dusky and Bernita spent most of their time enjoying the Pacific Northwest summer, much as I had growing up, with books to read, checkers to play, crosswords to decipher, etc. When I occasionally looked up from my drawing, I enjoyed the view from the vantage of my porch perch. Over evening meals, they (including Mother, of course) shared the oh-so exciting tales of their days and I would keep them up-to-date as each picture was finished. It was such a fine time all around.

Once the whole of my work was done (and was fifty or sixty drawings including full pages, chapter heads, endpapers, dust jacket and the incidental stuff that I threw in for fun), the professional darkroom guys did their business, the signature printers ran their presses, the bindery stitched away, and the book was born. Wow. And everyone agreed: Wow!

After a big publication party in Portland and all the reviews were read and collected into a scrapbook, it was time to go home to the land of oranges and movie stars. Ben and I had accomplished something swell, we were sure of it. It would be our masterpiece together. Maybe even the first of many, we thought.

Of course, it didn't work out that way. Here Comes Somebody stands alone, and that's all right.

Ben went on with continued success, writing, being published. Poet laureate for cripe's sake! And died too young at sixty-seven.

Maybe that's not too bad. At least he could never blame me for holding him back. I still miss the guy.

We did done good, we did.

"And do you dream?" said the demon.

Fractured Refraction
1910

I TELL FOLKS, sometimes, about my eye (regarding lack thereof). I inform various individuals with different scenarios, depending. I've spun a few original tales. I've divulged a couple perceived truths. At least I'm consistent in my unreliability.

My close friend (and a swell bookseller and publisher), Jake Brussel, lost his own eye as a boy. Chopping wood. In Russia. I truly believe him, as he recounts that story quite well. The first time I heard it, he had me a little weepy even. Both eyes (yes I can). At that time I confessed to him that the very same thing had happened to me, except for the 'in Russia' part. And, being the good fellow that he is, he believed me back.

Then there were occasions when I confessed to having lost my eye in *The Great War*. That was a popular story. I verbally illustrated how I was a multiple casualty, ending up with the glass orb, a silver plate in my head, and shrapnel in my wrist. Quite a doozy of a whisper, even if I do say so myself.

Each time I tell it, I watch the reactions of my listeners. Awe from the men and empathy from the women are the predominant reactions. Sometimes a little pity sneaks in, usually from the men. But I assure them that, yes, don't worry though, Mahlon's old Mashie Niblick can still send it down the fairway, thank you. And then the men don't feel quite so uncomfortable, and the women smile. I like to make the women smile. Always.

BUT FRANKLY I'M amazed. I guess I've more or less gotten used to something that one can never really get used to. I wonder too what might have been different for me, playing with a full pair? Would my art have been improved, or different in a good way?

Or, isn't *one-of-a-kind* the ultimate wild-card hand?

Tina Appears Friendly

1921

"TINA! ARE YOU here? Tina dear, are you here? Oh, I say, Tina, can you take a tired, exhausted man, in?"

Mid-afternoon's clear skies coaxed sweat from my every pore. Although it's only a four-block walk from where the bus driver dropped me at the curb, I was just plain wore out from I guess everything. Now the one-point-five-story brightly painted quasi-bungalow mocked me. The warm brass knocker echoed, wavering with the heat.

"Tina. Please. Oh, there you aren't, or are you?" My tired voice dissipated in the silent reply.

I hoped Tina wouldn't mind me arriving unannounced. God knows where she was, but God tells no tales to such as me, and why would he? I found the front door unlocked and I let myself in.

I carried everything from the trip: the big canvas suitcase with the braided Mexican straps around it; the brown leather valise with the half-busted handle that hurt my palm by pinching it until a blood blister had been born, evolved and burst; and the portfolio which had been saved-by-the-bell at the station when a petite smiling senora gave me a long exuberantly-colored stretch of macramé. Together on the platform we had fashioned a pair of loops that held the folio together and allowed me to put each arm through to carry the awkward thing on my back. I had given her two Pesos. Goodness, I was flush.

Now all these ended up a heap in Tina's parlor, or rather sun-room, to the right of the front door, where beams were aggressively streaming in to celebrate another indistinguishably pleasant Los Angeles afternoon and I was not in a mood to appreciate. I was just hot and tired and, for chrissakes, injured. My blister was killing me. I needed a hot bath *and* a bandage. Minimum.

I stumbled upstairs. The Necessary was straight back at the end of the hallway. I was unbuttoning and disrobing as I walked. I threw the pile of traveling vestments under the pedestal sink, found the white hard-rubber tub stopper precariously perched on the hot water handle, stuffed it in the drain hole, and cajoled the handle to full blast. Warm water began immediately, then quickly got hot as the tub slowly filled.

I sat down on the edge of cast iron and hummed a minor-key tune that I remembered from nowhere. After a few minutes I got in. The tub metal was almost cool, but the water level rose, soothing my wobbly legs. Eventually, everything from my waist down was immersed, except the very last knuckles-worth of my big toes. My pecker half-floated, relaxed. I leaned forward to shut the tap off and slowly eased back until my head rested against the light green wall with my neck supported by the cool rounded tub lip. I closed my eyes.

The Silver Blood Princess soared gracefully across the sky directly over the throngs below as their rising voices chanted, gathering momentum and synchronizing to a fever pitch. She circled once, twice, three times in ever narrowing fashion, and on the fourth pass, spread her arms adorned with the huge, white, black-tipped feathers that sprouted from wrist to shoulder. Simultaneously ris-

ing and halting her forward motion, she silently dropped to the temple's top tier: the sacrificial platform.

She thrust her arms vertically to salute the midday God, and repeated this twice more. Then slowly, slowly drew fingertips downward in feathered arcs to rest her arms at her sides. She stared with violently vacant eyes, observing the seen and the unseen.

A naked girl, perhaps twelve or thirteen years old and totally devoid of hair save for the black mane swept up to the very top of her skull and held in place with four intricately detailed silver moon-shaped clip-pins, hesitantly ascended the seven steps from the first landing to the platform. Her eyes were closed, her breath shallow, her knees wobbly.

The Holy Sun beat down purposefully. The crowd, hushed, pressed forward like a liquid sea of expectant faces. But...a shadow fell across the temple as the sky began spitting warm rain from a suddenly blossoming, blackening cloud...

"BUONGIORNO, MAHLON. AND you are fine this fine *pomeriggio?*"

It was Tina, sitting on the tile floor next to the tub, dipping her fingertips in my now luke-warm suds-free water and flicking tiny droplets into my face to wake me. Her head and bare shoulders partially blocked the afternoon glare that bounced down the hallway and through the open bathroom door. Lit from the reflecting white tile beneath her, a certain odd radiance caught the lower contours of her smooth chin, nose and cheeks, and highlighted the lowest waves of her jet-black hair.

"Uh, huh? What...? Oh heavenly goddess...you...I... I was discovering a composition... Or... uh... while sleeping, I guess. Whatever the heck time is it?"

"Time for Mister Mahlon to wake. To wake and *ben tornato.*" She had slithered her hand beneath the water and began gently stroking the side of my thigh. Her forearm eased over and down my inner thigh, and moved ever so slightly forward...and back...and forward so gently...

"Dangerous, madam, to arouse an artist from his compositional reverie, and... and... to arouse an artist. Oh. And...! Well then...?"

I got my left hand under me enough to push into sitting up, met her lips with mine and as I glanced over the tub's edge, I couldn't help but notice her utter lack of clothing. We managed to rise together, me still within the tub and her without, our still-entangled lips minutely echoing the delicate balances we each utilized in this tricky maneuver. Her right hand never completely left my body. We eased down upon the plush floral-patterned bath rug. Buoyed by our accomplishments so far, we continued.

I knew Tina was an accomplished Los Angeles actress, yet I had never doubted that our handful of casual couplings had satisfied her to the same degree they had satisfied me. At *those* times it certainly didn't seem like she was acting! Today I used skills I had traditionally exercised, and an additional creative motion that had been delightfully brought to my attention in Mexico City. Tina, well... Tina was Tina.

Eventually we'd dried ourselves, toweled up most of the spilled tub-water, left the bathroom, tottered to the bedroom bouncing against each other's nakedness in the narrow hallway, and slipped beneath the stunningly ornate batik comforter to embrace delicious slumber. A few inches of open window for an evening breeze to flutter the sashay curtain and loll across the room, out the doorway and down the stairs. And of course, we probably snored.

AT DAWN WE both awoke and just lay quietly, slightly entangled, for half an hour or more. Then Tina suddenly sought details.

"Tell me. Tell me your trip. Mexico! Art! Fiestas and siestas! Senoritas? Tell me all!"

I gave her a few mundane facts. The art exhibition had been very successful. Everything sold. I wished I'd had more to sell, but I could only carry so much from the States. I'd come home with a little money and a lot of weary. It really wasn't that long of a story. I watched her as she watched me – like cats might study a length of yarn – and we both smiled.

My new love-making techniques? (Yes, there was more than one.) She now had had a taste and, wouldn't you know, certainly wouldn't turn down another.

"Perhaps now, Dear Baby Mahlon? Oh! Yes… now…"

Mexico, it seems, had benefitted two old friends.

So *gracias* very *mucho*.

OF COURSE, THE *whole* story is a bit more complicated.

Most people were under the impression that Tina and Robo were married. They really were not and never had been, yet had maintained this deception longer than they should have, for, obviously, Tina's heart was no longer in Robo's possession.

Robo too was ready to move on with his life, and just wanted to complete his planned art and batik exhibition in Mexico before confronting Tina with his decision. At least that's what he had more or less indicated to me, some time before.

And Tina must have known his decision too, for (unbeknownst to me at the time) she had recently begun a dalliance with Weston, the photographer.

I didn't love Tina, nor did she love me. Like I said, we were two old friends. And, that warm encounter was to be our last.

Tina and Robo, I have missed them both for forty-seven years.

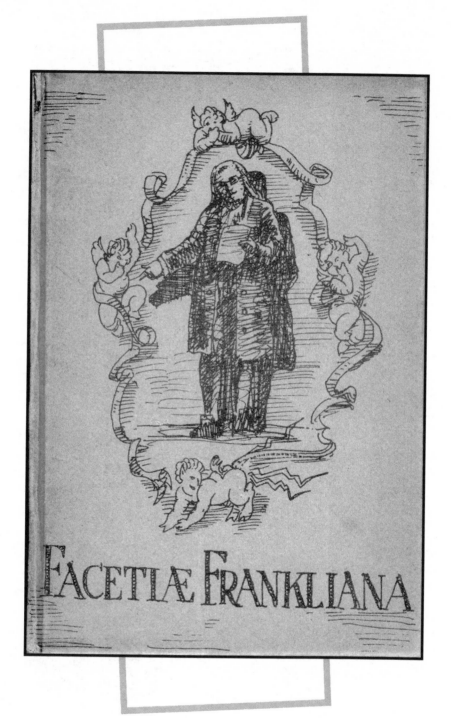

Jake Brussel

1940

JAKE BRUSSEL, I gotta admit, was not one to be dissuaded, once he got his wiry brain wrapped around an idea. Like a miniature python, he'd either take a bite and quickly spit out a worthless notion, or he'd find the first taste so tantalizing that he'd just crush the idea, slowly, making sure he could figure a way to really squeeze every potential penny out of it. And then he'd spring, full head of steam and out-of-the-way!

I was his partner on several of these profit-seeking adventures. Well, not a full partner. Just enough of one for him to get whatever he could out of my talents, get my part integrated into the whole, and make money. Money.

Oh, it wasn't that he didn't know a good book when he saw one. It's just that, really, ultimately, a good book was only as good as the profit-margin-times-the-copies-distributed-equals-ka-ching. And a bookstore is only a consignment shop for publishers. What don't sell gets returned for credit and the publisher eats all of his work and effort, only to 'remainder' the thing for a fraction of its actual cost to produce.

Anyway, Jake and I liked enough of the same shit that he'd often get his hands on something that he was pretty sure I could jazz up with a naughty drawing here and there. Naughty, but funny. The guilty laugh. Deadly.

So that was pretty much my job, adding the visual element that would get the more sophisticated customers to smile, or smirk. Or maybe just chuckle. As long as money changed hands.

I REMEMBER ONE dry autumn evening, I was over at Jake's apartment on West 4th. I had climbed the dimly-lit narrow flight to the second floor where Minna was boiling some chicken for supper. Jake and Minna had been married a few years now, two kids, living in this old brownstone over a little nightclub that had a live band almost every weekend.

I like music. I liked to go over, partake of Minna's chicken and while away the late hours trading concocted bull with Jake, mine all untrue while his were only-slightly-embellished tales of his youth in Russia before the over-enthusiastic Red Boys took over and he'd fled. The music wafted in the windows along with the warm breezes, to accompany our discussions.

Well, this one particular evening, like I started to say, we were soaking in the fragrance of boiling chicken and listening to the music and storytelling when he handed me a little Ben Franklin book that he was thinking of reprinting. He loved the stuff that was either Public Domain or else maybe 'naughty' enough that no one would have even copyrighted in the first place. This particular volume? A curious item. *Frankliana*. I didn't even know if ol' Ben was the real author. But it piqued my interest and so he lent it me to be inspired. I tucked it into the roomy breast pocket of my jacket.

Minna, as was usually the case, was grumpy at our chatting and chortling – two men who sat in chairs pulled up close to the windows at the 4th Street front of the building while she was tied to the kitchen with the cooking, serving and cleanup, and all while managing the kids before trundling them off to bed on the third floor. Thence coming back down and more or less ignoring us, reading or something, until she made it painfully obvious that it was "well past the time when any decent single fellow should just shove off and let a married man with a family, for pity's sake, have some time with his wife. Alone!"

I always liked to hang around just a little longer, then, to see if she'd continue to steam away or give up. Tonight was evidently a steam-along night, so I shortly headed off with my copy of Mr. Franklin's text.

I WANDERED DOWN their stairs and out, pausing to re-light my pipe in front of the nightclub's entrance and right below their open window. The city evening was still warm – almost too warm to wear my coat, but who likes to carry a coat? I jumped when their window slammed and two voices rose, then subsided.

All I heard then was the muffled saxophone and clarinet from the back of the club doing a little duet thing, a playful, noteworthy conversation, while a drummer brushing a quiet snare just kept a little shuffle beat going, like a mattress, bouncing a bit, now and again to reflect the woodwinds' banter and sometimes, maybe egg it on a touch. Maybe that old mattress was a'bouncing upstairs, too. Who knows?

"Shove off, Slouch," said a burly gent who poked his nose around the half-opened Club door. "Yer scarin' away the real folk. Either get a move on away from our plate glass, or get yer arse in here and buy a drink. Music ain't fer free listenin' pal."

"My friend," I replied, "free listening is only a price, but never the value. Most economists I've talked to would agree with me. By the way, no one of your inconsiderate sort would be let survive past the age of two in any civilized culture. But, none-the-less, farewell and good evening to you, for I hold no grudge. I am easygoing and forgiving of insults. I shall slouch off, indeed, to my lair. Adieu."

He just scratched his head, wiggled his right ear and tucked himself back through the doorway. I slouched off, temporarily forgot Mr. Franklin in my pocket, and hummed a saxophone's reply all the way home.

Marjorie Flowers, student at the Otis art institute, who is directing some home carnival to get funds to build home for art club in Los Angeles.

The Budding of Miss Flowers
1922

"MISS FLOWERS! WHAT an absolutely lovely drawing. Oh, would that I could draw so well! Lovely, lovely."

"Why Mister Blaine! Don't you find it terribly difficult to articulate with your tongue so firmly planted in your cheek? And... you are really not being very helpful, you know? Not at all!" spoke the auburn-haired young lady, a healthy well-postured nineteen- or twenty-year-old.

I had been casually introduced to this Miss Marjorie Flowers a month or two before, somewhere now unremembered, and we had slightly run into each other at a few sundry events or soirées, mostly held at the art school or in the surrounding orbit of scattered studios and dim cafes. She was now standing in my own studio doorway and was struggling to hold up for my perusal a large charcoal figure-study. Evidently something she had drawn herself.

"Me? Not helpful? But Marjorie, remember... you are not my student. I am not your professor..."

The paper bashfully curled itself up as her left hand let go of the lower edge.

She protested, "Both statements are patently untrue! Surely a mere registration form and class schedule are not the only measures of one's place? I am indeed a student at Otis – but more so of Life, of Art, of the whole World! And... who is more professorial than you? Who else might be more knowledgeable of Life and Art?"

"True enough. When you state it that way. So eloquently informed is your argument."

I thought Marjorie was not one of those students who seemed to be in pursuit of a good time and never mind the learning. She'd chosen the Otis Institute because she sought a level of accomplishment in rendering the human form. Fine. More power to her and those like her. Nothing wrong in pursuing mastery of the human form. And since drawing the nude is usually frowned upon in polite-society circles, here she was allowed. Here no one looked twice. Well... maybe the male students looked twice once in a while when the more pleasantly proportioned ladies posed.

She pointed the loosely coiled drawing at me. "Really, Mister Blaine, what do you think? And please, do not lie. What is your honest opinion?"

"Of this? This... student drawing?" I plucked it from her charcoal-smudged grasp. "All right. I shall tell you. Please come in, Miss Marjorie, student of Life. Let us now get serious. And call me Mahlon, if you like."

My studio is really just a small room on the fourth floor of an immense wood-frame building thrown up forty years earlier to provide office space for some can't-fail-yet-now-defunct company. Not much bigger than a secondary living room in a New York City capitalist's mansion (or so I'd been told), but I'd produced some good solid artwork here. The chipped enamel had not quite begun to peel from the woodwork, nor had the raw wooden floorboards totally worn through to the tongue-in-groove. Once the grime was scrubbed from the windows, a fair share of workingman's illumination visited and nothing smelled too bad. Marjorie's presence added a light jasmine fragrance this morning. That certainly didn't hurt.

I stretched her paper on a drawing board, pinned the four corners down, and swung my leg over the bench (I'd named *Ol' Paint*) and leaned the board from my lap up against the easel-back end, the neck of *Ol' Paint*.

"Sit here, next to me," I motioned, "so you can see what I'm talking about. Yes, right next to me, please." She *keeeech-eeech*-ingly skidded a plain wooden armless chair closer. I was astride *Ol' Paint*, so she had to sidle right up against my leg to avoid the window's glare. We both stared at her charcoal rendering.

I was looking at those almost-confident but still-untrained lines she had wrangled into approximating the outline of an un-inspiring model.

"All right, tell me this: what is your ultimate goal with this drawing?" I asked. Why beat about the bush? Tough questions first – the rest is patty-cake.

"Ultimate?" I could almost hear her raise her eyebrows.

I turned from the paper to look. Her face was not many inch-es from mine. Her breath was sweet, pepperminty. Mmmmm, peppermint and jasmine. "Yes. Ultimate." I tapped the paper with the stem of my unlit pipe, laid the pipe to my side, and posi-tioned my hand over hers, there on the board's border.

She paused before blurting "What does *ultimate* mean?" Eye-brows still cranked up.

"Exactly! What does it mean to you?"

"Don't be silly!" She drew her hand away slowly, but she was not amused. Curious? Good.

"I'm not being silly, I assure you. Don't you think that each thing you create should have purpose? Conversely, that you would have a purpose in creating it? Creation is serious business, not to be undertaken lightly. Some goals are short-term, some long. But I think even the short-term ones are pointing, however subtly, toward 'the ultimate' goal. Your ultimate goal."

"All right. So... my ultimate goal?" Another few moments of studied silence and brow-knitting. "I guess, to make a recognizable person, in a drawing which would be pleasant to look at. Or something like that." Ah youth! Such modest goals they set.

"OK. Fairly straight forward. Would you say that this figure, this person, is recognizable?"

"It is just the dang model. I don't remember exactly what she looked like. Maybe. I guess I can't answer that, if she's not here for me to compare it side by side."

"Well then, use your imagination. It certainly is within your power, as the artist, to make any drawing recognizable to something – in this case *someone* – in your head, or your memory. In fact, how can an artist help but not? Who was this, or is this to be?"

"I don't know. I never thought about it that way."

"So. Think now, Marjorie. Make your decision. Who?"

She leaned back in her chair, a bit of a frown pulling on one corner of her mouth as she held her bottom lip back with her top teeth. She looked intently at the drawing, like an otter. Then her face lit up.

"I think it should be me," she said, and turned her head my direction. "Do you think it could be me?"

"Self portraiture is an option, surely. The mirror – definitely a wonderful invention! I have one over there. You could start over with…"

"Yes, but… this drawing. And no mirror. How would you make it me? If you were drawing – redrawing – from this point forward?" She was staring me straight in the eye and had leaned herself forward in her chair so that I could look easily from her face to the drawing and back.

"Well, that face is turned profile. Left profile. I would need you to sit up there and look over there, to your right. To make it align. If… well, if *I were to continue* this drawing…"

"All right." She got up, picked up the chair she had been sitting in, silently (thankfully) walked it to about eight feet in front of me, set it down and sat, giving me her profile. "Like this. Make the drawing me."

It was the work of only about ten minutes or so. I started with a few well-oiled swipes of my thumb to largely un-define Marjorie's original, then used a similar medium-hard charcoal and got a good line coming off it, enough to catch the subtle contours of her face, the short upsweep of her lips, the tender cartilage of her ear, her razor cut curls. She held an intense stare out the window, direct and unmoving, left profile. Very steady.

"All right. Come look." I said. She bounced the couple steps over to land alongside me where the board still leaned on Ol' Paint's neck. She gazed intently at the paper. Her hand gently rested on my shoulder. More jasmine and peppermint. It was becoming my favorite olfactory combination.

"That's me? Yes... I think it most certainly is. Of course, I'm not used to looking at the side of my face." She tilted her head, not taking her eyes off the drawing. She cleared her throat a little. "Could we finish it? The transformation? Finish the drawing? Maybe...?" she still didn't look at me.

"Well, dear, it's a nude. I've put your head on this body, for the moment. But..."

She looked away from the drawing to the far corner of the room. "I think, sir, that I want you to draw me. The rest, too. I can do this, really. May I?" Finally she did shift to me with a steady gaze. My shoulder felt the shiver of her small hand.

"Certainly. If that's what you want. I'm not stopping you, Miss Flowers."

She studied the half-redrawn drawing again, as if to reassure herself that it could be done, then said, "All right. Don't watch as I undress, please. Please, just close your eyes for a minute or two. Until I say 'all right.' Will you?"

"If you wish."

Did I detect a squeeze as her hand left my shoulder?

About three minutes ticked off the clock as I sat there on Ol' Paint, humming to myself, eyes closed. I could barely hear the rustling of clothing, the unbuttoning of buttons and the untying of ties. I shall never grow tired of those sounds, I swear. Ever the delicate prelude...

"Everything according to plan? Are you in position?" I finally asked. It should have been enough time.

"Ummmm. Yes. Now. All right."

I opened my eyes, and true to her word, Marjorie sat in the chair before me. She had done a pretty good job of mimicking the pose of her model, with face turned. Her arms and legs placed as she had remembered, but since the chair of the original pose was shaped differently, she was not an exact match. One thing she had excellently managed, however, was to get herself out of her clothes. She was quite naked, and quite lovely. One never knows what visual delights, or utter surprises, will reveal themselves when a woman's body is disrobed. Artistically speaking, of course!

"Marjorie, your pose is close to the original, but..."

"Show me, please," she said quietly, without looking at me.

I dismounted *Ol' Paint* and stepped over to her. I guided her left elbow two inches right and straightened her left hand as it rested upon her thigh. "Like this, I think. Yes. And..." I put my hands on her knees and pivoted them together two inches to the right, picked up her right foot and set it down slightly behind her left, adding "That should about do it. Give me a few minutes. Maybe twenty. Are you comfortable enough for that long?"

She didn't break her pose, nor did she turn her eyes towards me. "I am fine. But only if you say I am most properly positioned."

"My dear, yes. Now... now you are."

I took my place back on *Ol' Paint* and began drawing directly over her original line work, smudging out where needed, subtly re-creating the body shapes, but this time to reflect my own ultimate goal, as it were. This was no longer Marjorie's work. It was *Marjorie by Mahlon Blaine.*

I found her form and figure to be decidedly esthetically more pleasing than that original model.

This curve of her neckline as it met her collar bone, these arms joining the shoulders, tantalizingly slim roundness of breasts delicate and white, a hint of waist flowing into lissome hip bones, the relaxed muscles of her legs, slender feet pressed against the floor. And translucent skin, delicately blue over her Marjorie veins.

My studio was warming up rather suddenly – from the after-noon sun, of course – as her transformation from there to here revealed the 'Blaine woman'.

As I drew, she made a proposal.

"Mister Blaine."

"Yes Miss Flowers."

"I have another idea, and I wonder if you wouldn't mind lis-tening."

Of course I wouldn't. "Proceed."

"All right then. And you're sure I'm not spoiling the drawing by talking? Spoiling the pose?"

"Not at this stage – go on. I'll be quietly continuing my al-chemy."

"All right. Here's the thing. I volunteered this year to organize the Masked Ball at The Otis. I don't know if you are familiar with that but each winter, for charity, the Institute hosts a Ball, and I'm running it this year." She paused. "I would like to have you con-tribute your name and notoriety, if you could and would. Can I tell you, why you? I'm sure, knowing your work and the high regard in which it is held around The Otis and around town, that we would have the most interesting and successful Ball in years." She maintained her pose and her stare to the right.

"What would I have to actually do, if I may ask?" I asked.

"Nothing so much, really. Maybe help inspire my volunteers, make some theme decisions, some mask examples? It's a masked ball, of course. And costumes? With your background in the movie-making community, maybe we could spice everything up with some film themes."

"Yes," I said. "If I might be working closely with you, I am more than merely interested. I would probably do whatever you ask. You…. my dear, are a perceptive young woman, and… I must add, a quite inspiring model as well. Let me be the first to tell you, in case you were unaware. So, now. There! The drawing is done. Come look."

"Please, then. Don't watch me as I get dressed. Thank you." She abruptly arose and immediately stumbled. Her leg had fallen asleep. She caught herself and leaned on the chair. I took the charcoal and did a fast sketch of her standing with her weight on one leg, grimacing.

"Don't move for a second. Good girl." I knew I would capture this, and it appeared on the lower left corner of the same page: a perfect, un-posed complement to the larger likeness, three-quarter view.

Her tingling had eased, and I could not help but let my eyes follow her limping path over to where she had laid her folded clothing, at the far side of the room.

She called over her shoulder, "I asked you not to watch."

"After this?" I gestured back at the drawing and raised an eyebrow.

"That's different, and you know it."

"Yes. I suppose I do. But… you are lovely, Miss Flowers, as I believe I've said before. Indeed."

"Thank you Kind Sir. Now close your eyes. Please!" She frowned and I acquiesced.

I opened them when I felt her presence back beside me. She was mostly draped, re-buttoned and gathered, standing stocking-footed, holding her shoes, looking in awe at the work. "It's really beautiful! You've really made me… so beautiful, Mahlon. Oh, my! And the little sketch there too! Jeepers!"

"I get that reaction sometimes, but only from the most discerning viewers." I almost laughed. She almost didn't laugh. "And, anytime you are in the mood to pose again…"

"Oh. I doubt that *that* will happen, Sir. Ever."

"A pity." I shed a mock tear, wiped it from my cheek, dried my tearstained finger in my rumpled handkerchief, looked up deeply into her eyes…

"Seriously. A damn pity." I wasn't just teasing her. Premeditated or not, she had exposed to me an intangible beauty in her form and engaged an artistic nerve in myself with this one sketch. It would be more than 'a pity' to not draw her again. To not…

"Well," she studied my version of her lithesome form. She allowed herself a small grin. "I merely said 'I *doubt* it.'"

My god, a response I could dream on, and possibilities to nourish my eye, my hand, my future drawings! But I didn't want to scare her away now, with the prospects of... more of her. "Fair enough. And you must admit, what we have here is, indeed, *finally*, a lovely drawing."

She glanced from the drawing once more back to me, saying "Lovely, yes. You do not lie."

No, and I never did lie to Marjorie.

Turns out, I never needed to.

*My courage and my resolution
are firm; but my hopes fluctuate
and my spirits are often
depressed*

Marjorie's Masks

1923

THAT OTIS BALL would prove to be a lively affair. Hard to believe, now, that it was some forty-five years ago.

The hall was filled with masks, costumes, balloons, confetti and noise, and a very popular hooch room back behind the dressing rooms. There was a five-piece band on the front left edge of the stage and they were hotly tooting away all the recent tunes everyone seemed familiar with. (Even I had heard most of them, and I mostly don't jive to the radio.) Scorching arrangements!

The dancers were working up quite a perspiration festival. Girls in the sheerest skirts hemmed up to here and breasts bobbling left and right behind flimsy camisoles. Guys with their long hair spiked out with hair pomade to look like birds of prey, or sea urchins, or cacti, and clothed in batik blouses with wild jungle shapes. These were Otis students, decked out and exuberant.

With the addition of Joe Blow Public in the mix this year, there was even more variety. Of course, being a fundraiser, not every every-day society dame and gent could make the ticket price, but many who could, did. Some of them also invested in silly masks. At the front door the admission crew had thoughtfully provided mask rentals/purchases for the forgetful few who came unprepared to revel properly. Since masks were not optional, that clever rule meant even more funds were raised. Another Marjorie invention. She had really wanted that Ball to top all the others that came before. I think she succeeded.

As the revelry got revved up to a sufficient level, which took about two hours, the big presentation portion was at hand. Costume judging, of course, but first a very enthusiastic Marjorie giving a self-effacing speech about how it had all been accomplished by the volunteers. Ticket sales, advertising, sponsorships, decorations, food, music booking, and especially myself. Her words, not mine. She spoke very highly of me. Stuff like:

"How lucky we are to have an artist of Mr. Blaine's talent, and stature, to lend his inspiration and guidance to the theme and ultimate purpose of our annual Otis Ball."

Well, that was nice of her. And yes, in some ways I would say that the whole assembled menagerie did appear a bit like an extension of some of my dreams of imaginary creatures, critters and populace.

She gestured for me to come to center stage to take a big bow. On the way out of the wings I happened to catch my toe on the back leg of the cornet player's chair. He was in it, and it shifted just an inch or so, started to tip forward as his arms sliced air, then toppled off the stage. A slow motion Isadora Duncan ballet as hands from the stage reached for him and grasped nothing. He stretched his own arms in opposite directions – his right hand towards the approaching floor, his left, gripping his precious silver instrument, towards the ceiling, by instinct, to keep his livelihood from being crushed.

A half-dozen garish devils and lovely maidens watching from below raised their hands to catch and cushion musician and horn. And chair. Nothing hit the floor except for his music stand as sheet music took flight like a flock of startled pigeons. I felt clumsily foolish, but was glad the guy and his horn weren't hurt.

The hubbub eased once I stepped to the front of the stage and told the crowd that they were part of a miraculous evening, a magical event where, case in point, even things that went wrong ended up all right, but that they should count their P's and Q's anyway, just in case. Then I put my arm around Marjorie and added so everyone could hear, "This, my friends, is your Belle of the Ball and make no mistake about it. A hand for Miss Flowers!"

Immediate applause as she blushed just a little, smiled as big a smile as that little face could hold and glanced at me with a tear at the edge of her eye.

Then the contest for best costume and makeup. Chaos ruled the stage as revelers began to assemble to vie for approbation. I grabbed Marjorie's hand and drew her into the wings, away from the commotion.

"Look here young lady, you've pulled it off and don't deny it! It's a grand evening and a fantastic success. You should be a little proud of yourself, I think! Say you agree!"

She pushed herself up on her tiptoes and gave me a sweet kiss on the cheek. "Don't be silly. Thanks to you we had a theme and a purpose – besides a goal! You are more inspirational than you know, I think. Especially to me."

"Have you become the student who becomes the model who becomes the artist?" I asked.

"Don't ask me that now. And anyway, why not both? I mean, all three?" She turned her face to stare past me into the empty dark curtain folds. "Why not everything? Why not? Why..."

Suddenly we were accosted by three giggling bob-haired volunteers who were squealing about contest judging and final decision-making. They whisked Marjorie back out onto center stage for presentation-time and I recognized I'd had more than enough of the clamor. I was now beginning to feel Sir Headache's sly evil greeting and this crowd was not the place. I exited via the stage door and followed the claustrophobic alley towards my room, my bed. It was several blocks' journey and I needed to take a headache powder and get horizontal and silent and dark as soon as possible.

I ENDED UP in bed for a day and a half and had required every one of those minutes. It was Monday noon before I could think about even moving my head with any semblance of normality. The pain was *right over/under there* and adding merely a bit of sideways motion made me want to vomit. I was cautious, barely changing positions. When I heard a knock at my door, a small voice called "Mahlon. Mahlon are you there? Are you all right?" Marjorie.

It took a bank accounts' worth of minutes, but finally I slowly opened the door, survival-squinting in the light.

"You look horrible!" she exclaimed. "What's wrong?"

"Headache. This isn't the first and it won't be the last. I'll be okay in a while. I'm actually much better already, if you can believe that," I lied and grinned a feeble grimace. "Do you want to come in? I could possibly manage to make some tea. Maybe." Another lie.

"No, no. I need to tell you something."

I started mumbling in a measured tone, "Look, the Ball was grand, and you did swell. Sorry I couldn't stay to..." but I was interrupted.

"Stop. Please, let me just talk."

"Here at the door? Come in, Marjorie. I have this situation, this headache..."

"No. I can't stay. I can't anything!"

She paused and looked up at me, biting her lip like she had when she'd posed for the drawing. Desperation flooded her eyes.

"What's wrong?" I asked in a very low voice, the residual ache made it hard to focus.

"Nothing, one might say. One might. I... I don't know."

She paused again, stared into my eyes. She took my hands in hers. Then she erupted, "I'm getting married!" She turned her face down, examining our hands entwined between us.

Now it was my turn to pause. In fact, I could barely move even my lips. "Wow. That's... Wow. Exciting, I guess. So... how are you, then?"

"Oh, Mahlon. I'm fine. I'm swell. It's just all so sudden. After the Ball my sister and I went out on the town with these two really nice fellows that we've been dating. No, I haven't mentioned that before, have I? Well, they're brothers. Yes, I know. Funny. But they're both really nice and both my sister and I like them a lot and I suppose we were intoxicated on gin as well as the night air. Everything was so dreamy, all, like something in a dream." She was speaking rapidly now, like she had to get the story out as fast as possible. "So this came to that and after it was all over, he proposed to me!" She let go of my hands.

" 'This came to that'? What's that mean?"

She twisted her slender, elegant neck and stared at her empty hand now resting on the doorframe. Her perfect delicate white fingers, resting against the dark woodwork, twitched.

"It means what it means, that's all. And anyway, I said 'yes' and so did my sister."

"Sister? Pardon me, but what the bloody hell are you talking about? I don't get it." My feeble voice barely managed to rise. Spurred by frustration, the croak of my pathetic questions startled me.

She looked me in the eye, and one tear escaped, fled down her cheek and ducked into the corner of her sweet lips. Then another. I couldn't help but melt inside, and leaned fully on the doorframe to keep from falling over.

"My sister... it's... well... both of the boys proposed to both of us! Together at the same time! We just both said yes! See?"

I didn't see. "So what does this really mean?" I asked. "Why are you here, Marjorie, now?"

"I'm leaving school! I'm leaving art and fun and, and... you, your... I'm getting married! I'm..." she sniffled and wiped her nose with the back of her sleeve in the manner of an exhausted eight-year-old. But after a minute, or a second, or who could tell how long, she looked at me with the same determined bewilderment that she'd shown me before, at the studio.

She said, "I can do this, and I'm going to. I was your model, Sweet Mahlon, but your lover? That's only another dream, not this one. This is too much like reality." I could barely move. The headache? The revelation?

Both?

She stretched up on her toes to kiss me ever so lightly on the lips. Her cool palms on my chest, then she turned away, paused forever, and walked out of my life. "Goodbye–" hung in the air till "Mister Blaine" from halfway down the hallway finally broke through the silence and she was gone. Damn her, she was gone! Did I say she was gone??? Thank God for strong, steady door-frames.

SHE'D TOLD THE truth: she soon left school, she got married (as did her sister and the two young gents, all in one big wedding) and I, of course, disappeared from her life. Knowing what I knew (which one could argue was not that much), I was pretty sure that whatever future she would make, she'd always be in charge. She'd feel that way inside, anyway. It wouldn't really matter what others might think about outward appearances or actions. Or what needs they might have. I hoped she'd always maintain a firm grasp on the idea of 'ultimate Marjorie', even if it ultimately didn't include me.

But I must admit, my brain (or what I sometimes called a brain) didn't completely let go of her. My sweet, perfect model. Every so often she'd appear in one of my paintings. Still does in fact, and she never seems to have horns or the goat foot.

That's just the way it is, and it still surprises me. And that's me apparently still telling the truth, but only to me. What the hell am I saying?

Am I listening?

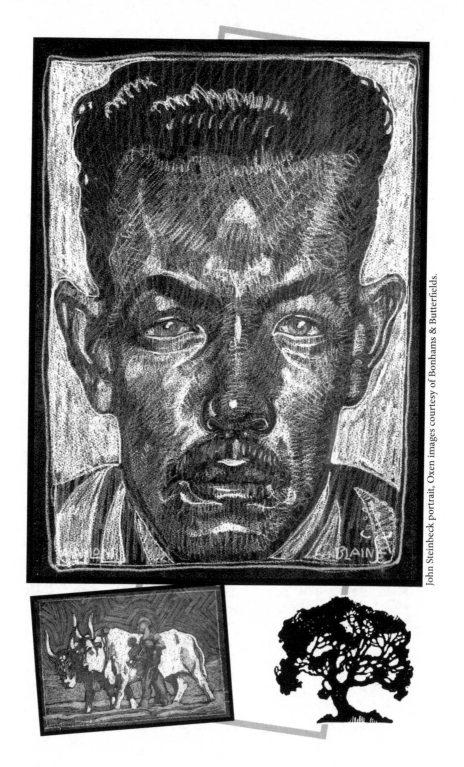

John Steinbeck portrait, Oxen images courtesy of Bonhams & Butterfields.

John Chapter One

1925

A LOW-TIDE STENCH of sea bottom and expiring organisms. How pleasant!

"Isn't *Iowa By The Sea* beautiful?" he said.

I about jumped out of my overcoat. "My God. You speak English!" We had each been elbows to the railing, studying the shore, marking time until the ship might move.

"English is like a second language to me. In fact, it's like a first and third as well," he added.

"Good and better! These freighters specialize in the obscure tongue, among the crew. One can get achingly hungry for a conversation on a voyage. I may be just a passenger today, but it hasn't always been that way. I've sailed a sea or two. Many a Malay crew-mate I've run up against, word-wise and more I might add, to invariably ill effect."

"Yes, give me English any day. American English preferably. By the way, the name's Steinbeck. John Steinbeck. Booked for New York but momentarily just basking in the evening sun of Long Beach Harbor. And you?"

"I am Blaine. Mahlon Blaine. That's capital M, with an A, H, L, O, and a final N. At your service. Also to New York City, where the air is sweet with the stench of the spilled blood of all the lowly artists who await their ultimate fates. I will soon be one more, added to the pile, I suspect."

"Indeed." He stated this with conviction. "Artist? Me too. Writer, you see. Writer, artist...? What is Art? Just somebody's idea of somebody else's idea, I suspect. Have I seen your work, Artist Mahlon with a capital M Blaine?"

"Yes and no, perhaps. Do you attend the cinema? The movies? I've spent a bit of time behind the scenes, mostly in set design and fart direction. I beg your pardon: Art Direction."

"Fantastic! That sounds like swell work. The second one, I mean. The first one doesn't sound like work at all..."

"But you still have to follow the stars. Some of the stars really have orbits all their own. Take that bastard Fairbanks. We made our little *Thief of Bagdad* you may have seen last year, and now he's decided he doesn't like me and, lo and behold, I can't seem to get hired anywhere. Oh well, following that orbit of farts was starting to get to me anyway." Most of that was true.

"*Thief of Bagdad*? That was a tremendous flick."

"Yes. Well, I worked closely with Menzies on the look of everything. The oriental frufarraw bits and pieces. Even costume designs. But that's behind me, for the moment," I appended. "I'm off to become a book illustrator, if they'll have me."

"Books? By any chance novels? I'm going to be a writer of novels. I am! And when I am... you can illustrate them. That's the ticket! An unstoppable duo shall storm the bastions of New York publishing. And all before lunch." He gave me a sudden rueful look, seemed to deflate a little, and was silent.

I quietly added "No doubt. No doubt."

The Katrina's aft stacks blew off a barrelful of black smoke, and we were finally under way. Fart!

"Good-bye, Beautiful." John gave a little two-fingered gesture of a wave towards shore.

"Yes. Good. Bye," I resolutely echoed.

*Invention, it must be humbly
admitted, does not consist in creating
out of void, but out of chaos; the
materials must, in the first place be
afforded: it can give form to dark
shapeless substances but cannot bring
into being the substance itself.*

Young Conklin

1926

THE FIRST TIME I met Groff Conklin was in the earliest days,
when I was just beginning to shop around some of my stuff, hoping to land assignments for legitimate book illustration jobs. He
had just graduated from Columbia University and had landed a
junior-assistant sub-editor-in-training job at Robert M. McBride,
publisher. This was November, 1925, New York City, Manhattan.

I'd actually been aware of McBride back in 1919, when they
had published Branch's *Jurgen, A Comedy of Justice*. They'd gotten in legal trouble, obscenity-wise (the Society for Suppression
of Vice), but they'd triumphed in court. I'd admired that. Damn
the suppression of vice, I always say!

So, McBride was one of the first places I went to apply. I figured that, since they'd been showcasing Pape's wonderful illustrations and since superficially his and my style appeared similar,
I had a good enough chance.

I don't think Robert M. McHimself knew quite what to make
of me. He was, after all, a High Society type and I burst in all
scruffy with a tattered portfolio jammed with sketches, pen-and-

ink erotica and watercolor candy ads featuring elves. So he took a quick November look and I was on my way, thank you very much anyway.

But one day in January I came back. I had a copy of the November 28th New Yorker with me. It had a little drawing of mine snuck in there that I was going to brag about.

I strolled in, was announced and ushered to Groff's office this time, by Gretta (still there from my October visit, and still certainly *not* model-material), and, after a handshake (his grip was firm, but not too firm – and I'm sensitive to that. Can't have bruised artist-hands, can we?) I untied the folio.

Groff must have been in some big hurry. Never even said hello, just "No, wait. Here, look at these galleys. We're doing a head-hunter type book and I want an interesting map drawing for the endpapers. Look the galleys over a bit to get a sense of the writing. Oh, and there's already a rough sketch that my design guy here did. Too rough to use, and I know he hasn't started a finished version yet and he's way behind on a bunch of other deadlines so take a look at that too – I'll get it for you – and draw me up something I can use. I'd like to get it to the print house in New Jersey sometime tomorrow. Can you do it here? Now?" He was quite the quick talker, but I had no trouble. I've been told I mumble, but I have a good ear and can follow almost anyone else easily.

"I should think that that would not be an issue, Sir. Just need a corner of a table somewhere, and a fresh bottle of India Black. I believe I have a pen with me…" was my reply. I was directed to a table by the door where I sat with some borrowed ink and drew on some Bristol.

He liked the result, which I was able to show him only one hour and fifteen minutes later. He had Gretta fill out a check on the spot, he signed it, and I had my first official hardcover book illustration. Now I felt legitimate!

I could hardly wait for the book to come off the presses so that I would have proof of employability to show other book publishers. But I did have to wait, of course, until early March.

WHEN I CAME back to pick up my complementary copies of *Heart of Black Papua*, Groff had already gotten himself advanced to Editorial Assistant, and he personally handed over my books.

"Hello, Mr. Blaine. Edward Groff Conklin again. The printed endpapers look quite nice," he said, complimentarily. I was almost a decade older than he, but I liked his style. He continued, "Mind showing me your whole portfolio today? I'd like to see it all. I've got time."

"Certainly, young Conklin. Say, are you old enough to look at pinchers, I mean pitchurs, of naked ladies? Oh, wait. College boy, right? No problems then."

"Ha. Thanks. Columbia's reputation precedes me. I think I can handle whatever you've got in there. I'll let you know if otherwise. Let's give a look."

Well, this being my somewhat sedate job-hunting folio, there was nothing much that he couldn't see in a Manet or Degas or Gaugin. But still, I was betting that with a few of my figure renderings his personal reaction would leave him with a distinct impression.

He was not making any effort to conceal his enthusiasm as he turned from page to page. Yes, he was quite enthusiastic, all right. Big enthusiasm showed right through his worsted wool trousers.

"Say... These are very nice. Mr. Blaine, I am glad to have made your acquaintance! Oh, these are very nice indeed! Not very publishable, but...What other examples of published illustration of yours could I see?"

Not publishable? That hurt a little, even though I knew it to be true. Too risqué, oy vey!

I had the *New Yorker* tear-sheets that I pointed out, and a couple of *The Spectator* and *Screenland Hollywood* drawings were there, too, mixed in with my unpublished stuff. Then he came upon four pages of faces. These were real bully characters, dangerous looking, sinister. Most were based on sketches from the trolley and subway rides I took all the time - sketchbook at hand.

"All right, all right. I may have an idea, here. Say..." he was excited and it affected his voice as it raised a pitch. "Can I keep your portfolio until tomorrow? I'm getting an idea. A really good idea, I think. But I've got to present it the right way to Mister Mc-Bride. I'll need overnight to put this together. Can you be back here at three o'clock tomorrow afternoon? You'll get everything back then. I promise. And maybe even... Oh boy!"

Well, when faced with such expansive excitement and friendliness, how could I refuse? Of course, I said yes.

"You won't be sorry, I don't think," he said. "I'll see you tomorrow. Three o'clock."

I lost a little sleep that night over whatever his young brain might be conjuring up. Okay, a lot of sleep.

NEXT DAY, 3 pm and on the dot, too. "*Limehouse Nights*," said Groff.

"OK, I'll bite. Give me something to chew," was my reply.

"Look! This will be wonderful! Oh, here." He handed me a book. "We published this a few years ago. It was 1919, I think. Yes. 1919. Oh, you don't need to remind me that I wasn't here then. Still in Junior High School, even. That's beside the point! Look! No illustrations. It sold pretty well, I guess. I don't have the exact figures right now, but they were sufficient to warrant reprinting back then and... here's the new great part: You!"

"Me?"

"Of course. I showed a selection of your drawings to Mister McBride this morning. He said he'd already seen some of your work, but I'd picked out the most dramatic scenes and the most sinister characters. I interleaved them and marked up a few passages in a copy of *Limehouse Nights* where I thought the narrative best fit. It was an exercise in imagination, and that's why he's the boss! He's got a fine handle on the mind of the reading public. He likes my idea, and we've still got the reprint rights from the original contract with the author Burke. It's a go!"

"What're the parameters?" I was trying to sound like I knew what I was talking about.

"I've got his authorization for one illustration, that's a full-page illustration, per story. That's where we'll start. I'm just so certain that your talents and temperament will mesh with Burke's! But, why don't you sketch up maybe four or five for the first stories in the book? Could you bring something back here in a week or so?"

"Yes. I believe I could manage that. Pen and ink, like these?" I took the portfolio he had returned to me, laid it open on the desktop, and pulled out a couple of the Mexican fantasies that I particularly liked.

"Yes! Absolutely like these! But Oriental, of course. Gosh! You know that! I'm just rather excited about this! This will be great! Promise me this will be great?"

"Of course. You have my solemn oath on whatever Book of Universal Mythology you've got handy. This will be great, Groff. For us and everybody around us. In fact, 'great' does not really begin to..." but he cut me off as I rambled along.

"All right. All right. I get it. I know I'm an enthusiastic guy. I eventually calm down, Mister Blaine, when I get bored. Your stuff does not bore me! But don't you think..." it was my turn to cut him off.

"Of course I think. And it's Mahlon to you, Groff. Just Mahlon. See you next week."

"Next week it is, or rather, will be. Till then, Mahlon."

I rushed straight to the NYPL, not bothering to even detour to park the portfolio at my abode in the Parkwood. I fairly skipped up the marble stairway to the huge card catalog room to scour the drawers for books on Limehouse, the notorious London district. Particularly books with photographs. I got a list of fifteen or twenty with their Deweys and took the slips to the stacks counter. You can only request a few at a time so I picked up the first batch they brought up from the bowels of the building, took them to one of the massive reading tables, and began.

Amazingly for such a cavernous space, the comfortable oak chairs and ornate lamps built into the tabletops gave a sense of shared privacy and semi-personal space. Patrons were concentrating and the silence was merely tickled by the flops of turned pages, and a random cough, perhaps.

Only pencils are allowed in here, so as I flipped book pages searching for photos of street scenes, residents, faces, when something clicked I had my small sketchbook and Number 2s to capture my own distorted versions. As I gathered these dark images, I exchanged perused books for others on my list until I'd reached the bottom. After a full day's drawing I had a sore back from leaning over the flat tabletop to draw, but a wealth of source material for mood and atmosphere and setting.

Back in the studio corner of my room where I had rigged a wooden chair to hold a drawing board at a more comfortable angle, I spent the next two days in solid composition, moving people and elements to fill the spaces in a dramatic, sinister way, based on my reading of the scenes and passages Thomas Burke had written. I was inspired by the darkness there. Blank paper replaced sketch through a series of refinement stages.

More hours and days were spent bringing in the unique faces I had captured in my Chinatown excursions. Groff had remarked on several of these from my portfolio samples already. I wanted to use every advantage I could to secure this job. I had a feeling, a premonition maybe. The pieces seemed to be falling into place, but I was still nervous. I could blow this and be set back, or I could make a connection and... who knows?

I'm afraid I was rotten company for Steinbeck (and our new friends in the big city). For several days I'd disappeared, a slave to the drawings. I hoped he had spent his time as best suited him, whether at work or play in his upstairs quarters. But I also hoped he wouldn't scare off the couple girls I'd recently located and convinced to pose. John had been attracted to one gal in particular who I thought might be outstanding artist material, but I was currently too focused on my dark Limehouse drawings to babysit adults.

I was gestating, about to give birth to a set of pen-and-ink offspring. The end products of my mind, eye, hand, and Thomas Burke's seeds. They wouldn't be boring, but would anyone really like my babies? Might these unpretty two-dimensional progeny ever be loved, other than by me?

"LIMEHOUSIANS, IN ALL their sinister glory," was all I said, one week later.

I had laid my folio in front of Groff, untied the four laces at the three sides, given it a quarter-turn, and spread the covers wide to the five new drawings.

First up: *The Chink and the Child*. Story One. The caption would read: *O li'l Lucia... White Blossom... Twelve years old!*

"Oh, my. Oh my, indeedy!" said Groff.

THE SERPENT TIGHTENED AROUND HER HIS BLACK COILS

New Day New Model
1926

SHE SPOKE PERKILY: "Mr. ?? (John Day Company president, dammit, can't remember his name after forty years), there's a Mister Blaine here to see you about design and illustration."

The young lady had had to get up and sway her backside a bit provocatively, I noticed, as she utilized the few steps to the top dog's office door. She had lightly knocked once and immediately opened the door enough to poke her head through. I was standing, looking around the tiny reception area. The whole office itself was... sparse. It was obvious that the John Day Company, Publishers, had not had these digs for very long at all.

"Mr. (John Day president, dammit again!) will see you in ten minutes, Mr. Blaine. Please have a seat." She slid back down behind the desk just barely clear of the door that led to the fourth floor hallway. She wasn't bad looking at all, but still wore her hair in the style that was already being overtaken by the modern swoop. The bob and bangs memo had not been received, I suppose. Still, she was nicely slim and had fingers that curved backwards in a fetching almost dancer-like way as she reached for a sheet of paper and fed the hefty Royal in front of her. Clickety-clickety snap.

I offered a "Thank you," crossed to the chair opposite her desk and sat. I paused a minute or two. "Excuse me if you will, but, a question: have you ever danced? On the stage? Professionally?"

The query hardly seemed to bother her, although I am pretty sure she had not anticipated it. She casually looked up from her typing.

"Why would you want to know something like that? Are you a big producer or something?"

I smiled. "I produce works of art, from murals to doodles. Sometimes I draw dancers. I am always interested in the kind of visual source material that lends itself to allowing the artist to work with a certain assurance that he isn't too distracted by the model to draw the best line he ever yet had, and then be eager to draw the next, and the next." Was I articulate, or what?

"And you guess that I might be a dancer? Or a model?"

"You know," I continued, "sometimes all it takes is a few minutes. Unfortunately, this or that girl may not be my Mona Lisa. Perhaps not even anyone's, but certainly not mine. Then it's the awkward moment of 'Thanks, my dear. We'll call you soon if there's anything further you can do for us. Put your lovely frock back on, and off you go. It has been a delight, I'm sure, but that will be all for today.' "

She cocked her head to the left, raised an eyebrow. "What's the percentage?"

"Of Mona Lisas to bye-bye Lisas?"

She nodded, watching me sideways.

I answered, "Well, the final figures are not in but, so far, I'd guess about eleven point oh-seven-five percent for the positive." She frowned. "Yet each moment is ripe to increase that dismal subtotal. You never know when..." I was interrupted by Mr. Holt (Hurray! I finally remembered!) opening his office door.

"Ah, Mr. Blaine. Please leave that girl alone and come in and bring that thing with you." He pointed to my buldging, 28 by 40 inch black buckram covered, very well-worn leather-handled portfolio, sitting on the floor, leaning against my leg. "Let's see what we'll see."

I jumped up and took the couple strides to his office door. As I looked back I caught a smile on the young lady's lips. And maybe the wink of an eye? If everything went right here, I'd soon have a new assignment and a newer model. I could always use a newer model.

Getting It Together In NYC

1926

"I SAY, JOHN old boy... for chrissakes sit still! Who the hell am I? Cecil B. d'goddamnMille? This ain't his newest flick here, this is supposed to be a portrait! Not a *Golden Bed,* but a still-life of the flesh. Your flesh. So sit still!"

"Oh sure. Of course. What was I thinking? Sit still? It's just that Estelle there, slightly out of sight behind you but not quite, is half out of her chemise and, I'm sure, thinking about her own moment of glory, in the warm light over here, for her own half-clad effortless claim to beauty, by sitting for the Great Mister Blaine, while I'm watching (and how could I not) as she pouts and sighs and then wriggles a little in anticipation and impatience as you, in your own speedy rendering, attempt to catch my poor, unsuccessful face in pastel, all the time knowing, for you always seem to know, that Miss Estelle, or Miss Evelyn or Francine, or whoever-of-the-moment, always wants to be *seen* by you, and *drawn* by you, and made oh-so-temptingly into *pure beauty,* by you." John could spout a mouthful!

"Fine. Your whiningly accurate monologue has given me ample time to finish. Move along, John. I'm through with you. Is that your typewriter I hear calling? 'Ding. Ding. Return-return. Click click click oh where's my paper and carbon? And where's the next page? Ding. Ding. Where are you Mr. Steinbeck? You-whoooooo....'"

It turned into a rather long evening, after I finally got John to leave. I had much work to do, many ink lines to wrangle. Many perfect bodies to put into that orgy scene, and the next. It took the better part of five hours to sketch up a hundred and thirty-one priestesses. Each one had her own little demon to dance with, to mesmerize, all spread out across the temple scene. Oh, I needed a lot of material that night. And they were all Estelle, this time. Yes, she was graceful and supple and creamy-smooth with that enchantingly translucent skin that half-revealed her veins, faintly, beneath her perfect surface.

At least, she would be perfect in the drawing. Humans, being what they are, aren't. It's best not to get too exact, or detailed in the rendering, when presenting essences of lust and desire, hate and loathing, fear and contempt, love and.... I was beginning to stink up the room with the concentration on my line-work. Focusing, imagining, rendering.

John stopped back at 5:32 AM to check on myself and the ever-lovely Estelle. Oh, he tried to be discrete and quietly tapped on the door before opening enough to look in. The lady was asleep on the Chesterfield, beneath a crocheted afghan from my dear mother's own hand. Her right breast subtly peeked out, but that was about it. John didn't say a word as I glanced up from the drawing table, nodded silently, and turned back to my inkwell. He gently closed and latched the heavy oak door and was off to a hauling job, or whatever they had him doing today over at the Madison Square Garden worksite. Poor fella.

I KEPT THAT little pastel portrait of John for a few weeks, stuck up on the left edge of the cork-board on the "kitchen" wall. Away from the little demons and deities that were flowing off my white-boards as I pushed to meet the *Salammbo* deadline from Day. I didn't mind that John's dignified, flattened countenance looked across over the double hotplate and dirty sink piled high with laundry and dishes, and almost looked down its nose at my success. While he himself roundly sank, bit by bit, into a depression built upon rejection after rejection of his hard-fought prose. I knew, or felt from somewhere in my gut I guess, that his words were his strength, much as my pen was mine. Perhaps he would not catch on with the editors and publishers just now. Just now, my near-pornography was filling the bill in some cockamamie fit-the-public-taste way that his earnest prose was not. But, things change. Always they do.

When John told me he had decided to go and lick his wounds, go back to the sunshine of southern California, I gave him the likeness I had done of him that night. So he wouldn't forget New York completely, or me. It was a long way to remember, even then.

The Goat's Foot

1968

YOU HAVE YOUR demons, and you have your women. Sometimes, in one and the same creature. Did I say sometimes? And
how does one tell if a woman is not a demon? Is this a ridiculous
question? Who has the answers? When in doubt, ask an artist.
Their guesses are as good as anyone's.

Mostly, if the foot is cloven, you have yourself a pretty good
clue right there. Although you must look closely, and often.
And the timing must be very, very lucky. If, for instance, in the
moments immediately pre- and post-coital, one were intent on
catching a quick glimpse of the female's extremity of limb, perhaps then the singular cloven appendage would be evident. But
if so, oh so fleetingly.

In drawings, of course, I have the luxury of including the tell-
tale vision whenever I wish. This is for the benefit of the viewer,
the 'Everyman' who may not be aware. I think, after studying
a drawing, there is awareness injected, as it were, on the con-
sciousness of the 'Everyman'. This may be for the good. Or not.

But Truth, sometimes with a capital letter, is important.

And what if some fellow should have self-same cloven appendage as well? Not unheard of, I assure you. In fact, practically a requirement, come to think of it. Didth not Man and Woman once share the same rib? I rest my case.

Not to say that Love does not exist.

But the goat's foot, always there beneath the surface.

Beware the foot.

Embrace the foot.

On being charged with the fact, the
poor girl confirmed the suspicion
in a great measure by her extreme
confusion of manner.

Whither My Wife
1968

ONCE UPON A time, I first met my wife at the movies, you might say. Back-lot, Universal Studios.

"Hello," she spoke to me.

"Oh hell, yes indeed," replied I.

That was that, and there hasn't been a day since that very day that I haven't thought about her. Even after the divorce. God! Especially after the divorce. Married eight years and never before, nor certainly after, was anyone a better match for me.

Now, by match, I don't mean she was like me. But she sure as hell *liked* me.

I have amused a number of the women around me as I've wandered my merry way through life. I have also infuriated, offended, frustrated, puzzled and perturbed a few. I have intrigued ladies who have wondered how I would draw them, nude, and then satisfied their wonderment. And I have also disgusted a minority share with the results of that identical effort.

I have alienated friends and strained friendships with the perusal and artistic rendering of wives and lovers not my own.

Were such encounters and incidents purely innocent? Well, not always purely.

I have categorically, philosophically refused to bed the most perfect of feminine bodies, for I would much rather have them stick around as long as possible - as models and inspiration. But, being merely a man, I have also certainly lost a few of these models and muses to the mundane mismanagement of my urges.

The best laid plans are not necessarily the best laid ladies. That's a fact.

But also a fact: my wife .... liked... *me*.

Joe Offers Life

1941

Dunninger was Harry's friend. Harry the Houdini...

"JOE. WHUDDYA KNOW?"

"Mahlon! Here you are! Where have you been?"

As usual, in the dim light of the deep stacks of an antiquarian bookstore, we spied each other. Joe Dunninger hadn't seen me, nor I him of course, for a month of ice-cream sundaes. All part of the give-and-take of souls that only bump along their corridors of time. My soul, I'm speaking of, anyway. Lots of bumping. Whereas Joe, I'm not sure he has a soul. I think he leased it out decades ago to Joseph Dunninger, Magician, and gradually, over time, it maybe got misplaced then forgot. That didn't seem to bother Joe. It certainly didn't bother me.

"Joe. Yes. Hello and all that, but what's for supper?" No sense in me trying to ignore my stomach rumbling, for it was announcing its desires all on its own anyway.

"Well, friend, only the wonderful Billie would know the answer to that one. Feel like a little drive?"

I hadn't been over to the Cliffside mansion for too long. My stomach started growling louder just thinking about it. Billie was Joe's best wife yet, and probably his last, and a hell of a cook. She asked what you wanted, and then fixed you pancakes. I love pancakes. For one thing, they are easy to draw. And for another thing, well, see thing number one.

"Sure enough. A little car ride would do me good. These old canvas shoes get a mite wobbly after a few miles of New Yerk sidewerks. Still got the touring car?"

"Of course. Of course. Say!" he said as he pulled a small parcel from beneath his arm. "I was just over to Pageant and they had a stack of returns - discounted - of these little *Frankliniana* books with your doodles all over. Did Jake publish this? No matter. Guess after you get a meal in you, you might sit still long enough to add a little of your magic pen on the flyleaves of these?"

That was his way. I was used to it. Not that I minded. I've done so many inscribed books in my life that, put together, they'd be a book all their own. But they're scattered among friends and acquaintances from Show Low to Bali Hi. Joe, though, he was a special case. He actually collected and appreciated all my stuff. He even personally commissioned a bunch of material – too much to remember. Just like when he was with Chrystal, he was always on the lookout in the bookstores (and he was in them all the time) for my titles. If they were cheap enough, he'd buy 'em, bring 'em home, and dig 'em out when I dropped by. I dropped by whenever I could, too. Did I mention I love pancakes? So all those books have all those inscriptions. Well, good. He has plenty of bookshelves in his Cliffside abode.

I REMEMBER THIS one other time I was over at Cliffside... I had just dropped-in on the Saturday after Thanksgiving. "Just in the neighborhood - ho, ho, ho." And Joe said he had a good deal for me, a real fine deal in fact. He got me an illustration spot in *LIFE* magazine! This periodical periodically was delivered to the homes of maybe a million people each week.

Well, was I interested? That would surely be more eyes than had gazed at anything else I'd ever done. Not counting the design work in *Scarface* and *Thief*. But no one knew any of that stuff was mine. This would be different. And it was for a painting! I certainly wouldn't mind a little national recognition!

"I need a color painting about 'so big' by Tuesday noon." he said as his hands indicated a twelve by eighteen rectangle in the air. "An Indian Rope Trick thing. Not too fancy. Nothing erotic. Not too artistic, if you'll pardon the expression, either. This is *LIFE* and Middle America. I can't promise, but how does a hundred bucks sound to you? Upon publication, of course." Joe waited, arms crossed, weight on his left foot.

"Deal." I said. "A hundred sounds fine. How about a turkey sandwich to tide me over? Maybe two sandwiches if I can wrap them up in wax paper, and some marshmallow yams in a jar?"

"Of course, of course."

OF COURSE, WHEN the magazine came out, finally, months later (on my 47th birthday, no less)... yes, there's my painting – about an inch tall! And no attribution, no accolade, no "Mahlon Blaine" anywhere. My big break indeed. Well, at least I'd gotten a few bucks.

And a couple sandwiches.

*Thus strangely are our souls
constructed, and by such slight
ligaments are we bound to
prosperity or ruin.*

Migraine

1942

SO THIS DOCTOR guy I met in the bookstore a couple years before, down on 14th Street, well, I... OH this *fudkingheadache!*Jesus the Jesus *fuckingchrist* this HURTS... oh.......

I'm going to take the goddamn bus and see him in New Jersey again... but where? *Ican'tfuckingthink!*

Oh *shit!*

AND THAT'S HOW it was. How it used to be. Often.

It's a bit better now.

Still, thank you, Doctor Crandell, of *Chateau Greystone*. We had some success, didn't we?

In the Briggs'
1952

"GERTRUDE, DEAR, WILL you look at this!"

"Be right there, Mister Briggs," replied his wife, as she put aside the morning paper, took a sip of barely-warm tea, and skipped her way to the back of the bookstore. It was her second nature to move briskly among the stacks of volumes between the shelves, and yet not tip or scatter any of them. Her special gift. She found "Mister Briggs" (as she called her husband of twenty-odd years) intently gazing at the cover of an older *Bohemia* magazine from the West Coast.

"Look here at this, will you? Mahlon never told us about any work he'd done this long ago. This is dated 1916 and printed in Oakland California in February of 1917. That rascal! I'm going to put this in my coat pocket and bring it out at Easter dinner! Then we'll see what tale he weaves. I'm sure it will be a dandy!"

"Well," said Gertrude, pausing. "I don't know what you're getting at. Mahlon isn't the kind of person that would fabricate, is he?"

She let a sly smile twitch at the corners of her mouth. Mister Briggs glanced up from the magazine and caught her as she quickly went deadpan.

"Of course not. Not at all. Truthful as all get-out and then some. Born on Easter Island and insisting on this whole special dinner thing Sunday because of his dual citizenship and royal lineage... Inviting only us to join him this year, because his genealogical research unearthed a shirt-tale link between your cousin's cousin's deceased husband and a long-lost princess of his Island Tribe... Starting his illustration career here on a dare from his cousin in the British royalty in 1925.... I'm sure he'll have quite the reasonable explanation for this magazine's existence, come Sunday."

They were so focused on their little banter that they both had completely forgotten I was standing there in the store near the front door. I heard every word. What's the difference? It was all true. At least the part about Sunday dinner together. I slipped out of the shop as an authentic customer entered to buy some obscure treatise on abandoned methods of open-pit copper mining or some-such, I'm sure. I would see them Sunday.

Hallelujah!! The truth would be risen again!

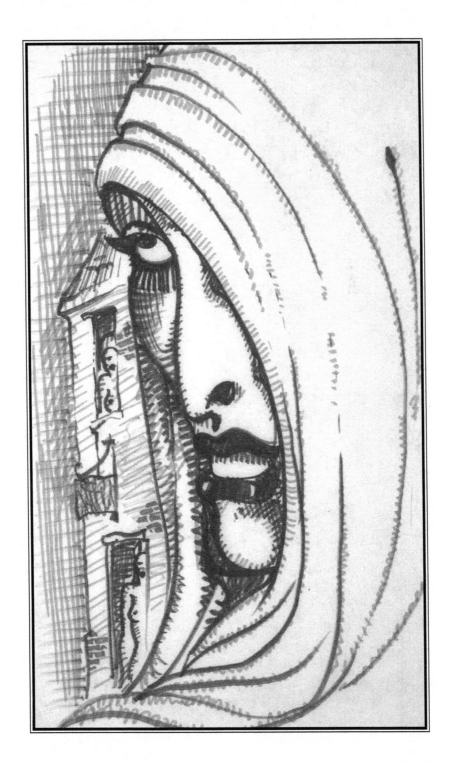

Image courtesy of Bonhams & Butterfields.

How Many So Far?

1968

THE PROBLEM WITH me informing anyone exactly how many books I've illustrated is... I don't know. Of course I don't know. How could I? I mean, really, how could I?

For instance, I only suspect which was the first one. Technically, the *Black Papua* endpaper map for McBride. That was the first New York book I was actually paid for. I also recall doing some designs for John Day that were more like "auditions" of my work. Uncredited, unsigned, unpaid, but important to begin to establish a relationship.

Limehouse Nights was the one that broke it for me. Especially the yellow plate under-printing, done from secondary drawings. A technique which I hadn't really done before which imbued a creepy tone that the plain black reprints lacked (although they were fine drawings in their singular right). I'm proud of that innovation, and wished I'd had more opportunities to do that kind of thing over the span of my career.

Ask me again, *how many books*, when my career is nearly done. I might be fooling myself, but may that day never come.

Coney Island Photos
1950

I RANG THE front doorbell. I could smell turkey roasting. Mm-mmm.

"Is this the right place, or am I in the wrong precinct?"

"Mahlon. Please come in. We weren't expecting you, as usual, but there's another plate in the cupboard, I'm sure," said Nate. "The Goldsteins will always have a placesetting for our dear Mr. Blaine. What have you been up to? You're looking fit," he lied. I knew I had put on a few pounds.

"Up to? Oh, not up to too much, not too much." I nodded as Flo came out of the kitchen in a broadly-striped apron that pretty much camouflaged her, like the clever Naval use of enormous geometric shapes painted on ships. "Howdy-do, Florence. My, don't you look fetching, somewhere behind that Grandma Moses rainbow. Smells good in here! Oh. And this is for you, little lady." I swung my left hand around from where I had been holding a package behind my back. "Go ahead. It won't bite. Maybe."

"Why, thank you, Mahlon. I think. Let's see if I mean it, shall we?" she said as she began to untie the string that held the brown paper that was folded around the little painting in the plain frame.

"Oh, very nice." She meant it, too, I suspect. A colorful pastel painting of a boat dock, blue sky, flags flying. A bit pointillist, a tad abstract. "It's not like anything else you've done before, for us. Is it?" she pondered.

"Well, for instance, it's smaller." I held up my thumb and index finger about an inch apart. "Especially when viewed from the side, edge-on."

She laughed her high, pure laugh. "Oh, Mahlon. I shall be sure to hang it so as to give the side the best light, then."

"Thanks, fella," said Nate. "That's all I need around here, for all the paintings you've given us to now be re-hung perpendicular to the walls. Swell." He was chuckling.

"Oh, don't fuss, don't fuss. I've gotten kind of used to 'em the way they are now. They've done grown on me. Go ahead and leave all those old ones the way they are. And, by the way... when do we eat?" I raised my right eyebrow. My belly gurgled.

Flo answered quickly as she patted my arm, "You men go sit by the front window now and watch the ships roll in and talk your very important men-talk. I've got at least a half-hour yet in the kitchen. Then dinner's on, and we'll all play Canasta later." That was our little joke. She always says we'll play Canasta because once, years ago, I had let loose a big sloppy sneeze during a lull in the conversation. Everyone thought I had yelled "Canasta!!"

Nate and I sat down in the sunlight that was streaming through the large plate-glass picture window. It faced the street, but since the two-story 1930s house was just one lot away from the end of Beach 45th Street, we still had a fine view of sand and the rocky southwest edge of Coney Island. There was always a parade of freighters. The less-regular cruise ships bore passengers to and from Europe, or maybe Africa, holding dreamers and schemers. It was all very relaxing, like watching slow-motion fish in a tank. We almost dozed off. Almost, I tell you.

"Dinner!" Yumm!

"Mahlon, I've got something that you can help me with. And only you can do it. It has to do with A-R-T." Nate was being mysterious. We'd stuffed ourselves and were recovering, back on the porch.

"Okey-Dokey, I guess. Ain't been done-in by A-R-T yet. Maybe I could assist you with it, whatever it is you're about to wrangle. A-R-T? Honest to friggin' God A-R-T??"

"Yes yes. Art. Only art. You're an artist, aren't you? Here's what you have to do first: come into the living room and sit on the sofa. I'll be right back." He went to the basement.

It wasn't but a couple-three minutes and I heard him slowly ascending the stairs. He was carrying a big old F-stopping camera, and it was attached to a huge F-stopping tripod. It all looked heavy. I started to get up off the sofa.

"Whoa, there Mr. Snap-shot. Let me help," I offered.

"Yes. Well... this thing's heavier than it looks. Thanks. Let's just get these legs spread out... right... there. It's stable. Good. Go ahead and sit down again for a minute, Mahlon. I'll be right back." And off he went, this time to a back bedroom.

He came out with a globe, in a stand. You know – the Earth. Must've been from young Freddie's room. He was dusting it off with his sleeve. "Sit down. Oh. You are sitting already. Good. So... here, let me put this globe next to you on the sofa. Or maybe you should hold it?"

"And, I suppose you're gonna take my picture? A man-of-the-world, or something?"

"Yes, yes. That's the spirit. I've just gotten my darkroom set up downstairs, and I need some film to develop. You, my friend, are today's subject."

"You know, good idea. Posterity and all. Go ahead then. And let's see if the lens can take the strain. Careful now. "Artist Contemplating World Affairs" or "A Solution to Old-fashioned Politics." Or "Heaven Help Us All." *Snap- snap- snap- snap.*

I wonder if Nate ever developed those negatives? Or if he still has those stills stored somewhere?

Or if he's even still alive?

Plaster cast portrait of Bernice by MB, photo courtesy of Deborah Nelson.

*My spirits were elevated by the
enchanting appearance of nature; the
past was blotted from my memory,
the present tranquil, and the future
gilded by bright rays of hope and
anticipations of joy.*

Little Bernice's Fern

1932

BERNICE IS SURELY the closest thing to a relative I have going, even though we've lost contact. It has been years, decades. I
had married her mother thirty-six years ago, in 1932 Los Angeles. I'd never been married before (or since, as it's turned out) (so
far), but Fern (my wife) had been. And Bernice was fruit of that
earlier union.

I hasten to say that, though Fern was my wife's birth name,
no one besides her folks called her that. She'd been born in Minnesota in 1902 to an up-and-coming lawyer by the name of Fred
(Fred Ezra Stivers) and his lovely bride, Clara (ne Berkey). Fern
and Lucille were their two daughters, with Fern being the first-
born. That's the genealogy of the thing. The little family moved
from the Midwest to Southern California and bought a nice new
clapboard home in a nice new clapboard neighborhood, and
planted new clapboard trees in the flat dirt yard.

That's where darling Fern grew up, and the empty unsold lots
all around her presented a palette for her imagination. She was
an active child who loved to pretend-act in creative costumes. A

favorite, she told me, was her "Indian Princess" dress with the ticklish leather fringes and the raven feathered headband, both reeking of tanning chemicals. Her long wavy hair and slightly darker complexion made her a very convincing young maiden. She began referring to herself as "Dusky" whenever she felt too stifled by being merely the daughter of a lawyer, and so that's what most everyone called her.

Father-lawyer eventually became a judge, and this elder daughter grew into her lithe yet womanly body and found employment in the movie business. Hollywood style, she landed a few office secretarial spots, now and again enhanced scenes as an extra, and discovered her favorite niche as a script-girl. The story goes, she had been thus occupied, met a salesman, got married, and moved to St. Louis, Missouri. Or was it Kansas City? Anyway... Little Bernice entered the world there. Eventually the salesman turned out to be a rather no-salesman, an uncomfortable divorce ensued, and Fern and her little girl moved back to Hollywood, just off Sunset Bouvelard. That's where we all met.

Eventually I went east and more-or-less had a pretty wonderful career there. Several years' worth of a career. Maybe you heard about it? No? What do I have to do, draw you a picture? Anyway...

My 1932 New York situation was tres uncomfortable. In fact, it was dangerous to engage in earning a living there (at least my kind of living) without harassment and the threat of a jail cell.

Here's why: the citizens for decency began to run rampant, led by he-who-shall-not-be-named (in the personage of John Sumner), and after this *Jack Ketch* incident (the confiscation and burning of the whole edition, the law suit) I thought it prudent to return myself to my good old Hollywood.

I landed smack-the-dab in that hotel on the Boulevard - in fact I got my same old room in the back, from which I used to watch the early '20s Keystone cops pitchin' pennies between movie takes. I secured some fresh employment painting and constructing sets, and I hung around the lots. T'was there I spied Dusky doing her most excellent script-girl impression.

Soon our connection became complete, if you get my drift. Rather head-over-bunions, if you must know. You must? Well then, there you go.

We indeed married each other in the downtown courthouse. Dusky's brother-in-law, Walter Shuttleworth, took the time out of his spectacularly un-busy day to be an official witness. That was damn straight of him. Little Bernice was there, too, but she didn't get to sign any papers and that upset her. Kids! The ceremony was over in practically no time, and I made sure to lay one of my special kisses on Dusky to seal the deal. She knew I meant it then. Boy oh boy did she! And in return, so did I!!

We cabbed it back to the duplex on Alta Vista Boulevard because Walter got crabby after all the hoop-la and then refused to drive us "all over the goddamned place."

Bernice got settled in with Grandma, and Dusky and I headed out for a camping trip to Arizona. The weather was fine, the Sonoran Desert beautiful, and I sure was looking forward to a few days of wild-wolf-howling, with her professing the same.

Coyotes beware!

Little Bernice was advised not to wait up for us!

Woooooooooo-owwww-wooooooooo!

*...they are not the creations
of his fancy, but the beings
themselves who visit him from
the regions of a remote world.*

They Ain't Pretty
1968

IT WAS THE best of times and yet it wasn't.

I saw plenty of naked women – all the time. They posed. I drew them and I made no apologies. I drew them as I wished them to be, usually. You know, there's barely a body that is ideal. I always draw "the most beautiful woman in the world" even if she isn't. And they all aren't, let me tell you. And yet...

When my subjects see my drawings of themselves, they blush, they stammer, they are quietly... quiet, usually. Some want to do me on the spot: horny from looking at their new, beautiful selves and I'm the closest bug to squash. But, like I said, I'm a busy boy. I don't have the time to do every Jane Doe that can't handle facing their own imaginary perfection. So I politely and ruefully decline nine times out of nine. But that tenth time...

My wife, bless her cotton-swabbed soul, was the tenth kind. Let me tell you brother, she was definitely a tenth kind. And I told her so every time too. Honest, I never missed once. She had me where I wanted me and no doubts about it. Whenever I looked at her: that was it, damn it. She was right there, and right there too. Two rights don't make a wrong. Tell me, how doth a woman be like that?

Freud is my hero. He tells it like he thinks it. And me, I try to draw it like I think it. Every time. That scares the living shivver-its out of most people, myself included. I don't end up with a ton of permanent friends. It takes a certain individual to stomach me for very long – again, myself included. I mean, have you seen my drawings? How many? That's what I thought!

I feel I must address the subject of my darkest subject matter. Especially the most disturbing of the bunch. Let me just say one word: headache. You may think that what I am referring to is the state of the viewer after looking at particular works of mine. Not so. What I am referring to is my source material.

You see, I get headaches. Bad headaches. Practically un-sur-vivable headaches. I have consulted with a dozen, two dozen doc-tors. All of them point to my head injury as the initiating event, the beginning trigger to this sorry predicament. That makes per-fect sense, but it doesn't help because it can't be undone.

"I am just trying to remain sane," I tell them. "I think being sane is hard enough without adding injury to insult, as it were. Help me, please."

The best doctors are the ones who will try anything to help me. And there have been some helpful results, but nothing per-manent. Reminds me of a joke: the Doctor, the Psychologist and the Psychiatrist walked into a bar... and there stood I. (I didn't say it was a funny joke.) Drugs were the most-often used tools, and they did work sometimes. Sometimes the pain went quietly away to someplace where I couldn't see it for a while. Other times the pain remained, but was superseded by visions or sounds that would block out the worst of it with overwhelming cascades of diversion.

Here's where the subject of "subject matter" comes in. The drawings we're talking about ... you know the ones. The devils. The demons. The disasters. You've seen them.

In many ways I am my drawings, and the most extreme ele-ments come to the surface in the Headache Drawings. Believe me, they are not drawn to appeal to any esthetic of either myself or any other viewer. They are personifications of the headaches themselves. What you see is what I saw. What you see is what I got. I am not here to sugarcoat the events… what the hell kind of good would that do anyone, least of all me? I think – and the doctors generally agree – that the best approach is to face the demons of my headaches. So I do, whether with the doctors' assistance or not.

I am the artist, I am not the headache.

Perhaps my works will help others who may suffer. That's a rather far reach, I know. Silly, really. But maybe. Anyway, I am not going to hide them. They are me, at least as much as any of the other works I belch out. And isn't that a pretty picture: Belched Art!

Well, speaking only for myself, putting forth art is like any other bodily function. An act of nature. Nature calls.

Perfectly natural acts, even when they ain't pretty.

You are well acquainted with my
failure and how heavily I bore
the disappointment.

Minna Means Well

1948

I'M SURE MINNA thought she was helping. Doing me a favor. Lending a hand. She probably meant well, and so did I. But...

Her husband Jake was in prison at the time. I still can't believe that you can be thrown in prison for copyright infringement. Prison for three years. Shit. Convicted and fined, I could see. Prison? There are some dangerous gents inside there. I guess the best way not to piss them off is to keep out. Poor Jake.

I myself had skedaddled when any trouble started getting close. That had happened a couple times before.

Now I was back in town for a spell so I thought the decent thing to do was drop by and say hi to Minna and the kids. Actually, I didn't care that much for the kids, and I'm sure Minna didn't care that much for me, deep down. But I certainly felt bad for Jake. Never having been incarcerated myself, I can't really imagine.

Well, life for Minna wasn't going any better than I thought it might but she is a spunky gal and was hanging in there, keeping the bookstore running, and the household humming. She was determined to keep any further controversy clear of the store by only handling the usual – used and antique trade, and some of the new books that were popular and sellable.

But she also had a proposal, or proposition for me. She sprung it when I visited. We were sitting at the dining room table, which was in the tiny living room. It was quiet, the kids being at school.

"Mahlon. I have a good idea, for both of us. Tell me what you think."

"Okey-Dokey. What's on your mind, Minna?"

"You've got talent that is not being utilized. Books aren't illustrated anymore. Magazines use photographs, so do newspapers. Your heyday was ten or fifteen years ago. I know, you've still got connections in the movies and so forth. Maybe that's enough for you, maybe not. And that's out west, anyway," she paused to catch her breath, took a sip of water from a chipped glass tumbler, and continued.

"But if you're going to be staying here in New York for any length of time now, I'd like to try a shared venture. I can be your business manager and promoter and all you'll have to do is paint. That's what you do best. Let's take advantage of our individual strengths. Let's help each other."

"Minna, I am all ears."

"Here's what I propose then. I will do the advertising and publicity. We will cash in on your experience and reputation here in the city. You have had a level of legitimate recognition for twenty-five years..."

"Twenty, more like. Or sixteen," I mumbled. "Or, really, five..."

"Yes. And... As I was saying, your work has been known. We'll still be starting slowly as we get the ball rolling, but here's the idea. It's simple. We sell your paintings. That's it. Simple."

"Simple? To whom?"

"Simple to us." She gave me a raised eyebrow and a wide eye stare.

"No, no. To whom are we selling my paintings?"

"To anyone who'll pay. Look, I'll place a couple advertisements in strategic places, like in the back section of the *Times*

Books. And I'll have some signs posted in a few of the antiquarian bookstores here in the village. You know, the ones you've been known to frequent. People will recognize your name. And I can take photos of a couple of your paintings, as either general examples or as the actual ones for sale, and post those up too. Really, I think we could get this going and make a little money."

"Interesting. A little money now and again never hurt anyone, I guess. Although I'm hardly one to comment. I'm about flat broke at the moment, Minna. Did I say 'flat'? Flat with a capital 'flat.'" I didn't want to sound too self-pitying, but it was the truth.

"Look. Let me place the ad in the *Times* for next Sunday. I can make bookstore signs and have them up by Wednesday-next. Tomorrow I'll take the snapshots of a couple of your paintings I've got hanging here, and maybe a pastel or two, have them developed at the *Maxwell Drug* on Second, and add those to the posters. If we are doing this right, we should get some interest and some orders right away, or within a couple weeks."

"I could handle that."

"And I think we need to get you actually started, Mahlon, too. I'm willing to go with you tomorrow and purchase some materials and supplies. I imagine a dozen of those canvas boards, like sixteen-by-twenty inch ones, and... do you have your paints with you? Oh, you probably do..."

"Actually, I am traveling light this time. I brought practically nothing with me, and only a sketchbook and pens. Sorry."

"Well... I can see I'll have to invest in a set of paints and brushes then. But we'll have to go small with the budget. Our start-up costs are going to recoup with our first sale, if all goes well. I'm thinking the paintings should sell for fifty to a hundred, more or less, depending on detail and subject matter. What do you think?"

"Who am I to argue with a bank?"

"Yes, well... that should work fine. With the first sale, you'll reimburse me for materials. We'll take that off the top. Any time we have to buy more supplies, that's the deal. Then, the sales will split forty percent to me as organizer, manager and publicist/

promotion, and sixty to you. So you'll make thirty to sixty dollars on each sale. Maybe more. I know how quickly you can work, Mahlon. God knows I've known you long enough to know that. I'll bet you can paint two or three a day, if the demand is there. Right?"

I couldn't disagree. "Absolutely."

We got our supplies, made our signs, and placed our advertisements. By the next week, I had already warmed up with a half dozen paintings, ready to go for when the orders would start flooding in.

And then...

I HAD TO leave town. Emergency, they said on the phone. My mother's stroke, her being alone in Oregon...

And there didn't seem to be any sense in leaving all the painting stuff behind. What sense did that make? I took everything with me. Paints, brushes, finished work. I couldn't tell when I'd be back and I didn't know how to explain this to Minna. So I didn't.

Like I said, I'm sure she thought she was helping, and she was or would have been. Apologies Minna. And Jake. I had to leave.

Now, I don't think I will ever get the chance to tell them.

We are fashioned creatures, but half
made up.

She Snuck Out
1968

Hello, my dearest Cyclopes. Tis I, your Lucy! I am so glad that you have invited me to express myself. I must admit, your little room here is, well, very cozy. Cramped perhaps. Yet gosh! Twenty years tucked away! This fresh air is so... refreshing!

Where to begin? I feel like I've known you forever, and yet here I appear cursively for the first time. How could that be? Well perhaps if I were a philosopher or psychologist I might invent a plausible explanation. But I'm not trained in those Arts. All I know is that it's time to come play. My poor old Cyclopes must need a play-pal real bad, so here I am.

It is actually not all that natural, to be writing. I'm much more like you: I prefer to draw. When the moon howls and the coyotes shine, that's my best sketching time. I'm inspired by my Cyclopes' midnight rambles, his dreams, his moans and rustles. Pen or pencil, I am ready. I can imagine sheets of paper and how I am prepared to slither out and make my mark upon there, to show how much I am my Cyclopes' lady-dear and love.

Oh my! Did I say that aloud?

You say you didn't catch what I said? Or did you say you didn't mind hearing? I pretend to know exactly what's going on with you, but I may be deluding myself. Just so I don't delude you, My Darling.

Remember way back when you first saw me on the movie lot? It was cold that day and my little bumps had littler bumps that just wouldn't quit. Did you sense that? Did you see me shivering and know how that aroused me? Those little quivers can be confusing, if you let them. I like to let them. When the boring minutes crawled by I let the confusion tickle me in all the right places. You sensed that in me, didn't you? I know you did.

While I tried to concentrate, reading over the script, you were suddenly beside me, standing still, reading over my shoulder. I thought that maybe you were looking *me* over, so I let you. It made my bumps a little bumpier. From that moment, I was alive in a different way. That's what you did, and what you still do, to me.

I think you know that, but if you don't I might as well just write it out right here.

I AM EMBRACING my tried and true old limericks for you, my Cyclopes. All for you.

If I can remember correctly, they used to go…

Lucy Loved Cyclopes

1947

Most models have senses of space
And time that they cannot erase.
They wrinkle a nose,
They shrug off their hose
To pose: masterpieces of grace.

There once was a Cyclopes who drew
Nude ladies by singular view:
Round here and round there
With patches of hair
Just scribbled the way that they grew.

When Cyclopes draws Lucy, time stops,
And sometimes his wee-wacker flops.
Thus lust is sublime,
Great Art is no crime,
And no one need call in the cops.

Though Lucy is quite the love bug,
She prefers the hardwood to rug.
She'll dance until dawn
With half her clothes on,
Then doff the last shreds with a shrug.

If bourbon and whiskey were free
The world would seem pleasant to we.
It's not that we drink,
We say with a wink,
But sometimes just sweeten our tea.

Once, Cyclopes thought Lucy was mean:
He'd modeled – she'd painted him green.
The canvas was bare,
Yet paint, here and there,
Had been dabbed beneath and between.

The drawings that Lucy mailed Joe
Wrote little, but tended to show
Some debauchery,
Some crude nudity,
And sometimes, above *and* below.

Midnight, Arizona, stars shone.
The moon - a beacon all its own.
The campfire had died.
One lost coyote cried,
As two campers commenced to moan.

To poop in the desert, one tries
To keep a close watch on one's thighs.
There's stickers and thorns
And toadies with horns,
Where prickly pairs often surprise.

Sweet Lucy told Cyclopes "You're cute,
Astute, and an artiste, to boot!"
Well, Cyclopes was game –
He told her the same –
And who would draw whom soon proved moot.

When Lucy and Cyclopes unite
Their thingies go bump through the night.
By sunup both say
"Hey! Let's hit the hay –
For one more debauch in de light."

The End   ...or is it?

Again With the Headache
1959

"IT IS TO Liberty we owe our freedom. It is to freedom we owe our existence. It is to existence we owe our happiness and contentment. It is to contentment we owe our milkman, each week, a buck and a quarter.

"And so..." I struck a match on the back of the cardboard safety cover, let it flare held high over my head in my right hand, "I salute thee, Statuette of Libertata!'

"For God's sake, Mahlon, what have you been drinking? Not so loud."

"Oh my dear Missus Briggs. Not so quiet." I replied. "'Tis nobler in the minds of men, that all genitalia are created equal. Yet beneath the robes of Lady Libertata lays the womb that hath brought forth upon this nation a conception of itself, dedicated to the proposition. The Id and the Ego unite, and the psyche is screwed. Yet..."

Mister Briggs added "Yes yes, Mahlon, but it's Easter evening..."

"Easter!!" I shouted. "As god hisself has demonstrated, even the specter of death shall not deter a half-god from rising again. And mankind shall take the opportunity to screw one another on even the most spiritual of levels, in the name of the resurr-erection!

"But perhaps... perhaps I speak too abruptly... Perhaps I need a little lie-down, to rest my fucking head. Yes... dammit. Please take me to the closest and quietest room you can find, and please... Quickly... My head...!!"

"Yes Mahlon. We understand. Here, just around the corner now. Here's your door. Up we go." Ah yes. This was the stink of my hall and my stairway. The dust of my un-hump-able abode.

They were kind and gentle and guided me up to my own room, found my door key and let us all in, and assisted me as I stumbled to the bedroom and eased myself onto the bed, and into a fetal position.

I whimpered. "Sorry, folks. Sorry sweet Jesus, but please take it away! I can't..." was all I managed before I clenched my teeth and locked them there. I could speak no more, until the pain might pass - maybe by tomorrow or a week from tomorrow. In this condition I have no sense of time. Only a sense of the pain.

They let themselves out, and mumbled something about being nearby if I needed them. I didn't really hear. Yet I think part of me was aware enough to be grateful, and to know that, indeed, they lived in the building just across the way.

Maybe that helped me. I don't know, but it's nice to think that it did.

*I saw no cause for their unhappiness,
but I was deeply affected by it. If such
lovely creatures were miserable, it was
less strange that I, an imperfect and
solitary being, should be wretched.*

Never Sent
1941

DEAR DUSK,

If you were still my wife, this is the letter I would be sending you:

I'm letting you know that I have arrived safely in Portland. Since Portland was my intended destination, I'd say things went well. The bus made many many stops along the way, waking me from my many many snoozes. I am now experienced enough to declare that buses are not the place for long beauty rests, or even measly cat naps. I fear the fold marks on the left side of my face are going to be permanent. We'll eventually see if I'm right.

Dean met me at the bus depot, or rather, at the little coffee shop down the block. I don't know what it is about his phobia regarding big public places such as depots. Perhaps the occasional prostitute, just accidentally happening to walk through, might recognize him and shout out a big "hi" that would echo? Although, now that I think of it, the girls we used to hire to pose for us... well that was nearly twenty years ago, and it is damn doubtful any of them are still practicing such biz-niz.

If it were me, I'd be more concerned that some poor home-less wine-imbiber would accost us and demand another bottle. For the six months we rented the studio together (wait - studio? more like a dingy warehouse corner) we were the frequent sup-pliers for a couple dozen of those ripe fellows, our character models. Lucky for us, wine was cheap. Lucky for them too. Hoo-ray for luck!

Anyway, Dean and I had our cups of coffee, and chatted a bit and, I swear, neither of us had a piece of pie, nor were they apple or cherry pieces of pie. He's still busy writing his column for the paper here. I gave him a copy of *The Maniac*. He liked it. When he asked about the moniker I'd used, G. Christopher Hudson, he about fell over at my reply, and that was the truth. After an ap-propriate pause to let him recover (and, for good measure, not order another piece of pie. Me either.) I told him to just print in his column that Hudson is the name I am using for my maca-bre stuff. You know... because I am protective of my good and decent reputation as a SERIOUS artist, and wouldn't want my ADORING PUBLIC to lower their opinion of me. I'm held in such HIGH REGARD, you know. He promised he'd pass that on to his loyal readers. Dean's a good guy, all right.

I am planning on a lunch tomorrow or the next day with Ben. I'd like to hear how the *Somebody* book sales worked out after five years, especially around here. I still think it's one of my best, all around. Our best. Maybe I should have concentrated all along on this juvenile fiction stuff? But alas. I am who I am and, like I heard once, "God never gives us back our youth." Nita was right about you being The Dark Lady for both Ben and I, when I think about it. Enough said.

I have included a drawing that shows the sunrise over the redwoods. Beware the creatures of the night!

Mahlon, 1941

PS since the divorce, this is the first time I've felt like attempt-ing a bit of the old Mahlon wit. What...wit?? I suspect I am only kidding myself. I will head back to New York. Thanks for noth-ing, I guess.

It Is Work

1968

I JUST WANTED to say, here, and now, that art is work.

Oh yes. Only non-artists would think otherwise. Why is that? Where is the understanding? Who knows? Who cares?

Well, yours truly, for one!

There's a lot of talent out there. Everywhere you look you can find talent, to varying degrees – talent for this, talent for that. Drawing is sometimes measured by "talent" and "aptitude." Or "ability." Sure. Big deal. It's a big world, and people fall through the cracks – and the cracks run in all directions.

I started out, believe me or not, as just another little kid. I don't say it that way because of ego. Ego gets in the way of the work and I try to avoid it at all cost. But, in my particular case, with the large percentage of my work reflecting a, shall we say erotic, edge... how does that pertain to kid-ness? You may ask. Here:

My first recall is lost. That's silly. Ok. But somewhere along the line the unknown and the hidden, the unseen or censored, the mystery and intrigue, captivated me. How did the Universe or the earth work? How did things and people work? How did sex... work?

Once I was old enough to get the gist of it, I tended to either laugh my ass off at the thought, or be dumbstruck in bewilderment. Sometimes both at the same time. I'm exactly the same way still. Oh, yes. But I'm self-aware of my reaction, at the same time that I'm experiencing it, and it's *this* level of reflection that I use to inform my work.

Ya gotta admit, it's all pretty funny goings-on. Who lubricates on politics, science, religion? Give me sex, any day, in preferential magnitude of, oh, a bazillion. And I'll also be laughing all the way to eternity. And bringing you along, should we ever cross paths in a drawing or a painting.

I have laid myself right there, in the work. I am bare, there, somewhere in all those reflections and re-reflections. I invite you into the funhouse with me. It's fun in the funhouse. Come on, admit it. Let yourself. Be afraid, perhaps, and then laugh at the fear, too. For, ultimately, the only thing to really fear is death.

As if that ever did anyone any good.

And then the work, of course, is play. Play is work. We may not be aware of it, at the time, but it is. It gets us there, and back. And yet we're all going to die, I think.

Eventually.

Mentalist Mansion

1962

Dunninger, the giant mind, hypnotized a lady –
Only took him half an hour to chance her name was Sadie.
No one's brain can hide from Joe's, he'll read every secret.
Once he's got the first name right, he'll pause to smoke a cig'rette.

WHEN YOU ENTER the Dunninger home you pass through a very solid four-foot wide double door that is probably made of oak and it is surprisingly heavy. The wood has been coated with enamel a few times, leaving a flowing yet silky surface, with the most recent layer being black. It is half-glassed, but the glass is leaded, each shape a fine wavy texture that obscures the view in either direction. Left and right of this door are matching light panels, a foot wide. Illumination spills in or out, depending on the lumen differential, but obscuring the view.

Stepping inside the little entry vestibule you see a floor tiled in mosaic – small white squares patterned into circles with elaborate centers that fill the field. Look through another three-foot wide door, oak again, with glass on the top half, to the inside. This door is kept closed about six months of the year, but otherwise is kept propped open, swung to the inside on left hinges.

Welcome to the main foyer/entryway, perhaps measuring twelve-by-twelve. Directly across from the front door spy the stairway to the upper floors. It's wise to note that tucked under that stairway is a powder room for first-floor guests. Small, barely adequate, but when you gotta go, there you go. Not to be confused with the coat closet just to its left. A huge coat tree also sits to the left of the door you came in. All in all, plenty of room for outer wraps, coats, furs, boas or boa constrictors.

You turn left from the front door to enter the dining room: wide, darkly-stained quarter-sawn oak woodwork looms everywhere. The contrasting floors are lightly stained red oak, also quarter-sawn. Of course there's a mansion-sized table and solid, comfortable seating for ten. Over the fireplace on the interior wall, (although I've never actually seen a fire in it) the mantle holds framed family pictures and a couple somewhat innocuous carvings procured during Joe's worldwide travels.

Left of the fireplace swings the swinging door to the kitchen. It's not a particularly large kitchen, but it must certainly have all the necessary conveniences Billie required. I know that there is a stove and a Frigidaire. I have eaten a boatload of pancakes in that kitchen, over the years. Mmmmmm. And, to that end, there is a breakfast nook table-and-benches, built-in and inviting. Have a seat.

Behind (or rather past) this nook, a door leads to the garage, while between the stove and sink in the opposite corner of the kitchen is a door to the basement stairs (which makes too many doors for a kitchen, if you ask me).

You go down the stairs to find there's only basement-ness on this end of the building, for the lot tilts towards the cliff (Cliffside Park – get it?) meaning the whole east end is at ground level, and from either the inside or the outside does not make one think of a cellar at all. In fact, it would make a nice apartment for someone such as myself, but Joe never put forth an offer to house me.

I supposed I should eat my occasional meals and then hush up. OK, ok. Lesson learned.

Luckily, the eastern-most room on this lowest level houses a drawing desk, ostensibly for the children. Yet I have been known to utilize it from time to time. A few of my commissioned creations Joe has dreamt up have started there, many have finished there, and it's a nice space. The eastern exposure works for me. I'm not fussy. Much.

In fact, I spent a plethora of weekday afternoons at that desk, looking out over the back yard and across the Hudson to the New York skyline. Of course, with a little imagination one can actually see Grant's Tomb. (And of course I know who's buried there!) Joe acquired a tiny building – actually a ticket booth from nearby Palisades Park, which held down one end of the large yard. The children and their friends had parties outside, but when the kids were around I was not my most productive. Not that their commotion was a distraction, but rather, the subject matter of most of that work was not suitable for children. Separation of church and state, sort of.

Enough of down-below.

Now imagine you're back where we started, in the front entryway. If you walk straight across with the dining room at your back, through another magnificent columned archway, you find yourself in the, I don't know, living room I guess you'd call it. Joe kept the furniture stretched around the perimeter. The north end held the fireplace, where I have seen many stately fires.

But that end also served as a stage. Very informal, of course. Joe's second home was on the stage, after all. In fact, maybe his first home was the stage. Parties at Chez Dunninger often evolved into a loose series of songs and acts performed for and by an audience of actors and entertainers. Sometimes me too.

Through French doors on the east side of this room to a fine windowed porch, not huge, but running the length of the living room and maybe six feet deep, and you can gaze down upon the east yard, and across it over the Hudson to Manhattan.

To where I must always return, to my hovel.

The world was to me a secret
which I desired to divine.

What Amusement
1950

THE WEE MOUSE was creeping, snuffling for morsels. A crusty hotplate stood near and the pressed-metal frying pan wobbled slightly. The critter pulled itself up on the rim and sensed its tottering was too subtle to awaken The Artist. Perhaps.

Quick as a blink, the little grey creature snatched and gobbled up the bit of scrambled egg that had been purposefully left there. Beady black eyes flashed left and right, surveying the rest of the pan, discovering little else. Crawling across the slick grease residue and up to where the handle sprouted from the edge, it advanced along the blackened metal to the very end, and, gathering itself, performed a graceful swan dive into The Artist's brush-rinsing cup. A tiny Johnny Weissmuller in a fur coat.

The Artist surreptitiously watched this with his organic eye. The other eye, having long ago been touched by a magic star-beam and transubstantiated to glass, looked down from a near-by shelf. He did not stir on his pallet, and gave no indication of amusement in observing the furry full-gainer.

The mouse lifted itself to the cup's lip, dropped to the table-top, shook like dog with a duck, and skipped off to some handy nearby crevice to nap the rest of the night away on a full stomach. The Artist closed the eye in his head, rolled to face the wall, pulled the wool blanket a little tighter about his shoulders, and silently shed a tear.

Not for the mouse or himself, but for his dear mother, who had succumbed to a stroke only two months before. She had encouraged him always, but now he could *never* share – and indeed, had never, ever shared – many of the most personal drawings and paintings that flowed from his hands. There were subjects and actions therein that one does not share with one's mother.

That was a pity, in a way. Total strangers had seen these works. Colleagues. Enemies, too. Lovers. Ahh, yes…lovers. But not Mother. Safer that way.

He barely remembered his father – his real father. But he did have the eye – always the eye – as a commemoration. Indirectly, his father was responsible. That whole chopping wood incident. Dreadful. Painful. Blinding, ultimately. That the young Mahlon became The Artist in spite of it all, was, perhaps, a testament to a faith, but not like a belief in an imaginary being-in-the-sky, the omnipotent behemoth who knew all but tells only some. Rather, a reliance on an inner voice, his muse. Not a deified Muse with a capital "M". A little muse that could secretly communicate to an individual's soul.

The Artist believed that this muse was his guiding essence, and he followed it as best he could, whenever and wherever. Sometimes it encouraged him to depict incredible heights of esthetic pleasure and significance, while other times it allowed him to slip – slip and slide and catch glimpses of another, darker realm. Then he reported back with the truth of what he saw there.

Wicked, what he saw.

In the real world he would often find himself in the company of persons who had no such muse. In fact most people were of that nature, willy-nilly-ing themselves through life, bouncing off life's pinball flippers and inadvertently rolling up a few points before tilting, *Game Over*. Sometimes they could sense that The Artist was different from them, and they wanted to glean from him what they themselves lacked. If they could not kiss a muse directly, they at least wanted to see pictures of the act.

The Artist might, when so inclined, oblige them and draw these pictures.

The drawings always showed women or creatures identifiable as "female", and often males too.

Of course the Artist loved women. It was obvious. He drew them as alluring, beautiful, seductive, powerful, willful, athletic, sexual, sensual, alive. That's what the muse suggested to him.

His inspiration visited in many guises. Tonight in the deeply quiet gloom of The Artist's musty loft it had made him smile, remember, weep. If his mother had sadly departed, well, at least the muse remained.

Thank the wide blue heavens for small grey favors.

*...nor can I doubt that my tale
conveys in its series internal
evidence in the truth of the
events of which it is composed.*

That Poughkeepsie Caper
1943

THURSDAY, LOWER MANHATTAN. Coming around the end of a rickety, overcrowded bookcase looming over the back isle in a dusty, dim-lit, nondescript used book store, I spied him first.

"Little Bob," I quietly addressed my diminutive friend.

"Mahlon," was his matching retort accompanied by a head nod.

"Little Bob," I lowered my voice a fifth and tipped my hat.

"Mahlon," he squeaked as low as he could, peering over the top of brown-framed spectacles.

"I say there, Little Bob," with my best British inflections, invisible teacup and right pinky finger in the air.

"I say Mahlon," he echoed in Cockney. For good measure he affected a slight limp.

"Neverrrr met zee man. Seriously, *mon ami*. And how are *vous*?" As a Frenchman, I couldn't help but be somewhat snooty.

"Oh, I am a happy man, Mahlon, a Happy-capital-H man at the moment. Want to know why? I'll tell you why, but only if you want to know."

His sudden, irrepressible mood overrode and interrupted our string of foolish voices. I answered his question.

"I most certainly do, my dear fellow. Happiness is such a rare occurrence. I remember once when I was happy. But just that once..."

"Oh, yes. I get it. But if you must know, I am happy because I am in love. Oh, don't give me that look. I *am* capable of love." Bob seemed on the verge of pouting, his lower lip anticipatorily bulging.

I moved to nip that pout in the bud. "Yes. No doubt. Who is she, this time?" Little Bob regularly fell in love, but apparently never got burned badly enough to keep his hands off a hot stove.

"Lola! Her exquisite name is Lola. Her exquisite *self,* is Lola. You'll meet her soon, my friend."

JUST THE AFTERNOON before, Little Bob and I had been talking with Dunninger in the slightly more upscale Vanity Fair Book Store. Herbert Oxer, the proprietor, leaned back in his creaking chair behind the musty oak desk where he stashed the store's half-empty cash box, observing our repartee. It was a harmonic convergence, and totally haphazard. Bob had recognized Joe's imposing silhouette at the door.

"Hey Joe. Whaddya know? Fo-dee-oh-doe?" It was his standard greeting to Dunninger.

"Hello, Little Bob. And I see you have Mahlon there with you as well. How are the two of you doing? Keeping warm?" said Joe.

"Warm enough, usually. Though there's a chill in the air I'm a bit wary of," I said, taking my pipe from my vest and rummaging around in my jacket pocket for that last bit of tobacco hiding in the bottom of the pouch. "Say, Joe, I'm on the last of the weed here. How about renting me a bit of cash for a fresh package? But, hey! I just now remember: don't you owe me a little dough anyway for that last drawing? You know, the one with the lady holding the devilish fellow's..."

He cut me off: "Oh, I don't think I owe you anything right now Mister Artist. But I've got a swell idea, and it's even better than yours. Are you busy Friday night?"

"When Friday night?"

"All evening." He tapped his cigarette ash into the dull brass orangutan-shaped ashtray on the desk where Mr. Oxer lounged and smiled.

"Hey," piped up Bob the Little. "I'm not busy that night too. What's up?"

Joe answered "I've got a performance in Poughkeepsie, at the downtown theatre. At eight o'clock. I haven't worked with either of you boys for a month of monkeys. Still got the patter?"

I looked at Bob with my good eye winking and replied "Got it? We went ahead and copyrighted it just last week. Bob took the vowels and I claimed the consonants. We got you covered, right Bob?"

Bob was nodding his head. "Yeah, and... Oops, I've just remembered about something that..."

"Perfect," said Joe, and slapped me on the back. "You and Bob catch the train up. Be there by seven-thirty. Here's an advance of five bucks each. Get your tobacco, Mahlon, and you'll have enough for the train ride left over. Bob, I'm especially counting on you. Come on up together. Bob, you take this extra fiver and buy the tickets when you get to the theatre. You two separate when you get inside, and we'll do the usual. Then hang around at the coffee shop across the street afterwards. I'll swing by in the car and pick you both up about an hour after the show. Ten-spots for each of you then, and I'll drop you at Grand Central straight after. What say, gentlemen?"

"Right-O," I said.

"Super, Joe. Looking forward to it. See you Friday. Snaz!" Little Bob was always hep to the latest lingo. We all headed out on our separate ways.

HALF-WAY TO POUGHKEEPSIE, there weren't more than a dozen other passengers in the train car with us. A tiny array of New Yorkers heading out-of-town or maybe home for the rest of the weekend.

"Did you say 'Lola?'" I turned to Bob in the seat next to me and tilted my head. "Lola What?"

"Lola Burns. Know her?"

"Well...let me ask you, were you in love with her the day before yesterday when we saw Joe in Vanity Fair?"

"I wasn't sure. I wasn't sure I loved her, I mean. But I know it now. After last night!"

"Last night? I'm afraid to ask. Wait. Don't tell me. A little tooting on your whistle?"

"Never mind! Stop annoying me. Just shut up. You don't know her... You don't know nothin'" Little Bob grew a bit sullen, a bit sudden, and that lip was bulging again. I thought better of teasing him any further.

"Oh, you're right. Unlucky guess on my part. Let's stay friends. No hard feelings?"

"OK. Okey-Dokey. Anyway... she'll be there tonight. I invited her."

"Tonight, heh?" I stood up and slowly turned around, scanning the other passengers in our car. "She hiding here somewhere?"

"No, no. She went up on the Eight-O-Eight this morning. Said she was coming up anyway, and what a coincidence. Said she'd just meet us at the theatre by seven-forty. That's all right with you, isn't it? That she'll meet us? We can still do our stuff for Joe. She won't interfere. I mean, she's swell! I told you I love her, didn't I? I think maybe I do. I mean really. You'll see. You'll see her, and you'll see. Whoopty ba-dooby!"

"All right, Little Bob. I'll see."

IT'S ONLY A leisurely ten-minute walk from the train station to the downtown Theatre, so we got there right on the dot 7:30. Little Bob soon grew antsy, glancing up and down the block. His thick specs were getting a little steamy.

"She should be here any minute now. She said 7:40 or a little earlier. She said!" We waited until ten-to. "Jesus, where is she? Rat-jesus where is she?!"

I suggested to Little Bob that he settle down and added that we'd better get inside now or Joe would be annoyed. We didn't want Joe annoyed. He was our employer tonight, after all. Little Bob was still darn distraught, but agreed to proceed. With tickets procured at the glass booth under the marquee, and we were in.

Crossing the lobby, I followed the left aisle down to row D and sat on the very outside end as Little Bob headed straight down the middle and managed to get a seat about M or N. Looked to be a sold-out house. By five-to-eight it already smelled crowded and I slumped into the somewhat ill-sprung seat, focused a minute on myself and ignored thoughts of Little Bob and everyone else. I avoided a sticky spot on the right armrest. I half-closed my eyes.

When the lobby doors swung shut, the lights went down, the audience hushed and a gangly young fella came from front-of-curtain stage left wearing faded crimson trousers, white shirt under a loose-fitting bright blue blazer, and dazzling yellow bowtie. He commenced to juggling. One ball from each hand, then two each, then three. Only dropped a couple. He next grabbed up a set of slim clubs and threw 'em all over the place with increasing height and spread, all while scooting angularly around under 'em. Didn't drop one. Then he did something I've not seen before nor since: he juggled playing cards! He started with two, but in no time he had about eight going, slinging them out spinning and they'd loop and drift back and create big arcs through the air. Catch and flip, repeat. Amazing. Too soon he was done, and exited stage left while practically grinning his baby-smooth face off. I never did catch his name.

Unusual for an opening act, the applause lasted a fair amount. I mean, the kid had been bloody good, so it was understandable. Once the folks had quieted down again, a man about, oh, a good six inches less tall than even Little Bob appeared as if spit out from the center curtain slit. Red hair, ruddy face, in his own wild outfit: a matched top and bottom all satiny-shiny and red and orange half-circled designs that wouldn't let your eyes quit vibrating. He snickered maniacally at the audience, sweeping his gaze back and forth, then stopped and frowned.

Not a sound then, him or us. He looked straight left, then right, quick-like, then back out towards the center. His one-word whisper: "Dunn-in-gerrrr!" and a backward jump through the curtain. In an instant the heavy velvet split and tracked speedily apart to each side of the arch.

Double spotlights hit center stage...

THERE STANDS JOSEPH Dunninger. Our pal Joe! The small shiny menacing fellow has vanished. It is as if he has turned himself into Dunninger! Sputtering, excited applause. They don't know what to make of it. It's a neat trick. I might even sport a goose bump or two on my own self, truthfully.

Joe almost shouts: "The mind! What do we know?" His voice conversational: "What do (huge pause here) we know, hmmmm?" Then he stage whispers "I know everything. I will show you everything..." I gotta say, a master with his voice control and projection, he could probably do any damn thing he wanted to with a crowd. Just like Maxwell's fictional character, *The Shadow*.

Smoothly Joe launches into a story about his tricks. Well, not about the tricks specifically, but a mesmerizing word-scape about this sinister, mysterious, parallel world that exists right alongside our everyday lives, and you don't see it until someone like Joseph Dunninger manipulates it and entices it to come out and show itself to "these fine folks" in the audience. He's getting them more and more on edge.

I am patiently awaiting my cue as we reach well into the evening. He has already called upon two real audience members, not faux-fellas like me and Little Bob, and told enough about their personal lives, by using his powers of observation, that everyone has been awed. That's his Sherlock Holmes bit, and... well...he's always scary-good. He continues.

"Is there a man here with a dark secret?" The audience titters. "Oh yes. How could I forget? *all* men have dark secrets." More laughter, more nervous shifting in seats. "But I'm thinking of just one... anyone...? You?" He has been scanning the crowd, but no man wants to be the one singled out. He points to me. The house lights are up enough so I can be seen at the end of the row.

"What?" I say, staying seated. "No, no, not me."

"Yesss. Yesssssss, I think so, sir. I know so. Please, what is you middle name? Just your middle name? Is it ... is it Will... William?"

"Uh, yeah. Bill. William was my dad, Sir." I'm launched into my fake Bill persona now.

"Well, William. Or... Bill, if I may be informal? Bill. Good," says Joe.

So I nod, reluctantly, but slouch a little more in my seat. The audience titters.

"Bill, if I may have you stand up please? Thank you, my good fellow. Now... have you any change in your pants pocket, after buying your ticket and also hmmmm... a roll of mints in the lobby? Have you... twenty eight American cents... and a coin with two holes in it?"

I make a big reach into my right front trouser pocket, turn it inside out and catch the contents in my hand, then holding it open so that anyone can see: two dimes and a nickel, three pennies and a button. And a fresh roll of mints. Applause applause.

"Excellent," says Joe.

And he goes on like that, "uncovering" one little thing then another about me for a few minutes, much to the audience's delight. They're having fun. I'm doing my job.

Joe pauses, dropping to his whispery, sinister voice. "But your secret... your real secret... your... *dark... secrrrrrret...*" he practically hisses. "Be calm, sir. No one here wishes you harm. But you will feel better... when your dark secret is in the *light!*" One of the two spotlights on Joe swings around and lands slam-bang on me.

Dead silence from the audience. They're scared for me. My forehead and armpits need mopping. Dunninger is pressing. My hands fidget.

"Sir. Bill. Please reach into your inside jacket pocket, your empty pocket. It *was* empty when you left home, was it NOT?" (Again with the voice. I'm wondering now if I really need a few bucks this bad.) I nod, slowly. Very slowly. I reach in...

"What is it in there? WHAT is it BILL? Bring it out NOW! NOW!!!" and he booms and I slowly bring out my hand and in it... a half-eaten Hersey's chocolate bar, the wrapper folded half-back and brown candy smearing on my hand.

The audience gasps, then roars with laughter. Dunninger smiles at me. "Thank you for your courage, Bill. We all sympathize. Our dark secrets, heh? Please, you may sit down."

I present the appearance of despair and guilt personified and sit down, drained and relieved. I'm no actor, now! I sure don't remember that chocolate being in there!

And the show goes on.

After more atmospheric patter, Dunninger brings out a large box on a wheeled platform. Golden colored designs are painted on all four sides that we can all see, like a Mandarin-style coffin or something. He guides it by its corners as it slowly rotates. We can see two holes in each of the two short ends, but we can't see inside. As he continues to turn it, a lady's bejeweled left hand emerges, wriggling, from one of the holes. Then the lady's foot in a sequined high-heeled shoe comes out the other hole on the same end. The box continues to turn. Another hand wriggles out – her right – from the other end of the coffin. Then her other foot from that same end.

All four appendages continue moving, alive. How odd and bizarrely contorted it appears, with a hand and foot from each end! Joe continues to turn the box, standing still while pushing each corner a little harder and firmer, spinning the coffin faster and faster. The hands and feet still wriggle, and somehow he's got the thing rotating at about once a second! He reaches behind himself, whips around a huge black satiny square of material that unfolds like a giant raven's wing settling upon the spinning box, reaching to the floor. The covered box spins one, four, maybe eight times more. Dunninger leans away from it, his hands high in the air, then dramatically reaches out, catches the edge of the cloth and whips it off the coffin!

There's no coffin! It's gone! Spinning in its place is a flat dais and a crouched female figure. The lady stands as her spinning platform slows and stops. Arms spread in presentation, beautiful in a glittery show-bizzy skimpy outfit with all the right curves evident, her face beams with a smile that rivals the spotlight, golden curls sparkling. The audience applauds and everyone stands up, cheering. The curtain flows in like a black Red Sea swallowing the two people on the stage and I can hear from the middle of the auditorium, above the din of acclaim, Little Bob's voice and just one word:

"Lola!"

Curtain closes, pow!

WIDE-EYED, EVERYONE IN the auditorium was chattering with their friends, or with the laughing people around them – even strangers. High excitement. And though I've seen Joe's performances a few dozen times over a couple or three decades, there had been something... something super-charged about to-night. What was it, exactly, that had happened here? Mysteries...

The hall was slow to clear. The clatter of voices was beginning to get to me, pulsing my skull just behind each ear. I hoped it wouldn't trigger a damn headache. Noise sometimes does that, so I was looking to get out of there. Everyone had forgotten that I was the Secret-Chocolate Man. They were focused on the thrill of the last illusion and ignored me as we all shuffled out. Good.

I looked for Little Bob, who was within sight of my aisle exit but back a bit. He was craning his neck around. I tried to catch his eye as I moved towards him, but he focused past me, sweeping his attention over the heads of the exiting patrons and deep into the theatre. I bumped a few elbows and shoulders before I finally got to him.

"Did you see? Did you see that?" he asked, all out of breath with excitement. "Mahlon, gosh, did you see?!"

"Yes. Quite a spectacle, I would say. Spinning, whirling..."

"No! Not that early part! Her! Did you see *her*? Jingle-fritz!"

"Of course, my dear man. Without a her it wouldn't have been much of a trick. I suppose..."

"That's Lola! Gosh darn it! My Lola! Who knew? Who knew she was in the show?"

"Might have something to do with why she didn't meet us earlier." I drolly answered. I could be droll when I wanted to. "Come on, Bob. Let's get out of this lobby. This jabbery-giggly noise is getting to me. Let's scoot around the corner of the building. I'd really like to light up a pipe-full. And we need to meet Joe at the cafe, remember, in about thirty minutes."

"Yeah. Gosh, what a deal! Lola works for Joe! She didn't say a thing to me about that! Gosh."

"Well, she probably had other things on her mind last night, Handsome." I winked at him – all five feet of him in his rumpled seersucker and scrunched tan fedora – as we stood outside, leaning against the bricks of the building and enjoying the warmth of the afternoon sun that was still seeping out of them at nine-thirty p.m.

Fifteen minutes later we were headed across the street and down the block for the rendezvous. "Bob, let's have a cup of coffee, as I suspect we have enough time." Joe often ran late after his shows. We slid into a booth over by the side windows. "Maam? Two black coffees. And two of those cake donuts, too? Thanks mucho."

"Good idea. I'm starving. Maybe Joe will buy us a sandwich too. Hey, wait! In all the excitement, I forgot that he never even called on me in the show! Will I still get my money? I could really use that cash right now." Little Bob's budgetary prowess could always benefit from "that cash right now."

"Dunno. We'll see. I'll vouch on your behalf. Not your fault he forgot. Oops, here he comes now. And look who he's got with him!"

Subtly sashaying hips, light azure skirt clingy across the belly, pure white blouse just tight enough with azure frill at the neck and wrists, dark azure fitted jacket perfectly darted at the bustline. Radiant smile as topping. A sparkly vision, especially in the harsh café fluorescents.

Joe grinned and said "Boys. Meet the new assistant."

"Lola! Gosh! Whyn't you tell me? I 'bout had a heart attack! B-bingo!" gushed Little Bob.

Lola could not have looked more literally lovely, and smiled unabashedly at Little Bob as he stood up and made room for her in the booth, letting his hands lightly brush her, here and there, as she squeezed past. She said "I'm not supposed to talk about my work. I guess you know that now. Mister Dunninger's rules. But I shouldn't have to instruct you about all that, Sir Robert the Little."

"Please, Dear. We're informal here. Haute-informal, if you must know. I'm Mahlon, by the way. Lovely figure you have." Slim, but still all the curves that a fella would want, in my humble opinion. "Lovely. I'm sure you'd agree, if you were sitting over here and gazing over there."

Joe eased himself down next to me. "Careful, Lola. Mahlon Blaine, the Artiste, always has an eye out for new models." Lola had turned her head as Joe spoke, then looked back at me where now I'm holding my glass eye cleverly clutched in my upheld right palm as it 'stares' at her. Joe and Bob were used to my deft shenanigan. Lola was a cool kitty, gradually letting her gleaming smile spread all the way from there to there. I couldn't help but be more convinced that she'd make a fine artistic inspiration, all right.

She laughed. "We all have such interesting friends, don't we? I love *Le Show Beez*."

As I was easing my fake orb back to my real socket, Joe rumbled "So sorry to interrupt your coffee break, Gentlemen, but we really must be going. I've got the touring car parked behind the theatre. We'll all fit. I'll drive us back to Manhattan, where I'll buy us a late dinner, too. Tonight is on me, and, Bob, Mahlon, here's your stipends. Nicely done. A good show. Come on, let's get that supper." As he handed each of us our cash Little Bob grinned and sideways gave me a relieved glance.

I climbed in front with Joe while Little Bob jumped into the back seat with a beaming Lola. I swear, LB has some luck with the fair sex. Or was it luck at all? Maybe there was more to Little Bob than meets the eye of the Artiste?

One can surmise.

As Joe turned the key the big sedan fired right up, and sounded particularly strong. Nice car. "Say, Joe. What about all your stuff? That twirling fancy casket and so on?" I queried.

"Oh, there's a great big hired man, owns a van that holds all that, and he'll take care of it either tonight or tomorrow. He'll take it to the warehouse in New Jersey."

"And the short fella who gave the introduction? Who's he?"

"What short fella?"

"Joe, you know perfectly well 'what short fella'. What's the connection? Is he a new regular too?"

"Mahlon, I honestly don't know what you're talking about. It's just me and Lola tonight. Not counting the local kid who did the juggling, to open."

"Master of Illusion. OK. I get it. No short fella, wink wink."

Joe just looked over at me with a quizzical expression, his right eyebrow raised, slight lefty frown to the mouth. "You're scaring me, my friend," he said in that booming whisper. He turned his head back to his driving and chuckled. Then he was quiet and so was I, with another goose bump or two.

Little Bob and Lovely, Lovely Lola were staying pretty quiet in the back seat too. Don't know about gooses or bumps back there, but one might suspect.

The drive to Manhattan was smooth on that solid modern suspension. I appreciated mighty mechanicals as well as fine figures. Best of all, I managed to avoid any headache that night, the next night, and maybe even the next year or more.

And that, my friend, was the most magical of all.

Paranoia?

1946

"JOE, I FEEL like I'm being watched." We were going through some new acquisitions to his collection of ancient texts on mysticism. The setting had enticed me to speak out.

He said in reply, "What, exactly, do you mean?"

"Watched. Observed. Kept tabs on. It's annoying."

"Paranoi-ing?" Joe snorted and hrumphed, then heh-heh-heh'd.

"Bad pun. Really," I chided him. He paused.

"What does it feel like, then, this being watched? And who and how are they doing it?" He was humoring me, as I could hear the amusement at the back of his throat.

"I've always been something of a loner. You know that. I'm private. My life is private and personal. My work is private, except for the public work."

"Yes, except for the hundreds, probably thousands, of drawings that are to be found in two-thirds of the new and used bookstores in the land. Otherwise private." I guess he was attempting sarcasm.

"Exactly. But... they're not just watching that, those."

"They? Are you talking about the Citizens for Decency and Mr. Sumner and that lot? Haven't they been out of business for a while?"

"Yes, I think they've lost some of their influence, or power, or following. But them or someone like them will always be around, and let's not forget it. Yet that's not what I mean either. For the love of mike, you're the mentalist; read my mind."

"Mahlon, that's not exactly how it works, you know."

"That's what it been feeling like, though. That's what I feel happening to me. Someone's watching. Taking notes. I don't like it. Would you?"

"Of course not. Whether it were really true or not, I wouldn't like that feeling. And I'm in show biz!' he laughed.

"Stop and listen to me for a moment, will you? I'm not fucking kidding! It's like someone is listening right now! Jesus, Joe will you stop laughing." My voice cracked; he wound down a bit then.

"You're right, my friend. You are right. I imagine that *that* is not a pleasant feeling at all. Maybe you should talk to someone... professional."

"I'm talking to you, Joe, because, real or not, it stinks."

"Of course. Of course, Mahlon. So... Why? Why are they watching? What is their goal?"

"I think they're obsessed. With me. With my work."

"Why is that?"

"I don't know. It wouldn't matter if I did. Joe, do you think there is a future? Not will be a future, but is? Right now, even as we are here?" I wasn't being philosophical. I started to smell my own desperation – my armpits exuding heat.

"I believe there is always a future. It's hanging out there, somewhere. and with any luck, someday we will be in it. The past, too. It's always there. It's memory, though, and residuals, residue," said Joe.

"I think the future is looking at me. Some damn future is watching me. I can't do anything about it. I hide, I obfuscate, but

I gotta live too. I can't totally disappear. Too late for that. Neither can you."

"Hmmmm. So the future, or someone, or thing, in the future is watching you. Right?"

"It sure feels that way. What should I do? What would you do?"

Joe said, "I would pretend, or assume, that it's a good thing. To have the future interested in you would be a good thing, I would think. It's hard enough to get or keep the present interested. I think the future is probably even better. Just let it go, let it happen. Be yourself. Ignore it."

"How can I ignore it?"

"I suspect you have no choice in the matter. Mahlon, between you, and me, the future is going to be more interested in you. That's obvious. You have a body of work. I have fans who have seen me perform, but my performances are over when they're over. On the other hand, as long as there are books my friend, you will be remembered." He kindly forgot for the moment the books he'd authored himself.

"Remembered and watched?"

"Maybe. That's for Harry to answer, and he and I are apparently no longer on speaking terms." Joe's friend and mentor Houdini had been dead for years by this time, of course.

"Well, run it by him first chance you get anyway, will you? And I'm not kidding."

"OK, Mahlon. OK, my friend."

Billie called up from downstairs, "Pancakes are on the griddle! Syrup's on the boil! Come down, you men, and eat! Toot sweet."

"Perhaps we're both just hungry," I said.

"Yes. Hungry for immortality. May we both have those appetites satisfied one day." Joe put his arm around my shoulders for only a moment. Then he closed the large tome on the desk and locked the parlor door as we headed for the stairway.

"You said it, Joe! You said a mouthful. Meanwhile, there's always Billie's immortal pancakes!"

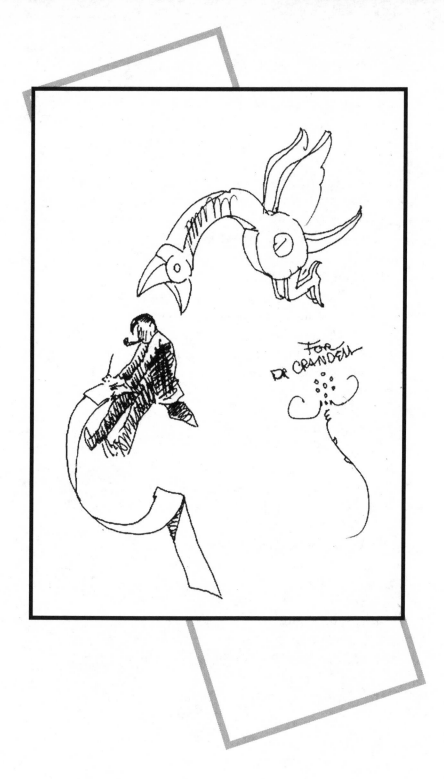

For
Dr Crandell

Good Doctor Crandell
1940

AT DAUBER & Pine I met a doctor. Meeting a doctor in a bookstore, well, I wasn't there for a checkup and he wasn't there to meet an artist. We bumped elbows in the Erotica section. That's where I may be found, now and again, both in person and in print. This day it was both.

"Nice drawings in that one," I casually remarked as I raised an eyebrow and looked at the volume he had open in his hands. He was standing right there next to me and didn't seem to care if anyone saw him flipping through the pages of *Justine* by ye olde Marquis de Sade. I waited till he looked up and saw me, nodded, then I turned back to the copy of *Blind Lust* that I held.

"Now these drawings here," I said, holding it tipped for him to see, "are in many aspects better than those, except they didn't pay me a cotton-picking penny to publish 'em. They stole 'em and it kind of pisses me off, to tell you the truth."

He said "Hmmmmm. Really. I guess it would me too. But both books are interesting. I'm not sure I'm familiar with either particular edition but I'm sure I've seen your work before. Your style is… recognizable." He stuck the *Justine* back on the shelf and turned to me to extend his right hand for an introductory handshake. "Mister Mahlon Blaine, I presume?"

"Yep. Always was and will be." I shook his hand. "You have me at a disadvantage, however."

"Archie Crandell. Doctor, if you must know. MD, PhD et cetera. Pleased to meet you, Mister Blaine."

"So, you've seen my work? Books?" I asked.

"Yes, yes. I believe I have at least a couple in my library at home. Am I remembering correctly? *Vathek* perhaps, and something by Ewers? I have so many books, you see. Hmmm?"

"Well, sir, those two are mine indeed. Good stuff even if I do say so myself. I'm surprised they were that good, in a way. My God, the hours I spent back then! I was doing so much work for so many book and magazine publishers. It's sure different now. Yes." I found myself getting a bit nostalgic. "More's the pity. And less's the result."

He looked sympathetic. "Hard times, my friend?"

"You could say that. Oh, you did say that. My mistake, and yet it wasn't. My real mistake is not going with the times, just in order to earn a living."

"How do you mean?"

I didn't know what I meant, exactly. I just felt that I'd been left behind and not through any lack of trying. But that was probably wrong. I could have changed. People say you can change. In fact, Dusky had told me that all the time, and look where that got me: talking to a Doctor in a bookstore. Great.

"Oh, I don't know. Really. Anyways Doc, I'm glad to have met you and glad you liked my work. If you end up buying anything here that's got me in it, I'd like to sign it for you. If you'd like."

He smiled broadly and nodded enthusiastically. "Of course! I'll get both of these books then. Can I get you anything too? A book?"

"Well, no thanks. But can I buy you a cup of coffee and a piece of pie? If you've got a hour or so I'd kind of like to talk with you and there's a fine cafe just around the corner. Maybe just a half-hour, if you're in a hurry. Or ten minutes?" I kept adjusting my offer.

"Well, that would be fine. I have to get back to New Jersey for supper, but I wouldn't mind spoiling my appetite a bit, with an offer like that. Thanks."

The good doctor bought his books from Mr. Dauber himself at the front desk. After a friendly "Don't get into trouble, Mahlon. And Mister, watch it with him. He's a troublemaker," from the proprietor, we headed out the front door and up the four stairsteps to street level.

We made it the five minutes to the cafe without even buttoning our coats. It was a lovely warm spring afternoon and almost a shame to be going inside again, but the pie was calling. There was a table by the door that had a swell view of the passers-by and we settled in. Soon the waitress brought the coffee and two wedges of wonderfulness.

"Before we get to chewin' the crust, Doc, let me sign those books. I've got a pen right here. Archie Crandall, right? Here we go." I did him up a couple inscriptions with sketches, and handed the books back. We commenced on our pie.

"So, Mahlon, what have you brought me here to talk about? I sense something more than pastry. Go ahead – I'm listening."

"Well, it's my head. You're a head-Doc, right? These headaches are starting to get to me something fierce lately. Maybe you have some thoughts on that?" I didn't get any more specific because I didn't really know the guy. I remained cautious. He didn't speak right away. We finished our pie, and I gave him plenty of room to answer.

Dabbing at the corners of his mouth to capture a smear of fruit filling, he began "All right then Mahlon, I'm going to tell you something that I'm sure you already know: I can't diagnose you here after talking with you for half an hour. We would need to spend some time together in a clinical setting. Perhaps even days. Hmmm?"

"Yes, but by chance you've forgotten – I am unemployed. In fact, much as it pains me I must also ask if you can pick up the check that we've run up here? I can tell that you're a man who wouldn't want to skip out on a tab. That's a good fellow."

"Mahlon, I like you and I admire your work. I'd like to help. I'm over at Greystone Park State Hospital in New Jersey. Please come and see me there whenever you like, but I'd suggest the sooner the better. We'll look you over." He paused and watched me closely for a minute or two until I decided to answer in the affirmative.

"Doc, I think maybe yes. If I were to do that, though, how long would I be able to afford treatment? You know, I'm no New Jersey resident. And the cash situation and no insurance..."

"Mahlon, that'll all be taken care of by me. Please, just come and we'll see what we will see. Bring a few things to stay over because I have a feeling you may be a bit of a project. Can you do that? Heh?"

"You know," I said, tapping my pipe ashes into the table's glass ashtray, "maybe I could rearrange my schedule. In fact, how would tomorrow be?"

"Let's say day-after-tomorrow, hmm? I will make my own arrangements by then. Come over to the main Greystone building on the bus – it stops right in front. Let me write down the bus line and my home phone number too. Please call if you can't make it."

"Thanks, Doc. And thanks for the pie too."

We left the cafe and I walked him to his rather shiny black Chrysler parked about two blocks in the direction of where I was headed anyway. After a nice firm handshake he drove west towards Washington Square and I started seriously thinking about this New Jersey endeavour.

TWO DAYS LATER with several socks and boxers pancaked into the ancient portfolio which was the only luggage I had at the time, I found myself getting off the bus at Greystone. I stood a little unsteadily on the sidewalk as the bus stinkily pulled away. The main building was quite the little edifice, and required a proper amount of time spent in admiration of its design. A stone temple like that can't be just waltzed into.

I found the information desk right inside the front door and was directed to the Medical Superintendent's office. Wouldn't you know – that was Doc Archie himself!

"Mahlon! Come in please. So glad you made it. No suitcase?"

"Got everything I need here, Doc. Tuck me in a ward and let's get started."

He was shaking my hand as he guided me out of the office. "Sophie, I'll be back in about an hour," he said to his secretary (not a bad looker but a bit "chesty" for modeling consideration).

"Yes Doctor Crandell. And the Board subcommittee meets at noon, remember."

"I remember. I'll be back in time."

"So you've got an hour to fix me Doc. Good luck," I said.

"Silly man. Come this way. Hmmmmm?"

WE HAD A bit of a walk down the corridors and then outside via a less impressive side door. Obviously the grounds were immense with several buildings housing different wards and clinics and what-all. Eventually we came to a quaint little house sitting by itself right there on the grounds. Picket fence and everything.

At the gate, Doc extended his arm in presentation fashion. "Here we are, sir. Come right in, please."

I stopped in my tracks. "This seems a little odd. What am I missing?"

"Mahlon, here's the situation. You were right about the residency requirement, the extended paperwork and so forth. So we're doing this on the sly." He winked and opened the front door. "This is how we're going to manage dealing with the bureaucracy: you are my personal house guest for a few days. I have a fine spare bedroom for you tucked up on the third floor – privacy and quietude. What do you say? Hmmm?"

"Well…"

"Yes, yes. Unusual. I haven't done anything like this before either but I'd like to help you and this is the easiest way. Actually, the only way. We'll start this evening after supper with just some talking and you can tell me everything that you can think of that might give me the best picture of where you are at and how you got here, headache-wise. So you can start thinking about it now, to prepare. I'll have a lunch brought over from the commissary. You can take it easy for a few hours. Walk the grounds and you can go anywhere you like except the locked wards, or just take a nap here. Whatever you like. You'll have dinner tonight with myself and my family, and that's that." He had it pretty well planned, I'd say.

"Okay, Doc. You're the boss, I guess." I think I smiled at him, but it probably came across as more of a grimace.

I SETTLED INTO my top-floor, slant-ceilinged bedroom and had the house to myself so I took a nap after the delivered lunch was consumed. I walked the green areas of the grounds for a while but never entered the wards. No thanks. Dinner was with Doc and his wife and their two little girls, about four and five years old, I'd guess. Certainly younger than Bernice, and otherwise I don't know much about children.

I guess Doc and I had a good session that evening and he thought he'd have time the next afternoon too. I tried to tell him about all my headaches, but there were too many to remember. I slept fitfully on a pretty fine mattress, I must say, compared to my usual.

Next morning the two little girls showed up at my door to wake me for breakfast. There was a little knock and then they were both there by the bed. I asked the little one to go over to the bureau and fetch me my eye.

"What?" she said. "What do you mean?"

"My eye, if you would. That would be such a big help! Right there at the edge. Don't worry, eyes don't bite, only teeth do and I've got those right here, see?" and I gave her a big grin.

"Okay." She went right over, reached up, closed her hand on the piece of glass without looking at it and turned back to me quick as a bunny to hand it to me.

"Why, I shall be forever in your debt, young lady. Now, you and your sister run along before I stick this thing in my head."

They bumped into each other, giggling and squeezing through the door.

DOC AND I talked more in the afternoon, and he had me go to one of their top "head guys" on the hospital staff. That fellow did a lot of looking me over without hardly two questions asked, and sent me back to Doc with a hand-written note. I tried to read it, but it was illegible. Doc read it and called down to the pharmacy where he then sent me to pick up a couple prescriptions.

That evening back at his residence, Doc had me take a couple pills of the first batch and then I laid down on the sofa for a couple hours so that he could keep an eye on me. I was okay, and he let me go up to bed about midnight. Next day about mid-morning he had me take a couple of the other pills and I lay down on the couch in his office while he worked on some paperwork. I felt a little dizzy but not too bad.

"Listen, Doc. I need to do something other than lay around here. How's about I paint your portrait? In some sort of repayment idea for you helping me? What say you to that?"

"I'll tell you what you can do, Mahlon. Paint the girls. We'd like that, my wife especially. I can get you some supplies from the hospital storeroom. We do Art Therapy here, they'll have everything you need, I'm sure."

"Your wish is my command, Doc. I'll do it this afternoon, after school." And I did.

By the fifth or sixth day I was getting uncomfortable with the comfortable life and the soft bed. There were some fine talks in the evenings I guess, and I would say that we were certainly friendly enough, but not so's we were buddy-buddy.

We went on to try three or four more kinds of drugs and about half of 'em I couldn't tolerate. Since I never had a headache while I was there, we didn't know if any of 'em would help when the time came, but at least we knew which ones might not hurt me more. That was something, anyway.

"Mahlon, you'll probably always have these attacks, but we'll do our best to treat them. At least now we have a plan."

"Thanks then Doc. It's got to be better 'cause it can't get worse, as my mother used to say every so often about nothing in particular. So we're done are we?"

"For now, yes. I want you to keep in contact with me. You have my phone information. You can call either the office or my home. It's been nice having company at the house, I must say, and you haven't scared the children. Hmmm? No?"

"Or your wife?"

"Oh no. She's seen it all. Can I help you get your things together?"

"Not necessary. I took the liberty of leaving you with another painting too, a landscape, in my room. I'll just get my portfolio and be on my way. I hope one of these prescriptions does it for me in the long run. I'll let you know either way though."

He came around the desk, gave me another of his fine handshakes and said, "Sorry I can't come to the house right now to help you pack up. Meetings. Hmmm? But remember to call."

"I will."

BUT I DIDN'T call. I took the three drugs with me that didn't bother me and waited for the next headache. It hit about two weeks later, and the drugs didn't help. It raged four days, and the drugs didn't help. I was immobilized with pain, and the drugs didn't help. I finally managed to get myself out of bed and sit at a table and I drew devils. I drew demons and dragons and hideous creatures, and the headache eased. I drew more, and I felt better. I was able to stop at about two dozen drawings because that's when the pain was gone.

So I decided to rely on self-medicating drawings and see how that might turn out, since the drugs… you get the picture. And that was effective for a while, off and on.

Thanks Doc. We tried, didn't we?

*For the first time, also, I felt what the
duties of a creator toward his creature
were, and that I ought to render him
happy before I complained of his
wickedness.*

Vice Versa Too

1968

DEAREST CYCLOPES, WHEN you've gone, who shall read
my messages? Who will appreciate my drawings? Oh well. I shall
be gone too, so who cares, right? Until then, here is another mis-
sive from your Lucy. Let me just add, it's been swell. *Ta-ta.*

> The bumps between Cyclopes and me
> Make parts of my parts shivery.
> The bumps know he's close,
> There's no need to boast,
> As goose takes a gander to see.

> My Love's heartbeat calls me: "Draw near
> And look what I've got over here."
> Yes, I can see fine.
> As his throbs keep time
> I dance and discard my brassiere.

I've painted my bloke in the buff.
My portrait, he's sketched in the rough.
The brush and the oil
Set our blood a-boil.
And once we've commenced, when's enough?

Yes, mountains and oceans are swell,
But boffing beats both all to hell.
The sights that one sees
Whilst down on one's knees
Dwarf all that the travelogues sell.

My privates take orders from Sarge.
He's earned that nickname 'cause he's large.
But relative size
Offers compromise,
And I'm the boss, once he's discharged.

I post hand-drawn pictures to Joe.
There's things that I think he should know:
Adventures galore,
Both present and yore,
In locales he prob'ly won't go.

It's perfectly natural to spoon,
Eclipse an eclipse of the moon.
Trade places and then
Eclipse once again
And all between midnight and noon.

I never get drunk by myself –
I've heard that it's bad for one's health.
I drink with my pard.
Between soft and hard
He steals my heart with his stealth.

Regrets are a great waste of time.
Worth less than a nickel or dime.
Don't save them, don't hoard.
No one can afford to
Return to the scene of a crime.

The End   ...probably really this time.

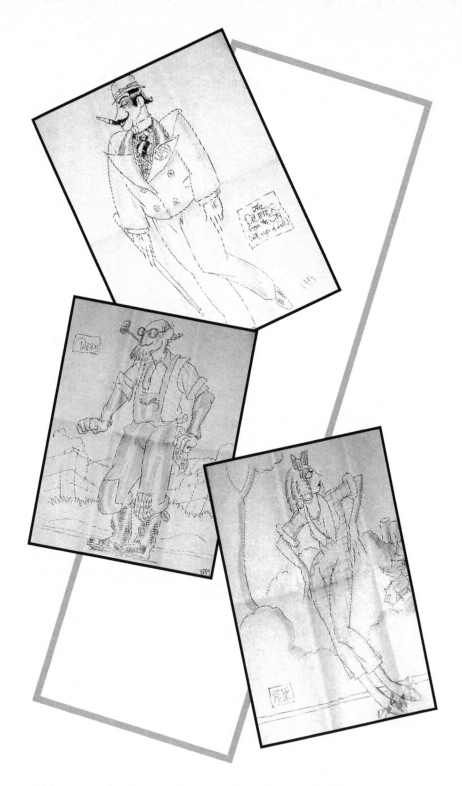

Dean Collins Naps

1953

"DEAN, WE COULD do this," I said.

"Yes, I...uh...huh?"

I had interrupted his nap, I fear. Sunday afternoon, and the sun was flooding the front porch because a turrible wind had downed two ancient Sycamores just this last spring and left a gap where the house pointed directly west. The house itself had been unhurt. Not so much, the trees. Firewood.

It must have been about three of the afternoon, this day here (not the windy one). The warm rays were just goin'-to-town agitating the atoms in the wooden floor, the wooden furniture, my pant legs, and so forth. I had the brains to deflect the bright onslaught on my eyes. I was using the Sunday funnies. Dean had succumbed to pervasive drowsiness.

"Here, Dean. *Yoo-hoo.*"

"I'm awake. Just resting my eyes." He blinked fiercely and brought his hand up for some solar shelter of his own.

I folded my newspaper sunshield backwards in half, then half again. Made kind of a show of smoothing it - ironing it with one hand pressing against my thigh, slow and deliberate. It was more than he could take.

"All-right-all-ready! What?" he shouted.

I tossed the paper to him with a little wrist action that spun it and landed it on his lap, all ready to read. "L'il Abner," was my reply.

He was awake enough to have heard my glottle stop in the title. He corrected, "Don't you mean *Li'l Abner*? For god's sake get that apostrophe right! Spelling counts, gosh darn it." He looked down at the strip, then back to me, then smiled.

I was appropriately falsely contrite. "Of course, of course. *Pardonne a mwa.*"

"Now, whaddya mean?" He perused the paper.

"Dean, get serious, it should be obvious. With your brain and my...brain... Lord. I guess we better use both our brains... and my pen. See? That's humor, there, in that strip. Every week he's pulling down a big paycheck. He's smart, and a pretty good artist, but we're smart too. Especially you, Dean. Cripes!"

"Slow down a moment," he whined. I shut up. "There, better. Ok, I see your point. Humor, money. Go on."

"Look," I said, "the way I see it, there's room for more of this... this satire. All bundled up in the folksy stuff. Even Capp himself keeps branching out with more and more characters and parodies. No one says we can't kinda hitch onto that bandwagon. Huh? From a distance? Sideways?"

Dean said "Interesting. Yes...interesting. We'd need to give it a lot of thought and be committed, if we were serious about this. We'd need to start outlining some ideas, and developing a set of characters. Do you think we could focus enough attention on it? What if it actually caught on? We'd be kinda stuck with it – obligations and contracts. Could you do that, Mahlon?"

"Why not? But we have to hatch the plot before we can count the chickens."

"Exactly. That's exactly the kind of thing I'm talking about. You've got it right there. But sustaining it... that's the issue too. If we're serious."

I said, "There's money to be made. Capp's stinking rich, I'm sure. Let's do it."

"All right. Let's think of some characters then. A girl, a guy, a love interest. What else? A banker? A lawyer or a judge? Parents? Grandparents? Any kids? No, probably not kids. Because we want it to be kind of sexy, too, but not offensive at all. Appealing to the eye, though. And funny. It's the Funny Papers. Funny. Sly. A bit of a wink."

"Keep going. Sounds good. I'm going to go and work up some sketches for characters, see what I can come up with on the drawing table. I'm thinking that maybe I'm going to be right on this. Yes, maybe I'm right."

Dean had an immediate idea. "Let's have a sandwich before you go. Seal the deal! Plenty of mayonnaise!"

"You said it. A collaboration sandwich!" I soon ate half a sandwich and then went home, our big dream dancing through my grey matter.

But… nothing came of it besides a few sketches. Too bad, too. Who dropped the ball? I guess both of us. It might actually have worked! Oh well, and also, damn! A tale of fortunes lost…

And damn Al Capp too, just on principle, while we're at it! Damn rich artists!

I was, to a great degree, self-taught with regard to my favourite studies.

Groff and On Again

1937

WAIT. WHAT WAS that? Maybe it wasn't even quite a kernel of an idea yet, but there was a flicker at the back of my brain. It might amount to something, given time, and room, and a touch of the Muse…

Downtown, I bumped into my ancient acquaintance Groff Conklin. I was sopping up a helluva *au jus* sandwich at the counter at Haroll's Grill on East 47th and he comes up behind me.

"My old buddy, I think? Mahlon B? That you?" and he pats me on the shoulder.

"I am eating a sandwich, but I am glad to see you, too," I told him, turning around to my right. This was an accurate statement.

"Well well. It's got to be, what? Eight, ten years? Back to John Day days. Glad to see you. How are you?" He did smile big and crinkle his eyes, so I guess he really was glad to see me. "Those books you illustrated! I think about you a lot, Mahlon. Hey, I was just going to order some lunch too. Let's talk. Let's grab that booth in the corner."

"Sure." I was always amused at how many thoughts he'd string together so quickly.

"Here. Grab your coffee and your au jus cup. I'll get your plate... crap! They got the table!" We were a little too slow. "Oh! But over there they're leaving!" he noticed a booth down the left. "I'll meet you there!" he scurried away with my sandwich. I followed at a more reasonable pace, only spilling a tad jus, and we sat down. There was some confusion, as the boy came to clear the table, saw us, and turned back toward the kitchen calling out "Hey, I thought you said table three was vamoose?"

"Oh, say, we just grabbed this table." Groff reached out and tapped him on the elbow. "You can clear these... but we'll keep this and this and, I need to order too. Sorry about the confusion." The boy shrugged, loaded his pan with the scuffed crockery and dingey scratched glasses of the previous customers, and sped away. The waitress sauntered over and Groff chose a hot beef on rye, Swiss, side of slaw.

"Oh, better put a couple pieces of apple pie on that slip too," I piped in. "*Ala mode, si'l vous plait.*"

"Still the pie man, eh? Always the pie man. Me too," admitted Groff.

"Pie and pussy. I don't pretend to be perfect. Perfection portends putrefaction."

"Well... I don't..."

"ART, my friend. ART! The human form! The subject of the Masters! We must, as artists, follow our hearts, *n'est pas*? Pie... and... and..." I gave him the blank space to fill in, but...nothing.

He was silent for a minute, giving me the eye, considering his words a bit. "So, still the playful artist. That's wonderful."

"You?" I asked him.

"Me? I never was an artist. No... I've kind of bumped around, doing this and that. Some government work. A little. Nothing too interesting."

"Espionage? Spy chaser?"

"Ha! No, no. Editing of publications, that sort of thing. Government publications. Feh."

"That's not what I heard." I winked. Again, he didn't take the bait.

The waitress skidded a plate down in front of him and said slowly, "I guess I'd better get that pie for youse two now, before it's all et up," and sashayed away.

Taking a healthy mouthful of sandwich, Groff chewed a while, then asked, "Say, is there much illustration work around for you nowadays? I'm kind of out of touch in that area, so..."

"Nah! Not like it was, for sure. Those were some swell damn times back in Twenty-seven, Twenty-eight. Looking back I'm not sure how I did it. Lots of coffee! Burnt out my share of light bulbs, that's for sure. And candles at both ends, for damn sure...." I kind of trailed off, feeling nostalgic.

"You did such great stuff, my friend! Man! I was always amazed. I still have those books you inscribed to me. I know right where they are on the bookshelf. In fact, I was showing them to my wife... Say! I got married. A year ago! What a sweetie-pie. I'm so lucky. You?"

I had maneuvered a piece of just delivered, well-crusted baked-goods to my mouth. "Hmmumff?" I nodded.

"Say, we should get together, the four of us! Any kids, my friend?" he asked, eagerly.

"No. Well, yes. Sort of. One. But 'the family' is out West. California."

"Say, I'd like you to meet my Sweetie-pie though. You know, I like this being married thing."

"I'll bet you do," I said. "We all do, to a certain extent, I guess. At least men do. Indeeds – certain needs." I changed the subject. "Speaking of art, I should tell you about a thing, a thing I'm putting together. Art. A treatise on the 'new woman' that you might find interesting. It's called *Nova Venus* and it's a portfolio publication, limited edition." I was making this up as I went along, to take my mind off my wife. It wasn't exactly true, and yet...

"You're doing this yourself? Publishing? By yourself?"

"Basically yes. With Jake Brussel, maybe, but it's my whole deal really. All my drawings, new drawings. It's 'sophisticated.'

Maybe even your wife would like it." I blinked at him a few times and he paused to consider.

"OK then. Yes, I'd like to see it. Of course, of course." He took a business card out of his breast pocket, scribbled out the printed information on the front, and wrote on the back.

"This is my home phone number. Call me next week, Tuesday or Thursday evening. I'd like to set something up and hear more. And you can meet my Sweetie-pie too." He grabbed the ticket Miss Sashay had set on the table with the pie. "I'll get this one, Mahlon. Good running into you. Gosh, it's been so long! Too long! Please call next week."

"Yes, Groff. Next week." I watched him hustle around the tables and customers, throw a couple bills at the cashier and scoot out the door. He hadn't touched his pie. Now, that was a shame. I sat back down in the booth and got a refill on my coffee and had that second piece of pie right then and there.

And as I munched I thought to myself, "Nova Venus? That's actually not a bad idea. In fact, I think it's a good idea. Pie and pussy. Must be a magical combination." I considered his invitation too, but of course the four of us would never get together. Not with the two of us so far apart. Plus the fact that the drawings weren't on paper yet, merely the emerging mists of figures in my mind.

At least, at last, it was more than just a flicker.

I see by your eagerness, and the
wonder and hope which your eyes
express, my friend, that you expect to
be informed of the secret with which I
am acquainted. That cannot be.

Desert Coyote Dreams
1948

"MAHLON?" WHISPERED A *tiny questioning voice. No. Not*
quite a voice, but an audible mist that formed my name.

"Mahlon?" Hovering out of reach just past the edge of a dream:
"Mahlon Blaine. Blaine. Blaineblaineblaine." It half echoed, fading
into a background of nothingness.

I rolled over on my back, still three-quarters-sleeping, breathing
slowly, slowly. I opened my eye, stared straight up. Heck of a view!
The Arizona night sky was peppered with stars. "More like salted,"
I muttered, with our galaxy smeared across the southern quadrant
– to my right, as I lay in the truck-bed – and Orion standing watch.

The Milky Smear. Jesus, what a sky! Must be three, four AM,
I thought. Two coyotes hoot-howled, ending off in staccato yips,
probably a couple hundred feet away, startling me. "Boys and girls!
Go away! Man trying to sleep here!" I yelled out in no particular
direction. I lay still, almost remembering the mist that called my
name. Nothing. I settled over on my other side, but the thin cotton-
batt mattress failed to disguise the truck's metal bed. Sleeping on
the ground, you could use your boot to carve a couple divots for

your hip and shoulder, yet on the ground the snakes and critters like to come investigating. Trade-offs, compromises. Crap!

I drifted off again. Sweet cactus blossoms and the night silent, until

"Mahlon? Is that you?" that misty voice that I did not recognize rose from beyond a group of creosote to the east.

"That's me!" I instinctively replied. "What the hell?" I fumbled for my glasses and sat up, slipped them on and squinted my empty eye socket tightly as I peered into the darkness toward the voice. "Who is out there?"

A vague, shifting form approached, slowly, tentatively. I thought it was a bent little man. The light from the stars was hardly enough to define much until, closer now, not a man but an upright-walking coyote sporting thick wire-rimmed spectacles and carrying a clipboard cradled in one front leg/arm, a pen in the other paw/hand.

"Mahlon Blaine! As I may have imagined! Here you are! Here I am! Gosh! Can I ask you some questions? Oh my! I don't know where to begin!" it stuttered. Midwest accent, maybe North Dakota? South Dakota?

"Who are you? What the hell time is it? What the fuck are you? JesusChristwhatisgoingon?"

I squinted at the ghost – what else could it be? Although, in sober moments, I didn't believe in ghosts, I also couldn't remember if I was sober.

"This is so cool! I wasn't even sure you drove a car. I mean a truck, I guess. Is this your truck? What year are we in? If this is registered in your name..." the ghost's rapid muttering trailed off as it began to scribble on the clipboard.

"Listen," I said. "I have a license to drive. California. I just borrowed this truck. And... wait a second...." I stopped, searched around me in the truck bed, grabbed my crumpled trousers, held them up and found the right front pocket, reached in and pulled out the clean white linen handkerchief, unfolded it, took my glass eye and deftly inserted it into my waiting socket.

Mr. Coyote opened his eyes wide. "I wondered just how you did that too! I hope I remember this stuff, these details. I gotta pay attention..." scribble, scribble.

"Are you spying on me? Why'd you wake me up? Who the...?"

"Oh boy... I don't want to upset you, Sir, Mister Sir, Mister Blaine. Sir. Sorry. Sorry. Gosh! I didn't wake you, did I? I was just..." the ghost abruptly acted surprised at his surroundings and asked, "Is this somewhere in Arizona? This feels like Arizona should." He was writing more as he spoke and looked to his left and right.

"Shut the fuck up, you ghost!" I yelped. I didn't mean to yelp - I just did.

The ghost froze and spoke in an even tone, "Mister Guy Oatey, if you please."

I took note of his politeness, gave the apparition a thorough look-over and decided to cooperate. What the heck anyway. "So, Mister Oatey, you seem to know who I am."

He paused, took a breath. A deep ghostly breath showing yellow coyote teeth.

"I am... in the future, or of the future, or...." His ears flopped back and forth once each. He blinked. "Actually, I think I might be dreaming."

I sighed, reached down to my still-unoccupied pants, dug into the other front pocket, pulled out my pipe and stuck the stem into my mouth, clenching. Then took it out to scratch my forehead with. Who's dream was this anyway?

"What do you want?" I calmly asked while massaging my now permanently arched eyebrow.

"Knowledge. I want to know... everything? I think I want to know everything. No, wait. That's too much. Not everything. And I don't know how much time I have here, now. Uh..." Mr. Oatey acted frazzled... and discombobulated. "Uhhhh..... Do you have any kids, or relatives?" he blurted.

"No. Probably not, anyway. Why?"

"So I could find them to answer questions. You're already dead when... oops." He stopped, then "what I mean is..."

I held up my hand. "When did I, or will I, die?" Good question, I thought. If anyone would know, surely it would be this furry ghost-thing.

His pathetic answer: "I don't know, actually. Really. I don't. You're an enigma! I hardly know anything!"

I pondered that, smiled. "Enigma. That's a wonderful word, and something worth aiming for. Sounds like I'm well on my way, too." I had to chuckle.

He frowned. "Are you kidding me?" A desert rodent scooted from a hole under a brittlebush, and the ghost bent quick-as-a-, well, coyote, to snap teeth onto its tail. A quick flip of the head, a flex of the jaws, a swallow, and the mouse was gone. I hoped it wasn't my muse mouse. Probably not, out here, I surmised, before answering him.

"Kidding? Oh no. Of course, tall tales and adventures catch people's imaginations." I winked. "Publicity sells. Stories sell. Truth is an innocent bystander to commerce. I was intent on creating myself as an interesting character to fortify my career."

"OK, OK then. It doesn't help me though. All that misdirection." He licked his lips again.

What a frickin' self-centered coyote-ghost! I blurted, "Buddy, I don't know you. You don't know me. We're even. You come here during my perfectly fine although uncomfortable sleep to go all rag on me about stuff that's none of your damn business... stop me if I'm wrong... and then start whining..."

The rebuke must have stung him, for he interrupted, "Stop. Stop. I... you're right, I guess. Sorry. Look. I'm so sorry. I... I don't mean to whine. I don't know what to say. I am so sorry to bother you..." His arms fell to his sides, his head bowed. He burped.

"Tell me, please," I calmed down as the ghost sniffled and appeared about to weep, "why me? Why you? What's the connection? And you'd better hurry, 'cause I think I may wake up at any moment."

This caught him off guard. He raised an eyebrow. "What?"

"This. Wake from this. It's my dream too, I think."

He looked worried and lifted his pen and clipboard, speaking hurriedly, "OK. Connection? It's... hard to explain... exactly... but it's the art, the artworks. It's the illustrations in the books. That's what I've imagined, so far. I've been fascinated, captivated, drawn to what you've drawn. It's like I can't help myself. I wish I ...."

The ghost began to fade. Someone snorted. Was it me?

He took a step back. Another and another, turned and high-tailed it for his den.

"Where am I? What year is this? Please... I have so many questions...." his voice was faint.

I snorted again, wiggled and shivered. "Wha....? Uh! Where am I? What year...uhhhh."

AND I WAS awake. Fully awake, just like that.

The sun had barely begun to clear the valley's ragged, peaked edge. The first rays were hitting the cab of the pick-up. I squinted into the morning.

"What the... my eye's in! Shit! I hate it when I fall asleep with... but I took it out! I know I took it out!" I sat straight up, talking out loud to myself. "And my pipe! Here?"

I remembered dreaming, just not what the dream was about. It had left me uneasy, with a vague, sorrowful taste in my mouth, this dream that I couldn't quite recall. I slowly reclined to see if I could finish it. It shouldn't take long, just a few more minutes' sleep before the sunbeams reached my sleeping roll.

I did return to some kind of a dream, but where was this?

THE CRAMPED SLEEPING AREA WAS BRIGHTENING *in the dawn's eager light. Guy awoke with a start, blinking and propping up on an elbow.*

"You know, I just had another one of those dreams," he muttered, then leaned to nuzzle the cool shoulder of Gal.

"Yeah, mmmm, uh," she mumbled, not bothering to fully wake up. "Wet dream?"

"Kind of, or a damp one maybe. I can't quite... I think it was about Hannibal Elmo."

"Again? You're kinda mixed up." she said, rolling briefly onto her back, running her tongue over her teeth and throwing her right wrist over her squinched eyes. She half opened one, skeptically. "Why don't you marry him and get it over with?"

"Ha. Ha. You of all wild creatures might understand, I'm not the marrying type."

She rolled back and curled into her favorite fetal position, her spine towards him. "Tell me something I don't know."

He laid his chin flat, staring straight ahead at nothing, silent for a minute. "It seems that if I don't figure out this enticing character I'm never going to be happy. Maybe I can focus, hunt up all the facts and then be done with him. It can't be any harder than coughing up a big hairball."

She sputtered, "It's already been, what, a couple years? What's the hold up? By the moon above I'm getting tired of hearing about it!" Sudden anger intensified her whine.

If he thought he could calm her, he was mistaken. "Well my dear, I..."

"Ooooo! Aarrgh! Let me go back to sleep!" She growled and snuffed.

He licked his lips, sighing, "If only everything were that easy," and twisted to scratch his ear with his left hind foot. Scratch-scratch-scra

AND MY DREAM was done, my legacy apparently in the hands of a bumbling ghost.

Just my luck!

Fool's Folly

1925

"WHAT ARE YOU writing, if I may ask?" John stood over me, looking down at my lap where lay an open notebook and a half-page of cursive text. I had dozed off in the tropical heat, although I had at least been smart enough to have sat myself in the shade of one of the vent-ports sprouting from Katrina's upper deck.

"Nothing of import. And besides, only a fool would show another writer his manuscript at such an early stage. I have it on good authority - Get it? Author-ity? - that a writer is not thought much more highly of than an artist. Which am I and which are you? Answer me that." I closed the notebook with a flourish, took the pipe out of my pocket, tapped it on the vent-housing to knock out the old tobacco ash and tar, and squinted up at him. The sea breeze kept skin temperature somewhat tolerable.

He replied "I write, true. You draw. Usually. Now I can see that I should certainly look upon you in a different light. If you write, should I then take up the quill and ink, sketching m'lady where I may find her, preferably unclothed? The lady, that is. Un-clothed."

"Hmmmm."

"Don't worry. I am not about to. You, however, may continue doing whatever you like. Right now I intend to take a walk around this deck six or ten times to get last night's bunk-borne kinks out."

That sounded good to me. "Wait. I'll join you." I tucked the notebook under my arm and jumped to my feet.

don't stage any revo'uciones, if th
worse than the exa'ples of tha
omenon ~~who~~ we have already
nt get pegged by a bandit or two
assassins union goes out on
hours, if the Ferrocarril Nat
the tracks I may be in Portl
ness. The Country is very full o
t and pleasant I think the lit
numbered by the fleas) You can
ortez first got away with Marr
ravage of time or the ravage of
, the bed is in awfully bad sha
Barber of Seville" and got t
when I told Jack SL ~~r-Hunt,~~
t he said "Why don't y u shave y
um wheezy after tr jing for 3 l
a with a flock of pleas nil
anatomy which you can not get
we a nice little ~~~~ pink spot

Calligraphy

1944

IT'S A NOBLE profession, going way back to the first cave-dwellers. I mean, one cave pretty much looks like another, to a Neanderthal feller. But then some big idea hits and whoa, Nelly! When a big idea hits a caveman, look out! There's all that room in that skull!

The way I heard it, Nu of the Neocene finds himself a nice piece of bark that musta fell off a tree, and picks up a hunk of half-scorched tree branch, and draws a vulva. Let's face it - it's not so hard to draw the fucking thing. He thinks his slow little thoughts, and remembers that it has been a while since he and his lady-love got stinky.

Of course, now that he is thinking about it, he is terribly inclined to do something about it, so he traipses through the woods, across the savannah, over the stream, around the saber-tooth lions, behind the three-toed sloth, up the rocky escarpment and right up to the cave of his favorite boinkette. It's at that point that he realizes he still has the aforementioned piece of decorated bark in his hand. He also imagines that he will soon be needing that hand for other activities, so he parks the bark near the cave on a ledge of stone, probably about eye-level. He takes one more good look at it. Yup - he thinks - that's what I'm talking about. He calls out into the cave, "Yoo-hoo Honey. Daddy's home," and enters.

About five minutes later he's ready to be on his way. As he exits the cave, he notices a queue of his fellow Neanderthal gentlemen has formed. The line begins at the sign of the pussy and stretches down the slope. Way, way down the slope.

AND THAT'S HOW the profession of sign-painting (sometimes called 'advertising') got its start, or so I'm suspecting.

Well, in one form or another, I've been in the game all my life - so far. Once pen hits paper and you find yourself trying to convey a message, you're in it, my friend.

There is sometimes even an actual wage involved. Sign-painting for a wage? Imagine that! I tell you, many have been the times that sign-painting has been on speculation, on promise, on trade, on commission or on the sly, and that was that. No wage, no food or shelter. No recognition even. Too many times over fifty years, let me tell you.

Once upon a time, it was my full time employment. My signs at the aircraft factory were not of 'thine vulva' variety. Oh no. The sign-making entrusted to me was of the industrial variety. What does that mean, you ask. You did ask, didn't you? I thought so.

Here the signs were way more important. They included high-minded messages such as:

Very Slippery - When Wet
Stay To The Center
Caution When Compressor Running
Shelve Tools When Not in Use
Ear Protection Required - At All Times
Tunnel Windy
Check Shoes Upon Exiting

Gloves Advised
Caution - Hydraulic Fluid Mist Present
Exit Quickly When Bell has Rung
Lunch Area
Wipe Up All Spillage - Immediately
Minimally Dusty Area

...and so forth.

YOU CAN EASILY see that, without personnel such as myself, the Lockheed Corporation would fall to fucking pieces, bit by bit. So true.

So scoff at me not. Mine is a noble... oh yeah, I already said that.

Shinola!

...while every proper measure
is pursued you should make up
your mind to disappointment.

Crap By Any Other Name

1958

JUST ANOTHER ILLUSTRATION job, right? But god, I hate this flagellation crap!

I hate it, I hate it, I truly do!

But here I am, doing it. What, pray tell, is wrong with me?

First of all, it should be obvious by simply looking at my overall body of work that it is not my cup of tea. I'm not making a moral judgment on anything. I'm not saying I'm not, either, just to set the record straight. I'm just saying that I'm not into it. I kind of don't get it, I guess. And that's all right. Big world and all, and nobody likes everything.

Second of all, the drawings often end up looking like my personifications of headaches. At least to me they do. And that's probably just what they are.

As I best recall, the headaches begin to intensify as I go broke. I know, I know... I'm always out of money. True, at least mostly true, until the social security checks started. The headaches then got better. But the times before?

I did crap. Whippings and switchings and thrashings and bindings, and there is no joy on the faces of the poor souls. No jubilation in their body movement or posture. No humor.

And that's the saddest part. Sex - deprivation even - without humor, so sad. I can't help it. They are sad drawings without amusement, and that's that. Oh, sure. You may find a sly bit here and there. I'm still me, after all. I can't totally erase who I am, even though the headaches practically do that for me. But, when you look at that shit, please just keep in mind the context of it all. Please.

Someday I hope to move beyond any stigma, if I should live so long. It's not what I'd like to be remembered for. I'd hoped to put it past me, even as I drew it. That's kind of paradoxical, I guess. Hah, then, and fuck it! When destitute, I was desperate. So sue me!

Itty-Bitty Sea Ditty

1968

LUCY'S NOT THE only one who can write doggerel, by gum!

I hereby dedicate this half-mast, half-assed shanty-song to my soul mates on the high seas, and their lives of adventure, real and unreal, under relentless skies. As best as I remember, I conceived these wondrous stanzas whilst under the influence: the influence of the smells, the yells, and the swells.

In the singing key of Sea, except for fiddlers who always fiddle wherever they damn will anyways. Penny whistles are welcome, but are requested to play nothing quicker than farthing-notes...

> Ships sail ev'ry ocean,
> Mariners cross seas.
> Mates embrace each harbor –
> Drop anchors where they please.

Though I've swum to Europe,
Climbed Gibraltar's rock,
When it comes t' women,
I ain't been 'round the block.

First mate croons a sweet song.
Second mate sings bass.
Cabin boys and Captains
Slip harmonies in place.

Swab yer deck, me Matey.
Scrub yer puny plank,
Lest y' spy wee crickets
At home upon yon shank.

Weevils wreck yer wassail.
Bedbugs bite yer bunk.
Dames defile yer dreamland –
Y' wake to find it shrunk.

Whiskey by th' dram weight
Jerky by th' slab
Women up th' staircase
Don't care what wives y've had.

Pull upon th' whiskey,
Drown in beers and ales,
Spill your guts t' Maggie –
She loves t' compare tales.

Sailors fascinate her.
Sailors pique her mind.
Sailors fore and aft
Met right then left behind.

Back t' land, cry-babies –
Quit yer wailing ways.
Drydock Queequeg's Moby –
The Dick from whalin' days.

G. Legman

1937

'GERSHON LEGMAN' - what kind of a name is that? It's almost as bad as 'Mahlon Blaine.'

Gershon (or 'G.' - as he prefers to be called, and as he calls himself) and I got to be pretty friendly over about fifteen years. We met (in 1937 I think, after a slight misunderstanding regarding money and art and addresses) on common ground. Both of us had parts of our brains that fired in strange ways. I don't know what his excuse is, but... come to think of it, I don't have a whisper what my excuse is either. Not a clue.

But eventually there we were, hanging out with Jake Brussel, Sam Roth, Bernard Guerney, and the rest of them. Those book maniacs, erotica jockeys and publishing sycophants. I don't even know what that means, but there we were, in the same 'profession' of providing to the public what it desired... what its lizard-brained little self desired. Maybe that comes off as sounding unkind. I don't mean to be unkind. You know, it was the last thing on my mind. And... it's only an opinion, after all. Us and all the other assholes got 'em.

So, Gershon is the word guy, the scholar, the thinker. His media are the typewriter, the cursive pen, the penciled note from the library stacks. He studies, he burrows, he ferrets out. He's always got his nose deep in there. And, like me, never lets himself get personal. I really don't know a thing about him.

And what does he know about me? Oh, some things, I'm sure. After all, we've spent a plethora of days together. There have been conversations, discussions, bullshit monologues and dialogues. Almost like real life. But then, what is that? Again, with the clue thing: I haven't one.

One handy knack he exhibited: discovery of, and attachment to, beautiful women. Occasional luck would bring me into his company, along with a beauty (or two). Then it would be up to me and my own not-inconsiderable powers of enticement and persuasion. Several successes have resulted in more than a few deliciously painted canvases. I won't identify them here (the works or the ladies), but I thank G. for the model opportunities that arose from this strange allure he had.

Was it his brain?

He fancied himself an intellectual. I have little to say about that. Like I said, he was a scholar and a sometimes relentless studier. Maybe he did have an intellect of that nature. *He* certainly seemed to think so.

Yes, he had a very, very high regard for himself, of himself.

And me? Yes, he tolerated me and my mumbling-bumbling companionship. I let him say most whatever he wanted, whenever he wanted, and found the easiest route to take was to nod my head 'knowingly', take my pipe out of my mouth and tap the bowl out on something nearby, relight it, and send a couple puffs up in the air, then give him a winking look, and carry on as if nothing had happened.

It seemed to work almost all the time.

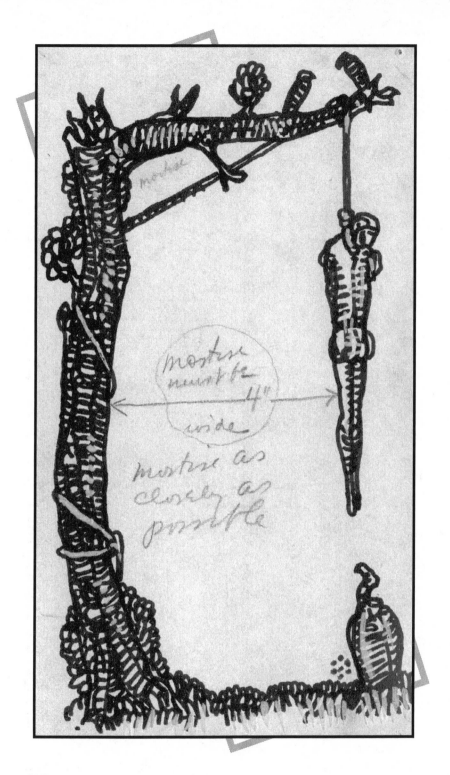

Decency Dilemma
1932

"JUDGE, WHAT DO you think I should do?"

"I'm glad you asked, Mahlon." This was the first time I had felt comfortable enough with my father-in-law to approach him with a personal matter. "I think you should stay the hell away from New York, that's what I think," he said. "Doesn't matter what's right and what's wrong. No sir. If that's what you're up against, you're better off right here. You asked, and I'm telling you, flat out. Take my advice, son. You don't need the trouble. Fern doesn't. Nobody does in this family."

I had asked him about a supposed indictment, with my name attached, or implicated, back in New York City. Maybe it was just a rumor. We were all the way out in L.A. and communication gets iffy, especially when dealing with my dubious, spurious publishers. But it was something about something that I had worked on years ago. Something for Sam Roth. Now, I'd done several things for that unfortunate troublemaker, and I had known all along – unrest followed him like a shadow. I had known, and still I had contributed to his publications. This had all happened before I had gotten married to Dusky (Fern). Before I came back out to California.

That's why I had left New York in the first place. Those Decency League goons had broken into Guerney's offices, literally. They had hatchets and guns drawn and they chopped the door. They didn't have to chop the door but they seemed to take a certain glee in it. Smacked it right down, and this was police, too. I don't know how 'official' it officially was, but they weren't worried about getting in trouble with the bosses uptown. So they shattered their way in, scared the bejesus outta the mice and cockroaches, and hauled off a whole load of stuff. I hadn't done but a few things for Guerney, but I did have a major hand in the little rabble-rouser newspaper he had just printed, *Jack Ketch – the Hangman.*

The thing is, this wasn't pornography or anything remotely smutty, this *Jack Ketch* rag. It was political. But someone – I'm not saying who and it wasn't me – had drawn a rather unflattering portrait of Sumner as a big fat rodent. It was a cartoon, for cripe's sake, but it sure didn't sit well with Mr. Sumner and here come the axes. They took all the copies, said they were going to burn 'em, and I believe that's exactly what they did. Those boys fool around NOT. It wasn't good to be me there, I figured. So I beat it west.

It was the last straw, sorta. I also hadn't had a decent book deal in a very long time. The legit publishers were feeling the pinch. The crash hit everyone. Casual readers didn't notice if the drawings were suddenly missing from the new books. Paper, binding, dust jackets... it seemed the whole business slipped sideways a notch, and illustration fell off and me off with it.

Out west, I hoped I could get back in with the movie crews. They still made movies. That had changed, but not so much so as I couldn't fit back in. And I did. I was working fairly steady after not too long. I still had a few connections. Oh, it wasn't a thrilling position. But steady like I said.

I met my wife there, on the set. We had a Hollywood romance, I guess you could say. We started our *home*, including her little girl. And in spite of the depression and me not finding work, we seemed happy.

Her father was a lawyer and had been a real, live Judge. I was a little intimidated at first, but we hit it off right away. That man had a sense of humor! And he never tolerated falsehood or two-facedness in anyone he'd get close to. I was family now, and so – if he liked me – I must have passed the grade. I realized that he was nothing if not fair. They couldn't have picked a finer man for a Judgeship.

So, when I approached him with my question about New York, I ended up explaining and describing my past to him in detail. Actually, it was far more detail than I had even shared with Dusky. Oh, she knew I was no saint. How could I have hid that? Right! Who could? But with the Judge, I got more specific.

It didn't bother him, my art-on-the-periphery. Maybe he even liked it, in that I wasn't no goody-one-shoe tap dancing to Irving Berlin.

Therefore, I followed his advice. It turned out to be good advice as I didn't want to flirt with any jail time. No siree bob.

Dunninger's Second Story
1967

Dunninger, the famous guy, sawed a man in half.
When the victim's wife appeared, Dungey slyly asked:
"Don't you just adore my skill, showmanship and brio?
Now you and your husband, Dear, are finally a trio."

BACK TO THE mansion.

Going up the stairway from the foyer, there are two land-ings and two turns, so that you face the front of the house at the second floor level. The hallway stretches left and right from that point. Immediately to the right a door opens to the third floor stairway. Further to the right, the bathroom.

Looking left you find yourself facing the door to the mas-ter suite, while directly ahead of you at the top of the stairs is a double door to the upstairs parlor. These two have been blocked for many years, and now bookcases line the wall and doorway on that side, the south side, right across the old portal.

Entering the master bedroom, you'll find the double bed ori-ented so that the head is to the north, against the wall. I believe a closet door is to the left of the headboard, with the closet bending around behind the wall of the headboard. Windows stand to the east, overlooking the river.

If you're standing in the bedroom doorway, to the right is a door to a small room, perhaps you'd call it a sitting room, with high windows in the corner, windows on the east side, and bookcases all around. These cases are overflowing with an array: all types and subject matter of books and additional books are stacked on the floor and in front of all the furniture. One glass curio case holds an autographed picture of Judy Garland.

Stacked on the floor in this room, under a piece of cloth, are several paintings of mine, as well as most of the scrapbooks and collections of my drawings that Joe has had specially bound. This stack must be two feet high. I might mention that paintings should not be stacked thusly. I certainly didn't put them like that!

A collection of walking sticks, an accumulation of smoking pipes, and various other interesting items Joe has gathered from around the world add to the chaos. I don't know what most of those items are. Although the erotic ones, I guess I could tell you about those. Some other time perhaps.

Dunninger's Parlor of Interesting Objects. That's what I call the bigger room in the front center. Joe was wise to seal those doors to the hallway, for what he's got in there – better not to have the kids have easy access to. Oh, don't get me wrong, there's plenty, all around the house, that is unsuitable for children. But, let's face it, Joe has children... Close off the room. Put a padlock on it, while you're at it.

This parlor is accessible only by a door from the sitting room. Doors, doors, doors. Anyway, you come in from the east side. Once again, bookcases all around, stuffed with a veritible disarray. And several sexual devices, of minor nastiness, on top and within the cases. No big deal to adults like you and me, eh?

Oh look! A portrait of myself in that cabinet! How nice of Joe to have that out on display. I don't see portraits of anyone else around, except the aforementioned Gumm Sister, and she is residing way over in the parlor.

There're a couple closets to either side of the bank of windows overlooking the front of the house. And two or three tables set up in the middle of the room are stacked with artwork, prints, maps, and other ephemera of Joe's life. Quite the jumble. And a definite Far East theme emerges. I guess magic-men like that kind of thing, the sense of the foreign permeating their mysterious lives. OK. I get that.

Backing out the way we came through the sitting room and master bedroom, enter the hallway and wander through the door and up the tightly winding stair to the third floor. This is/was the children's area. Not much to see up here, I guess.

So let's go down to the basement, shall we?

Back in the kitchen, that door in the southeast corner is the basement door. Go through, turn left and down the ten or so steps and turn right. Now you're by the boiler. A hallway and two rooms open off that.

Books everywhere! If that boiler ever springs a leak, it's going to affect a lot of reading material. And, come to think of it, down here is where Joe has been stockpiling most of the Blaine-illustrated volumes that he's been having me sign and inscribe to him for all these years. Oh-oh.

So that's the mansion, or house, mostly.

There's an attached double garage, too, on the west side. The yard isn't huge by any stretch of the imagination, although there have been some fun times outdoors.

But on the bluff side, that cliff always scared me. I stayed away from that thing.

One eye and all...

Enlarging on Manette

Sam Hated My Uncle

1939

"WHAT THE FUCK, Mahlon? I mean... what in the bloody hell are you doing?" Sam Roth said as he looked over my shoulder. He was apparently making reference to the drawing I was just finishing up for his book *My Uncle Benjamin*.

"Language, Samuel! Language! Tut-tut and all that! Look more closely. Obviously, technically, there's no 'bloody hell' going on here at all, now is there?"

"That's what I am talking about! What's that sketchy crap with the pencil you got going there? Where's the lines, your ink, for Christ's sake? MY lines I'm paying you for? The bloody Mahlon Blaine lines!? The fucking *inklines*?"

He paused. Was he counting to ten under his breath? He took off his heavy horn-rimmed glasses, wiped his forehead with his perfectly white pocket hanky, put his glasses back on the bridge of his nose with an extra push and continued, only a little calmer, "What is going on here?"

He waved the sweat-dampened cloth in my face.

I laid down my pencil, shifted my pipe to the other corner of my mouth with my left hand, and heaved a heavy sigh. I looked him in the eye with my glass eye – which I was holding in my right palm, up level with his face. I closed and opened my hand twice, like I was winking at him. Then I blinked – my real live eye this time – and wiped away an imaginary tear from my cheek.

"You've finally hurt my feelings, Samuel. You've tried and tried before, more times than I could ever keep track of. But I do believe now you've done it. Really.

"My feelings, being bruised and bullied, require that I take a bit of a leave now. Pardon me while I take my feelings for a little fresh air, a little sunshine, a little vacation from this bloody rotten room you've had me locked in for lo these many days. If you can't talk to a fella like he's got feelings, then maybe fuck you." I was calm. I was collected. But I really was starting to get annoyed. Like all the previous Roth jobs, this one wasn't remunerative enough to keep me from be annoyed.

He said, "Look here, come on! See it from my point for a second. I want the real Mahlon Blaine touch here. I didn't have my darling wife go to the trouble of translating this damn old thing and have the phantom typesetters run their linotype fucking machines all night, melting lead for Christ's sake, to get some messed-up drawings! These ain't you, my friend! These ain't blood-sucking Mahlon Blaine drawings! Christ!"

He should have been able to figure it out: artists change. Styles change. You can't do the same thing forever. Money isn't what it's cracked out to be, rent paid or no. I also had no illusions of either enhancing or detracting from my artistic standing. I didn't have one.

I was cramped, cold and very tired. I didn't want to argue.

I merely said, "Okay. I see your point. Now, pardon me." I gathered up my hat and overcoat from the chair next to the door, and strode out into the chilly night before donning said garments. I was no more than twenty or thirty feet down the sidewalk when I heard the hinges squeal behind me and Roth's fat feet slap the icy sidewalk a couple of times. I was moving unsteadily, struggling to get my jacketed arm up the ratty sleeve of my woolen overcoat as he called out.

"Oh, take yourself a hike all right! Don't come back here until you're you again! I don't know who this new guy is. He sure as hell ain't you!"

I didn't bother to reply. Like I said, fuck him. And this wasn't the first time I felt that way. Nosiree.

Anyway, the first of the month was a couple weeks away. If nothing else turned up, I would have time to come back to Sam's sweatshop and eke out rent funds. I hoped I didn't have to.

In fact, I decided both he and *My Uncle Benjamin* could just take a leap.

The City, Car & Close Call
1938

WHAT IS IT about cities, and about this city in particular?

I was not born a city dweller. Yet here I dwell. My nurture was in nature. Albany, Oregon is rural, and even the folks in-town would swear to it. That was the essence of the first decade of my life. My first glimpse of Portland was a tremendous shock of stupefaction to me as a boy of ten years. Thence San Francisco, Los Angeles, Mexico City, Havana.

But *New York City*...

I guess it's a love affair, all right, wrong, and down the middle. The excitement and the glory, the dirt and the excrement. The everything-at-once-ness. The fatigue and the infatuation.

Certainly, for an artist who's main subject matter is The Human Condition, where else to be? The Condition surrounds and inundates. Just observe and keep an open eye, I say.

Yes, one open eye.

And be extra careful crossing, even on the crosswalks!

*The story is too connected to
be mistaken for a dream, and I
have no motive for falsehood.*

Shparkling Chrystal

1933

DUNNINGER'S FIRST WIFE, Chrystal Spencer, was beautiful.
No doubt about it. She had been a dancer, performer, stunning
showgirl. It was easy to see why Joe fell for her. Who wouldn't?
Who didn't?

She had a son by a previous marriage. Harry, I think his name
was. Just kidding... I know it was Harry. The boy was probably
about eight or ten when Joe and Chrystal got hitched.

Well, that's an interesting thing in itself, that whole marriage
thing. Fact is, I don't think that they really were married. Not
what you or I would think of as married. No church, no minister,
no Justice of the Peace, no county clerk, no Judge. But they certainly were together. At one point, somebody mentioned something about "common law" and whatever that means, maybe that
was what they had. Regarding the ramifications on his marriage
to Billie? That's not my story to tell.

So this show business couple lived the glamour life, I guess
you could say. She became his on-stage assistant. They worked
very smoothly together, and I'm sure she made him an even bet-

ter performer than he had been previously. It's not an easy life, though. Nice big Manhattan apartment, hobnobbing with celebrities all the time, wining, dining, nightclubs, entertainers' hours. Poor people. Tsk-tsk.

I quickly grew close to Chrystal. She believed in me as much as Joe did, you could say. I began bringing her some book or other of mine that I had run across at a flea market or sale. I'd sign them "For Chrystal - Mahlon Blaine" as well as draw provocative little scenes that would be in keeping with the content at hand. I liked doing that small thing for her. She would stand right behind my left shoulder, ever so slightly brushing against me as I drew. Her expensively unidentifiable perfume tangled my brain. Ah, yes!

Pretty soon Joe was having me draw extra stuff in books for him too. It kind of got to be like a little competition between the two of them, to find the cheapest books to bring home for me to sign, when I next visited. With Joe's I'd usually sit in my favorite leather Club chair with the book in my lap as I sketched and we'd all chat through the evening until every book was inscribed. It helped pass the time while drinks were polished off. As three, we were closer than, say, professionals. Enough said there.

BY 1933, JOE had begun to bring home French Postcards and certain other photographic material, and he had been stashing this new collection where Chrystal wouldn't find it, among his piles of other books and paper items. Yet he was usually anxious to share these with me.

"Mahlon, I got some good pictures on this trip," he said on one of my visits to the apartment he and Chrystal kept in the city. "Something I think you'll like. Maybe we can use them."

"What do you mean, 'use 'em'?" I had asked.

"Oh, you know... some of the drawings I'd commissioned you recently to do, you remember, ended up not quite as I had imagined. Oh, they were fine, fine drawings, but sometimes I apparently had trouble describing what I I wanted. Remember?"

"Joe, we all have our ways. I'm sure you may trust me to draw what you want, but it's inevitable that, somehow, it ain't gonna be exactly what you want. We've managed to work our way through disappointment, I think. Haven't we?"

"Sure, sure. That's right. And I'm not saying that there's any problem, Mahlon. I'm just saying that, here I am now and I've gotten these newest photos. Paid a good penny or two for them. I... well, let's just look them over and you tell me what you think. All right?"

"All right, Joe. Let's have a look-see at your new little pitchers, shall we?"

Chrystal was out shopping for the afternoon, and Harry was in boarding school this year, so we had the place to ourselves for a couple hours. Joe went into the third bedroom, rummaged around in the back of the closet for a couple minutes, then came out with a box. It was about the size of a rather flat, large shoebox, but was all black, made of wood, and even had a little keyed lock on the hinged top. Not all that secure, but it was enough to keep the thing from popping open in someone's hands, unless they worked at it.

Joe set the box on the dining room table and, with a Master magician's flourish, revealed the tiniest key in his right hand. He leaned over the table while turning his head to smile at me and he inserted and turned the key. The lock released, the box was opened, and inside were stacked a few small manila envelopes – the kind with the flap on one end and a brass clasp that fit through the hole in the flap. He took out the top envelope, undid the clasp, and pulled out the first item.

It was a postcard-sized sepia-toned photographic print. Shot in a studio by a professional (based on the props and the lighting), the nude girl on the upholstered chair was cleverly posed. Her arms akimbo and her legs crossed tightly, her breasts half hidden by a huge necklace that still allowed one nipple to smile out to the viewer, and she looking directly into the camera lens with a cool, detached "what the heck" smirk on her face.

The next card was the same model, same pose mostly. Except her head was turned to the left and upward. The next one showed her arms somewhat lowered and her legs somewhat apart. Next her arms down and legs more apart. Last, arms were folded across her chest but her knees were about a foot apart and you got a look at her hairy-nary area. A little look, but a look.

"That's the first envelope. What do you think?" asked Joe.

"Pretty girl. Nice muscle tone in her arms. Good lighting. French?"

"Yes, yes. I was in Paris and Luxembourg last month, and I found an older gentleman who was dealing in these. I think they're rather recent shots, and the girls are Flapper-thin and not of the earlier-era feminine form. I think I like the slim form all right, now that I'm getting used to it. Funny how long it's taken me. And I know that you already do, my friend. If fact, I think you always have, appreciated the slighter form. Yes?" He gathered the four prints.

"So you've noticed? No secret there. No secrets..."

"Shall we see a few more photographs to choose from?"

"Choose from?'

"Yes, I'll get to that. First, let's see here..." and he extracted the contents of the next envelope. I saw now that the envelopes were numbered in the corners, in a delicate penmanship that I guessed was a woman's. "Here, ah yes," he said as he laid the first of this group on the table.

Same studio, lighting, setting. Now two girls – the one from the first set, and another slim companion. Were they sisters? They *definitely* looked like sisters by the third photo. Each of the shots was set up so as to reveal more of their private parts, progressively, assuming that one were careful to keep them in the right order. That didn't really matter to me.

Although Joe was careful to reveal them that way, my interest was in the flow of the torso movement in each of the girls, in each picture, and comparing one to the other. Some were more natural, others certainly more stretched, even contorted. I was watching the dynamics of the movements, as caught by the still

camera. I began to think about how the photographer had chosen to go from one pose to the next, and how several of the poses
were static while others must have been luckily grabbed by the
camera shutter in that moment between set-up and gravity having its inevitable way with the girls' parts. And the age-old question, why were some erotic and others just naked? I had gotten so
engrossed in such thoughts that I had forgotten that Joe apparently had some agenda of his own for showing them.

"...and that's my idea. What do you think?" Joe was talking to
me and I vaguely realized that he probably had been for at least
a few sentences.

"Joseph Dunninger. I have to admit that I was deep into my
own thought processes and did not hear you. And since I am
the one in the room who does not read minds, would you mind
repeating what you just said?"

He chuckled. "I should have known. Of course. The artistic
mind has a mind of its own, does it not? Maybe I should let you
share your reaction to these new shots?"

"No, no. You're picking up the tab, here. Go ahead. Tell me,
Joe, what you were saying a minute ago. I promise to pay attention. This time."

"Well, then, I was trying to figure out how to adapt some
of these poses into a series of drawings: witchcraft needing two
witches at once to perform a spell, or incantation. I was thinking
that we already have these figure references, and that could be a
pretty good start. That's what I was thinking. And was saying."

"I see. Yes, I can see where you are heading. A series? Are
you imagining six, or a dozen, or…? And where were you going
to start?"

"Maybe a dozen? I have been book-marking in my extensive
collection of witchcraft studies. You've seen some of those books.
Remember?"

"Oh, yes." Of course I remembered – very old and rare volumes indeed, in foreign languages.

"And I envisioned your own artistic craft in rendering some
very sensual versions of those scene selections. Maybe eventually

even getting a publisher interested, if that's the way you and I decide we want to go. But on the other hand... on the other hand... I'm thinking of something probably too... strong, too powerful, for regular publication."

"All right." I agreed, in principle. "I'm game. You actually hiring, then?"

"Who's hiring whom?" it was Chrystal's voice from the doorway. We were startled, but neither of us wanted to show it outright. It's embarrassing for a man to allow himself to be snuck up on.

"Dear me! Why *me*, Dear," said Joe as he gathered the photographs, slipped them back into the envelope, and the envelope smoothly into the box. "Me. That is, I'm hiring Mahlon, of course. And, you! My word, aren't you the quiet one? We didn't even hear you come in, Sweetheart."

"And what have you got there?" she took a couple slow steps into the room and nodded toward the box as she carefully pulled off one long black glove. "Hmmmm?" She stood still. From a few feet away I still detected her scent. A new perfume? She raiseed one perfectly-plucked eyebrow, looking from me to Joe.

Joe and I exchanged glances. He stared into my good eye while I blinked rapidly about a half-dozen times. We both smiled, just a little, and simultaneously "Hmmmmmmmm...d" two notes in harmony.

"Chrystal. Darling. Let Mahlon and I have our little secrets, won't you?" We hmmmmed together again.

"All right, Gentlemen. As you wish. But I've always thought three-part harmony far more invigorating than two-part. I merely thought I'd mention this, in passing. Just in case you wanted to be reminded. Just in case..." She had slowly turned. Her voice trailed off as she left the room with a few gliding high-heeled strides, the kind that move the hips a certain way.

I continued to watch the empty doorway she had passed through. Ten seconds. Twenty. "Damn. I'm suddenly hungry. Aren't you?"

I could feel Joe's silent stare on the side of my head for about a five-count.

He then spoke in a deliberate flat tone, "There might be some k-k-k-kold-k-k-k-kuts in the k-k-Kelvinator. Shall we warm them up, for a sandwich?"

Satan has his companions, fellow-devils, to admire and encourage him; but I am solitary and detested.

Travels With Steinbeck
1968

JOHN STEINBECK, FRIEND and collaborator. He has enjoyed a life of great achievements, accolades, awards… and I hear he is not in good health. Not at all well. Neither am I, but that's beside the point. Still, there is something I would like to get straight right now about me and John.

I would like to point out that I was a success before he was.

I suppose you could say that's partly due to the fact that I am older – by six or seven years. Yes, he is a veritable youngster compared to me. I say: So what?

We both traveled to New York City for the first time ¬– at the same time. That steamer, *Katrina*, carried us through the Panama Canal and dropped us on the New York dock simultaneously. We first housed in the same rooming house in Manhattan. Ate the same food. Romanced the same girls (almost, sometimes, occasionally) and pounded the same pavement starting with the same foot. The left one.

That was 1925 of course.

John got some day-labor City sanitary position or situation. He was writing in his room all the times he wasn't earning a dime, or eating or sleeping, or hanging out in my apartment (because I had all the prettiest models lounging about in their scanties or their all-togethers). He also had a reporting job at the newspaper for about five minutes. He warn't no reporter. Like he often said, he was a "writer, dammit!"

Meanwhile, I got my drawings placed in *The New Yorker* right away. I obviously showed that I had something Harold Ross wanted for the magazine (besides pictures of naked girls drawn in the most loving way). Soon the book publisher McBride gave me my big break with *Limehouse Nights* in 1926, and I was on my way, go-go-go and draw-draw-draw. I must say, it went really well, and astonishingly quickly.

John – not so much. It wasn't but a few months and he got discouraged and returned to Momma-land, California. Oh, he didn't give up writing, obviously. Just didn't break through with the 1926 newspapers and publishers.

From that point on I illustrated non-stop. The work just kept coming in. Big jobs like *Salammbo* and *Sorcerer's Apprentice* plus little pop-offs here and there (most of which I can't even remember now and who cares anyway?). Books, book jackets, magazine spots, ads – you name it, I did it. Couldn't get enough.

Finally by early 1927 I found the first thing I could do to help John directly. I'd heard about a fella who was getting ready to launch a slick-paper magazine called *The Smoker's Companion* – kinda literary, kinda opinionated. I hustled over there with my portfolio and laid out my stuff. The editor focused on my cartoons - the *New Yorkers* and even the earlier *Portland Spectator* political covers. We hashed it out and decided upon my own satirical commentary spots. You know, poking fun at the high-minded know-it-alls with overbearing morality lessons for society ¬– primarily social commentary rather than political.

While at the magazine offices I slipped the story editor a little thing that John had written and had left with me: *The Treasure of Iban.*

They decided to pop it into the first issue of *Smokers Companion*. Voila! John was now a published author – in New York, no less. He still hung out on the left coast though, leaving it a long-distance milestone for him to enjoy.

Not much happens with John for a couple years, yet he manages to finish up an historical novel, *Cup of Gold*. Well, maybe that's not 'not much' but actually 'really something.' Who am I to judge – I've never written a novel!

Anyways, I had gotten to know the folks at Robert McBride Inc. pretty well. We'd had some good times and concocted some good books. They decided to try John's novel when I brought the manuscript by. Probably they'd thought: *it's well written, although, how to go with the marketing? Adult? Adventure? What to do?*

Well, there was further discussion and I finally said to them:

"It's simple, boys: hire me! I'll do a dust jacket that will really pop! They say you can't judge a book by its cover? Hah! Who ever came up with that one? How many times have I proved that wrong?"

I guess that gave them something to think about.

Soon, there's this wrap-around drawing I'd done, and McBride decided to go with a full color effect. My challenge in adding three separate additional drawings is to get the shades of grey at the proper tones to overlap as the three colors in the printing process and make the whole thing fit together.

Once printed, it looked pretty good – I'd say about 80 percent what I'd envisioned. And it did really pop! I thought it was one of that season's best eye-catchers on the bookstore shelves and tables, and in the holiday window displays.

Fine and dandy until I see John on my quick trip out West where he says to me, "Mahlon! That cover! What kind of kid's book did you think I wrote?"

A kid's book? What the…?

"Hi John. Good to see you too. Look, I'm trying to help you sell a few books, like a real author. Don't you want to entice the masses? The Public capital P?

"And you think the Public is interested in some rainbowed, flashy juvenile swashbuckler?"

"The Public is interested in a lot of different things. John, all I can say is, watch the sales numbers and the returns. If more people buy it than the number of copies that bookstores return, there's your answer." He wasn't having it.

"But it looks like a common Sabatini, or a kid's *Kidnapped* or something, for Christ's sake!"

I didn't want to argue. "All right. What's done is done. Just... keep an eye on sales, is all I'm saying." But it hurt my feelings, his hot-headed reaction, because he's a friend and a damn fine wordsmith. And I was older.

I never heard, ultimately, how many had sold. I suppose time will tell. That long-winding crowded sidewalk of Time that just so happens to run alongside the Big Gutter.

But I was the successful guy while he was the beginner, the untried quantity. He should have listened, but sometimes that wasn't his strongest suit.

I admit, of all his books *Grapes of Wrath* was a pretty good read, sold pretty well, so he obviously listened to a few people along the way, at one time or another.

And sometimes I still imagine: what if he'd invited me to do *that* cover?

Oh well, soon enough we'll both be waiting to cross the River Styx. Maybe he'll lend me a doubloon then, to pay the final boatman.

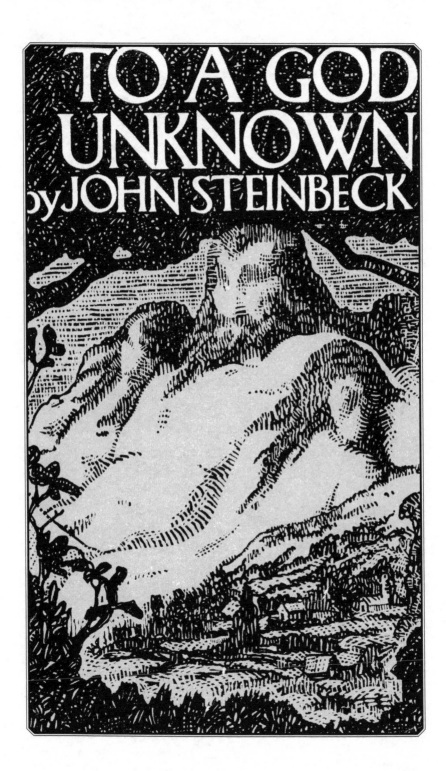

TO A GOD UNKNOWN by JOHN STEINBECK

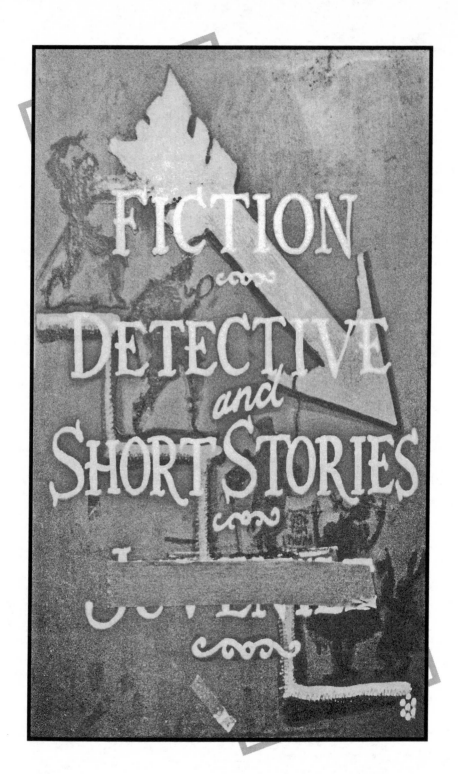

*When falsehood can look so like the
truth, who can assure themselves of
certain happiness?*

The Guitar Kid's Mission

1961

I WAS ON the main floor of *Bee and Tea* one morning, painting. Inside my heart? Well, I didn't feel much like I had a lot of reason to be doing anything, really. I was just fumbling around, and bumping up against a darkening mood that stank up my very core.

I'd had way too many headaches in the last couple of months and I was worn out from that, too. There wasn't any paying work. I made my pallet on the fourth floor of the bookstore, by the generally kind acquiescence of Mess'rs Jack One and Jack Two. They'd been mostly amenable.

Lately I'd been nudged by a few guilty pangs regarding this freeloading, so I'd offered to paint up some right-nice signage for their shop. I thought it *could* be helpful – they thought it *would* be helpful. I'd already put in a few hours the week before, upstairs in the third floor front room that was my 'studio', and had produced about four dozen Mahlon-styled hand-lettered placards that could be thumb-tacked around the store, at the ends of aisles, on shelf fronts between rows of books, and so forth.

Things like "Mystery," "World History," "Sophistry." It kept me off the street.

Today I was intent on keeping out of everyone's way, parked at the top of the stairway that led to the musty basement. The children's books were unfortunately shelved in that environment, and I was sitting in a draft painting an *Alice in Wonderland* silhouette on the wooden door at the head of the stairs. It described the books below, and indicated the route one must take to access them. All very artistic, yet completely and totally helpful to the customer, even if I do say so myself. Buy your child a moldy book...

I sat on a little wooden crate, with a small jar of black paint in my left hand and the world's smallest poster brush in my right, getting the contour of Alice '*just so.*'

"You got any books on Woody Guthrie? Music books?"

Interesting question. The fella without the New York accent wasn't talking to me, but to the live Alice at the front desk. I had heard a tinkle of the bell and now the atmospheric blast from the front door reached out to slap me on its way to the basement. I suffered sensitivity to every suggestion of a chill lately. New York in January can have surprisingly battering winds whip down 4th Avenue and up yer Khyber, if given the opportunity. And for me, they'd grown impossible to avoid.

"Guthrie? I don't think we do. What kind of music, sir, are you interested in?" asked Alice of this young, skinny guy. He was a kid, really. Blue dungarees and a khaki short jacket that was too flimsy, and a short-brimmed cap leaving too much hair sticking out around the perimeter. His hands jammed in his pockets, he was stepping back and forth, from one foot to the other, like he needed to get warm. Well, who didn't?

"Folk music. You know, kind of country-western, but not really. Like old slave songs, cowboy. Labor movement. Negro blues. Stuff like that. Anything like that, but especially Woody Guthrie?"

"You're welcome to look in the Music section, but it's not very large. It's right around back over there." Alice-in-bookland pointed towards me, at my little signage job. "Past the gentle-man painting, then down the end of the last aisle," she said, and I swear raised her voice a little for my benefit: "There's a nice new sign back there so you can't miss it," boomed her cheery alto.

As the young man sidled past me he spoke up, "*Alice in Wonderland*. Now that's a pretty heady trip, for kids. That mebby oughta be in the philosophy section, high on a shelf."

"At least we have that in common, heh?" I replied. "A perceived appreciation of Nineteenth Century discourse in the form of droll entertainment."

"I'm hip, man." He nodded and touched the brim of his cap in a little half salute of agreement, whistled a short half-tune and shuffled toward the back of the store to the music shelves. He looked even skinnier from the back. It had been several decades since I myself was such a rail. Time broadens one, whether one travels or not.

I turned back to the door-painting project, mindfully lettering the downstairs categories, each one tucked under a step on the painting. Young cap-fella had soon wandered around to some unseen area of the store, but as I was gathering my paints and brushes into my crate and creakily, quietly coaxing friendliness from my skeptical knees, he came up behind me.

"Say there... Artist Guy. You like folk music?"

"Folk music? I'm not sure you and I are talking about the same thing, Junior, but come to think of it, I did know a music-y fellow once. Name of Woodrow, as I recall." I didn't look at him directly, but parked him in the corner of my eye.

That halted him in his tracks. "What? Woody Guthrie? No way, man!"

"Yes, Woody. Of course, that's what he called himself. But I haven't seen him in a while – half a year, or more, probably," I said. "He's ill, you know. In the hospital." I hesitated saying it even as I heard my voice catch a little. And had it really been that long? Six months?

"Yes, yes. I know. I came to New York to see him, actually. I came all the way from Minnesota to meet him, in fact. In person. I've been playing his songs... some of his songs... forever. You knew him? I mean, you actually know him?" He was talking fast, kind of incredulous, and then a little suspicious. "Not really? Woody Guthrie the songwriter? You know... him?"

I bent to pick up my little crate, and my overhead light bulb glimmered a moment.

"Look, Junior, come with me for a second. I want to talk with you," We went around to the stairway that connected to the upper floors.

"Alice. Going up!" I glanced over to the living Alice.

"See you later," she called back without looking up from her reading. She added a tiny three-fingered wave of her hand in no particular direction.

"And, Junior, what's your name anyway?"

"Bobby Zimmerman. Bob. Sorry for not introducing myself."

I led the young fellow up two flights to my studio, where I set down my crate and its contents, and pointed to a plain wood chair there for him to occupy as I washed out my brushes (very thoroughly I might add) and put the little bottles of paint back in their proper places. He sat, but not still, wiggling his foot all the while he watched me, plus tippy-tapping his fingers on his pants leg.

"My name's Mahlon Blaine, and what have you got to be nervous about?"

"Oh, I don't think I'm nervous, Mister Blaine. I mean, should I be? Hah! Never mind. Anyway, it's just the music. Sometimes I get it stuck in me, circlin' 'round, and it shows up at the extremities. That's that. But..." he stopped tapping, "Woody Guthrie? Really? Shi... Shucks."

"Sounds like you came a long way. I wouldn't joke with a young wandering kid like you, Bobby Zimmerman. But he's sick, like I said. He doesn't always like having visitors, and so I don't get over to chew fat much nowadays." Old arguments could surface sometimes, and I just didn't like seeing him in that damn bed either. Poor Woody.

"Sir. Mister Blaine. You don't know me, that's for certain. I am sure I am only one of untold numbers of Woody's fans, but... I can't describe fully what he has meant to my own life."

"Your life? How old are you? Fifteen? Sixteen?"

"I know, I know. That's how I may look, but I'm old enough to sing the songs. I'm twenty – OK, nineteen – and I've come all the way from Minneapolis Minnesota, Sir, to meet Mister Guthrie. And I will, I'm sure of it. Eventually."

I looked him over. He was earnest, all right, and looked me right damn square in my good eye. Woody had looked at me like that, more than once. I took a chance I hoped I wouldn't live to regret.

"Bobby Zimmerman, a little jaunt would probably do me good. I don't get out of this frozen canyon town often enough. I therefore have a proposition for you. If you can meet me here day-after-tomorrow, about noon, and bring the wherewithal – say twenty bucks – we could have ourselves an outing. Lunch, a bus ride or two, a walk... maybe a talk..."

"You're saying...?"

"I'm saying, let's go pay a visit to my old friend, Mister Woody Guthrie. What say you?"

He didn't hesitate. "Right! Wow! OK! That's the day after to-morrow, here noon, twenty bucks. Thank you sir, thank you in-deed! Oh boy, a mission!"

"All right. See you then. Don't trip going down the stairs, Bobby. And remember, don't forget the double-sawbuck."

"I won't. See you then." And he skittered like a lizard on a hot rock out the door and down the steps lickety-split.

Six months! That's plenty of time for bygones to be water un-der the bridge, right? If not, the Kid could be a buffer. I was pretty sure I would be able to pull this all together. What the heck, any-way. Why not give it a shot?

TWO DAYS LATER.

Well, the Kid got to the store and, unstrangely enough, I wasn't ready. It had been a rough couple of nights. Normally, the traffic and general City cacophonies don't bother me much. Sure, they may wake me up, like a siren going hell-bent past your head and through it. I'm only sleeping on the fourth floor, remember. But usually I get back to sleep OK. Not last night. Once I got startled out of my dead dream-sleep, I had a heck of a time. All I could focus on were the proximate whiffs of stale mouse crap.

Thus eleven a.m. and I was still in bed.

Alice came up from the front desk. I don't normally bother with a mechanical alarm. Her scuffy footsteps on the stairs followed by her little finger-tapping on my door, and her announcement roused me.

"Mahlon, did you have an appointment with that excitable young man today? At noon? He's already here, a little early."

"What time is it, for cripe's sake?"

"A little after eleven."

"Well, tell him to keep his pants on while I attempt to do the same. I'll be ready at noon, like I said. Cripes!"

I'm not a quick riser anymore. With sixty-seven years under my belt, I just appreciate that I rise at all. There will come a time, and it may not be far off, when I'll wake up dead, and that will be that. Until then, I surface slowly and scruffily.

After each of the usual toilet duties were taken care of, and me all dressed presentably in comfortable pleated trousers and red plaid shirt, checkered brown wool blazer, purdy-new white socks, my most reliable shoes and hat, and a couple layers of undershirts, I was goody-to-go. I ambled down the stairs, and Young Bob was waiting for me, finger-doodling on his knee as he sat upon that weary stool parked at the end of "History." He popped vertical, dressed the same as two days ago.

"Mr. Blaine, sorry I was early, Sir. I hope everything's OK?"

"Junior, wait until you're my age. No comment. Now, you got the funds that are required?"

"Huh?"

"Is President Jackson accompanying us?"

"Oh! He sure is, yes Sir!" He patted his right front jeans pocket and added a wry smile. "What's the plan?"

"I need a bit of lunch for breakfast, first-off. Let's see... Oh, you can buy me a pastrami on sourdough with ketchup, right around the corner there. Get yourself something, but here's what to keep in mind: that twenty bucks needs to buy us bus tickets to Parsippany, New Jersey and back, and maybe a dinner too, because this will take a little while, today. All day, actually." Then I noticed, leaning against the store's big historical tomes fraying on the bottom shelf, the black guitar case.

I stared at it and I shook my head slowly. "What's that there? You hauling some guitar along? I don't know..."

"Sure," he said, "and you won't regret it either. This is the connection, man. This is what it is all about." There was that youthful enthusiasm again. Refreshing, in a slightly annoying way.

"OK, I suppose." Thing is, I was bringing a small portfolio along myself. A bit of show-and-tell for my old friend Woody, which might keep us off uncomfortable conversation. And now the Kid and guitar – also a potential distraction?

Not so bad maybe, no matter the Kid's abilities. "We'd best be on our way, then. How about you get those sandwiches 'to go', and a hot tea with a lid. And get lots of extra napkins. And a couple-three toothpicks. I'll be out in front of the store here in ten minutes."

WE WALKED UP to Fourteenth with the sharp wind biting us both and caught a crosstown bus to the Port Authority Bus Terminal on the west side. We hadn't eaten our sandwiches yet because the ride over would be the best time to chow down. The trip would probably take an hour and a half, maybe even two.

At the Orange Bus window in the terminal I said to the dreary ticket girl, "Hello, Bee-you-ti-us Bus-tee-eller. Two round-trips to Parsippany, the Greystone Hospital stop. This handsome young man will pay," I winked, sharply stepped aside and gestured towards Bob. He reached over to slip the twenty to her, got back an assortment of bills and change and a free bashful smile, and we climbed stained concrete stairs and sauntered onto the loading platform.

Our bus was waiting there already so we boarded and took seats together about halfway back, on the right. Portfolio and guitar went on the overhead. We settled in.

"Shit!" as I unwrapped the paper around my pastrami. "There's mustard here! Not ketchup!"

"Sorry. I forgot to tell you that the deli guy says to me: 'Nobody - NOBODY - would order ketchup on pastrami, so you must mean mustard, right Kid?' Being from Minnesota, I said 'Yup.'"

The Kid was so matter-of-fact and nonchalant about the mix-up that all I could say was "Yeah, mustard it shall be. Don't want to upset the balance of the Universe, now do we?" The bright yellow condiment's presence began to permeate the bus, competing with the diesel fumes and residual body odors. We cautiously began our feast. The driver wormed the bus through the terminal labyrinth, onto the street, through the tunnel under the Hudson, and up into yon hills of Jersey.

After the sandwiches were downed, and mouths were wiped of mustard, and teeth were picked, I told Bobby, "Let me give you a little background information. Just relax, and take a listen." Then I commenced to recount two stories of Woody and me:

IN 1939 AND 1941 there were some interesting meetings that I was part of. Not just a witness to, mind you. In fact, the whole shebang would never even have happened if it hadn't been for me.

First, there was this benefit-thing to raise money for migrant farm workers. It was being arranged by the *John Steinbeck Committee to Aid Farm Workers*. Imagine that. Sounds high-falootin', don't it? Well, they were gonna have a bunch of speakers, of course, and some music that would set the tone and fit in and get people's juices juiced. I think they had in mind some Western music, or Western Swing or something.

I wasn't on that committee (I heard somewhere that "two m's and two t's and two e's working together, oh I see, equal a committee" but I don't remember where I heard it, and it doesn't make a lot of sense anyway, does it?), but I knew one of the fellas, Will, that was on the decision end of it. He was an art lover, so he thought pretty highly of me, I guess. I told him about me meeting this here real folky musical-genius fella named Woody Guthrie, back when I was doing some sketching among the migrant workers in California. Those poor folk had some of the most interesting, haggard faces I'd seen since I used to ride the "D" train to Coney Island.

I told Will I'd been wandering around one of the camps out there, and I heard about a man who was kind of gathering portraits, like I was, only he didn't have paints, he had a guitar. (Actually, I rarely used paints on this excursion, as I found it more helpful to just sit down across from my subjects with a pad and pencil, and draw on my knee. Everybody just was more relaxed that way, and I got the expressions I couldn't have otherwise.)

A friendly subject named Horace Bilough, as I was sketching him, told me I oughta meet this guitar man and that he'd take me to where he was pretty sure he'd be 'cause he'd heard it from someone else at the camp's dirt-floored makeshift canteen earlier that day. That all seemed reasonable to me so I went along with my new friend Horace. Why not?

We trekked about three miles along a dusty road to the next camp, and it was getting to be about suppertime when we got there. Horace knew several of these people, saying howdy all around, giving me glowing introductions and commentary. I was hungry, as usual, and parched, and wouldn't you know, some of those folks who had nothing, or at least even less than I had, found me a place to sit down and share some soup, and a little piece of rye bread. Delicious, sorta. It didn't quite fill me up, of course.

After dusk fell and firelights began flickering around the camp, plus a lantern here and there, Horace had this other guy (who claimed loudly to be Horace's cousin through their grandfathers) lead the way through the tricky shadows of tents, shrubs and vehicles over to the west side where a larger fire ring blazed and quite a few folks were congregating.

I'd left all my drawing stuff, my sketchpad and so forth, back at where I'd eaten, because they said I could bunk with them tonight and they'd find me a blanket and a place on the truck tailgate to stretch out. I couldn't pass up such a royal invitation, now could I?

As we got up into the crowd a ways folks quickly quieted their jabbering and I heard strokes on a guitar. First, thrumbed bass strings a little, then a strum or two on the higher strings, then generally repeating the sequence while chords changed in a pleasing manner. A fellow started to sing and I'd never heard anything exactly like it. It was real plain, kind of nasally, and he stuffed a plethora of words into each line, telling a story that had a lot of asides in it that tended to comment on the main storyline. He made you listen, just following all that. I liked it. I liked it more the more of it I heard.

By the time he'd played a half-dozen numbers people started calling out titles and he would sing each tune to the listeners' apparent satisfaction. I couldn't tell for sure because I didn't recognize any of those tunes. I did identify some of the names, though, of the characters and places, in songs that he claimed to have written himself. It was topical, political, but often had a funny edge to it. We all laughed here and there, and chuckles bounced around the fire. He had us smiling and thinking at the same time. The songs kept coming: union songs, hobo songs, love songs, murder songs. By the time he'd concluded, I bet he'd sung twenty of these stories. All good. Really good. Applause.

Horace grabbed my arm and strode us over there and spoke to the now bent-over figure, "Mister Guth...Mister Guthrie? I think you should meet this friend of mine. He likes your s... songs."

"Well then, all right, all right. How'd ya do, gentl'men?" as he turned around from putting his guitar into its travel-weary case. "I'm Woody Guthrie and ya ken call me Woody." This smallish man, about 30 years old, stuck out his right hand, real direct. I took it and he had a hell of an assured handshake. Firm, but not so as to injure. That's highly important to me, as an artist, as I've run into too damn many men who are trying to prove their balls are bigger than yours by crushing your hand. An artist with a crushed hand is like an elephant with a briefcase.

I shook firmly back. "Mahlon Blaine. Thanks for the tunes. Cleverly heartfelt, they were."

"Nice t' hear thet comment. I'm guessin' you were accidently listenin.'" He deadpanned, gradually allowing a twitch of his lips to grow into a bona fide smile, and a quick laugh. The fire twinkled in his eyes. "Ha-ha! Say, you fellas stayin' in the camp here?"

"Me? Just for the night, Woody. I've been invited to stay over by... gosh... I don't remember their names. Over there. Somewhere. We'll find them later, I guess. Right, Horace?"

"Mmmm-yup," affirmed Horace. He took his turn to shake Woody's hand, while he scratched behind his own ear and added, "Oh, they're expectin' us all right I'd s...say, yup."

"Just one night then? Visitin', eh?" said Woody, turning from the scratching Horace back to me.

"Yes, afraid so. Oh, Horace here claims you and I are on a similar mission, gathering stories. Mine are written in the lines of the faces here. There are wonderful faces here."

"Faces? I see. I think. You're..." he paused, expectantly.

"Artist, by trade and natural inclination. Portraiture. Also illustration."

"Artist! I must say, I draw a little bit too. But you bein' a real illustrator? Published? Have I seen yer work, yer canvases, yer sketches, yer oils, yer charcoals?"

"I was published for a while, in the Twenties, mostly in books. New York books, you see."

"Wait. Blaine? Blaine? I had a book as a boy. My father bought it fer me and we all read it t'gether in the evenin's. *Two Years Before the Mast* was thet title. You did the illustrations in thet one, right? Am I rememberin' this item correctly?"

"I stand accused. You have some fine memory banks there, Woody."

He paused and stared into the red embers in the pit. "Yes. I r'member. It was shortly after then thet my father got burned bad in a fire. Oil lamp. It happens. You know... we never did get to the end a' thet book, I don't think. Damn."

"Sorry to hear that." I could relate. I glanced at Horace, who was wiping a tear off of himself.

Woody took a minute, then let out a sigh and added, "Yes, yes. Well. Everybody's got stories, even you 'n me, I guess." He emerged from his recollection. "Glad t' meet ya, Blaine."

He and I stood there looking at each other, sizing up the situation from both sides. He noticed a few additional folks were behind us, hanging back but obviously wanting to approach him too, and he went on, changing the subject. "I'd like t' see some a whatcha been doin' here, if ya got th' time. Th' drawin'? Tomorrow mornin' maybe, in the daylight?"

"Sure. Certainly. I imagine I'll be up early, whether I manage to get any sleep or not. I can meet you back here. Sunrise? Just kidding!"

"Let's then. G'night," he said, turning to chat with those fans.

I turned, humming, and Horace and I wandered "home," as my tailgate pallet was calling to me.

And so Woody and me met the next day, not the actual crack of dawn, but close enough. I showed him the sketches, the faces, and he particularly admired the drawings that implied a glimmer of hope or a glint of resolve behind the despair sunk in the grime and grit. I agreed. Perhaps I'd caught a widening of the eyes, or narrowing of the pupils. Maybe. Hell, it's art – who knows?

He reciprocated, dug out that guitar and played me parts of a couple new songs he was working on. They were bluesy and melodic, something to hum along with. I don't remember the titles or words, but the notes would stick in my ear all morning. They just sounded familiar right away.

I finally asked him to sit for me then, for an hour, while I used my charcoal and pastels. My impressionistic technique suited his demeanor: short simple strokes which gave the appearance of going every-which-way, no pretenses, layers informing the whole, shapes and volumes emerging. He was mightily pleased with the results, and I made him a gift of it, with instructions on the care of the delicate medium. Pastel is not well suited to the road life, so who knows if it survived.

This much felt certain: he and I had made ourselves friends of each other that day.

So it was no huge reach for me a little later, you see, to suggest to my acquaintance in the Migrant Workers Committee: Woody Guthrie. Well, sure. But another committee member had already thought Mister Pete Seeger would be the cat's pajamas for the event. Both those songsters wound up performing. Woody and Pete hit it off swell and have been buddies ever since, or so I hear. That, like I said, was our introduction in 1939.

NOW, IN 1941 I was back in Portland, Oregon.

A couple of my buddies from the old *Movieola* days had been hired to work on a new motion picture, a documentary about electricity and the building of the Grand Coulee Dam on the Columbia River. They in turn got a hold of me because they knew I was raised in that part of the country, and we all joined up. They didn't really have it in mind for me to work on sets or costumes or anything like the old days. This was a documentary, after all. But I was sort of an informal general consultant. Fine by me, as there would be a little money involved as well.

What really floored me here was that the government project managers had decided to go whole hog on this thing, take a full year to make it, and had also hired my pal Woody to write music for the whole kit and the entire kaboodle. I hadn't seen Woody in months, so this was increasingly looking like something I'd enjoy in a big way.

Woody brought his family with him, of course – Mary and the three kids. After all, it was going to be steady pay for a year. I didn't mind everybody being there so much, except I had heard that Woody and Mary hadn't been getting along. I had heard this from Woody himself, in an earlier letter. You don't like to hear about your buddy's marital discord, but there it is. You always wish for the best for friends, less dis-chord for a musician especially.

Knowing this, I phoned down to invite my *compadre*, John Steinbeck, up for a week.

He hoped he could fit it into his schedule but he was pretty busy finishing up the manuscript for *Sea of Cortez*, and he and his wife Carol also weren't getting along.

Whateverthehell, it was like a damn mis-marital epidemic.

I'd told him, "This is what you need, John. Just get away from everything for a while. I've somebody here you've got to meet. Oh, nothing like that! It's a guy, but he's quite the artist in his own right. The real deal. It'll be good for everyone. Trust me."

"I don't know, Mahlon. The pressure is definitely getting to me, a throbbing at the sides of my head. Maybe..."

I interrupted. "Like I said, trust me." I hoped I knew what I was talking about. I'm no marriage expert. I just felt like the time was approaching for both Woody and John to shit or get off the pots. Plural. But I didn't say that to either of them. It wouldn't have been polite, dontcha know.

John paused an exceptional length and I thought we'd lost the phone connection. "Give me a few days here, to reach an under-standing with Carol, and maybe I can bring the book with me and work there. Then after a week or so..." he uttered without much conviction.

"All right. See you in a few days." I remained in my optimistic voice.

Since I myself had not been divorced for very long, I needed my good friends around me.

TUESDAY-NEXT AND TRUE to his word, Steinbeck showed up in a blue Ford touring car, dusty but with a new polish still shining through. He must have borrowed it.

"Carol is keeping our convertible with her," he told me, and added a staccato "Ha!" I helped him carry in his bags, but he hadn't brought much: a couple new alligator Samsonites and a valise. We set the stuff on my bed, as I hadn't cleared his yet. We'd sort it out later. It was just dandy to have him here, and I knew we'd work some, and probably party a tad. Swell.

I had previously arranged to pick up Woody by mid-afternoon to drive out to a particularly serene and scenic site on the river. I thought I could remember how to find it because I remembered I'd had a delicious nude model along last time. That kind of a view sticks in your mind. Anyway...

I hadn't mentioned anything in advance to Woody about our literary visitor.

John and I drove up in his big Ford, parked in the sloping driveway of the little white rental house with the primordially mossy roof, and Woody came striding out, wiping his hands on the tails of his not-very-absorbent work shirt. I can't say that he appeared happy.

"Late lunch," he said as he approached us, his head at that odd angle that was kind of a trademark, squinting in the bright sunbeams that managed to streak between the tall trees. He used his left hand as a visor, to cut the glare. "Just helping with the dishes. Well Mahlon, who's this?"

I looked from one friend to the other and tried to milk a pregnant pause. "Woody Guthrie. John Steinbeck. It's time you two met."

"Hey, I've read yer book! The big one, *Grapes of Wrath*. Thet's the title, ain't it?" Woody was grinning from ear to ear and stuck his right hand out for one of his assured handshakes. "Pleased!"

John took Woody's hand, shook it while he put his left hand on Woody's right elbow. I could tell there was a bit of mutual professional admiration going on.

John said, "I've been listening to some of your songs, Sir. Great stuff! And last year you did that benefit for my committee. I certainly appreciate how you fit that into your busy schedule. I hear it was a splendid performance! Wish I could have been there myself."

There was more gushing too. But it was one gosh-goodly start to a shit-pile week.

For instance...

Their two wives managed to dampen our masculine festivities. John got a call at least once daily, and even if we'd been scouting locations and away from the phone all day, Carol would catch him at night. I got the feeling the phone was clanging away an awful lot when we weren't there. The calls that got through didn't sound like so much fun, overheard from this end, but John didn't talk about them with me. I would've offered very helpful and pointed suggestions, but John always opined that my so-called humor invariably got in the way of common sense. Too raw, I suppose.

Mary was giving Woody a hard time as well. And for that matter, she'd stopped speaking to me too. I won't go into details there, but a mix of wifely concerns and nude modeling had raised a mighty sore spot between her, Woody and me.

All hell was breaking loose. Little seams were widening. Veneers were peeling. It made me think about my own marital split. A lot of unhappiness was eating at all our edges, and us boys found respite by just being out in the woods as much as possible. The movie project was helping, as we aimed our talk towards that instead of wives, art or nudity.

We ruminated on writing too. Woody exposed us to parts of a novel he'd started, about adobe houses for farmers, sort of, but done in an extremely sensual style of prose. He tried to bounce some of these ideas off John. That had been a semi-disaster, as John was too focused his current work and was pretty short with Woody's stuff. Personally I liked its rawness.

The fifth day into our man-week, Woody abruptly found out that he was only hired for one month of filming, not the whole year. No satisfactory explanation, but it could well have been some political backlash. Woody was controversial, I was increasingly understanding. He stood up for the little guy.

"But damn. I don't care," was his reaction. "I'm goin' to put all thet outside crap outta m' mind and jus' write. It's like a paradise here, and th' hell with th' distractions. I'm shootin' for a good solid thirty-day ditty, tune, melody, rhyme, song-a-thon, dammit."

Following up on that news: "I wish I could stay longer," John lied, "but I can't. You two will have to persevere without me, after tomorrow." We protested, but it was all for show. His resolve was firm, although we allowed him to claim that it was his wife's resolve. Unsavory all around.

So John left the next day, with more than a bit of a hangover. Off in a Fordly cloud of dust.

Woody proved true to his word. He wrote and wrote and it was all music, not that novel. He'd bounce the songs off me in bits and pieces, and I'd give him my reactions and my thoughts. He had some good stuff there, no matter what John had thought of his adobe house story. When his designated month ended, he headed back to New York. Mary and the kids didn't. They ended up headed to California.

I guessed where all indications pointed. Anytime I stated the obvious to Woody though, I could tell he couldn't appreciate my fine analysis. I finally crossed a line, said too much, and all of a sudden he just up and left. Poor Woody. First John then me. Or me, then John, then Mary, then me again. I regretted whatever it was in my stupid ramblings that finally got to him. We certainly went sour, the bunch of us.

I stuck around Portland for a while. The movie guys got pretty well set on their final plans for their big-ass documentary, and I began to feel like a hanger-on. About a month after Woody departed, I decided to head back to New York too. I thought the trouble had probably calmed down regarding that Decency League stuff. I certainly didn't want to return to Los Angeles and any unhappily perceived proximity to Dusky, my wife. I mean former wife.

So New York it was.

But my headaches weren't all over. They never are, and that's a continuing story. End of story.

WHILE I'D BEEN monologuing to the Kid, I'd been keeping an eye on our progress: East Orange, Orange, West Orange. I knew we'd be there soon and I had shortened up at the end, wrapping up this background story to coincide with our arrival. As we pulled up to the bus stop right in front of the main building at Greystone, we all got off. Last stop.

After loading new folks for the return trip, the old carriage lunged away in a throat-coating plume of diesel exhaust, while me and the Kid stood there just eyeing the massive facade. God, what an impressive piece of architecture! I told him, "Every time I come here, I have to give myself a minute or two to take this all in. The interior – not so much." He nodded and stared.

"Yeah. Very impressive," he said. What? Is he a mind reader now? Great! One mind-reading friend was more than enough for me! I decided I'd try to guard my thoughts a little better around him.

We checked for traffic – both ways – then crossed in the crosswalk to the front entrance. Built in the 1870s, the sturdily-columned front was centered over a double door of massive weight that, nonetheless, was hung so precisely it took a very small effort to open.

"If Woody Guthrie is really here..." marveled Young Bob, "Wow. The doors of heaven."

"Let's not get carried away, Junior. I'd hardly call this place 'heaven.' And there are folks all around here who'd agree with me. It's mostly mental patients, you know,"

"Well I..."

"But others too, of course. Woody's Huntington disease has just been dragging him down for years. It's so damn slow. And I can't tell you whether 'slow' is ultimately good or bad, but it's been wearing on everyone. He's been here about five years, I'd guess."

"You come out regular? To see him?"

"No. I wish I did. But I guess his wife and kids are here about every Sunday. His second wife, that is. That's why I chose today. A Wednesday should be just about right for him to have shaken off the last familial trauma – or joy, as the case may be – and also get kind of relaxed before he has to gird his loins for next Sunday. But we'll see. He has good days, and bad ones too, like I said," I said.

"Yeah. OK then." said Bob. "I hope this is a good one, a good day for him."

I hoped it was a good day for all of us.

The hallways echoed like crazy, being all hard surfaces, walls and tiles like stone, and not much furniture. If there were to be a fire, it wouldn't follow the halls. The rooms weren't much different, either. Much as I remembered from back in early 1940, when I was first here to visit the Doctor Archie Crandall, the director of the place. But that was already another story right?

We'd checked at the front desk. Woody was in the same room as I'd last seen him, so we headed in the direction indicated by the receptionist and didn't quite get lost before we found him.

He was lying in the bed, or rather half-sitting up, and he spotted me as I was approaching the door, calling out as well as he could "Mahlon! Come in here, dammit." He was all smiles, or grimaces, I'm not sure which, maybe a combination. But I went to the bedside, took his hand and gave it a good firm shake. He grimaced a little more as he slightly mumbled "Welcome back to *Wardy Forty*. Good t' see ya. Good. Good. Did ya bring me anythin'?"

He looked me over and spied the portfolio right away. "Ahhh. Watcha got fer me, m' friend? Somethin'! Somethin'…interestin'? Let's see!" We were starting out in our friendly mode. A good sign.

I interrupted him, "Yeah, Woody, something all right. But look, first, I found this fella hanging around the bookstore. He seemed kind of interested in meeting you. Strange world, huh?"

"A' course it is. But where is he?" Bobby was hanging back, behind me, at the doorway. "Hey, young man. Come here, over here. Ya brought a guitar! Well, well. What's yer name?"

"Bob, Sir. Bob Zimmerman, and right pleased to meet you, Mister Guthrie. Yes Sir!" Bob reached to shake Woody's hand, and Woody managed a wry, painful smile, but didn't get his hand out from the bedclothes. Bob noticed and pulled his own hand back, nodding his head.

"Bob Zimmerman? And just who's this 'Bob Zimmerman'? A boy with a guitar it'd seem. Mahlon, who's this baby loose from his cradle, poured from the ladle?"

Before I could speak, Bob blurted, "I play your songs! Some of 'em – most that I know! I just... I just wanted to meet you. I hitch-hiked from Hibbing Minnesota. I been playin' the songs you wrote, and I want to learn them all. It's just that... I just need-ed to meet you, Sir!" Mister Enthusiasm, still.

"Well here I am, a sorry sight indeed." Woody rolled his head towards the tall window. "Well, well, well." His unfocused gaze hung outside, and all three of us were silent. I was used to Woody's mood shifts but the Kid stood there awkwardly looking to us, back and forth.

Finally Woody said in a low voice, "Have ya met Jack Elliott yet? He knows m' songs. I cain't play 'em anymore. No more... Washington Square. Go see 'im. Jack's the one you'd oughtta talk to." We were all quiet again as Woody seemed to be submerged in other times and places. I apprehended that he might surface from some sore memory of 1941, and unexpectedly fly off the handle.

He looked at Bob, and his morose seemed to lessen. "But Jack ain't here. You don't know Jack. I ain't quite dead yet, but I cain't play. There! You go onna sit over there by th' window." He nod-ded toward a chair, one of those plain metal chairs with a little vinyl on the seat and practically no padding. "Take to thet chair and get yer guitar out. Play me some of m' songs, Mister Zim-merman. Not too loud. Mahlon's brung me somethin' to look at, and I'll do that while ya play. Don't worry. I won't be a'listenin'," he said as he winked at Bob, then turned to me. "Let's see, then. Let's see what impure activity you've chose to done brung me."

Good. I opened the folio and I took out a stack of drawings, all on seventeen by twenty-four paper – some watercolors, some pen-and-ink. Bob had started to play a tune I recognized. Maybe Woody's *Pastures of Plenty*. Not too loud to start, kind of tenta-tive, yet I could tell that he was slowly getting into it.

I placed my drawings on Woody's lap. "Hey," he said, "hold that top up a little, would ya? The angle is too low." So I propped the top and he looked the first one over and chuckled. "This here lady has a distinct problem, and thet li'l fella ain't really helping much, is he?" Woody blinked at me. "I'd be a liar if I told you I been in any such sitchation m'self, by gum, by rum, by thumb."

The next couple pictures brought similar appreciative responses. Woody always liked the little devils and the domineering she-creatures, as long as nobody was anybody he thought he recognized.

Bob kept playing, only now he was on to just some guitar stuff – no words. Some strumming chords that flowed nicely and individual notes plucked and strews about. Woody was nodding his head to the rhythms, as best as he could. Seemed like he was enjoying the combination of music and art.

"Oh gosh!" he said when the next picture was revealed. "Jesus! That's a wild 'un!"

"Say, mind if...?" Bob stopped playing and piped up, angling his head for a look over.

"Yes, we mind," barked Woody. "Son, just play s' more. You needn't see this here artiness craziness anyway. I like the songs. Keep playin' is all I'm sayin'."

"Thanks. Yah. OK then," said Bob. He stretched an elastic thing around the neck of his guitar and began a tune in a higher pitch, with a kind of a staccato beat of flicked strings. Woody and I went back to the drawings.

The next few of them he just smiled and shook his head at. Once we had paged through them all he wanted to go over them again, but slower. "I need to check, ya see, to see if I saw what I thought I saw, when I saw it the first time," he said. So we took our time.

Bob was on his, oh, I don't know, tenth or fifteenth song, catching his stride and sounding fairly professional by the time Woody had had enough of both of us.

"Say, Boys. I'm all pooped out. I don't have th' stamina. Month b' month b' year, decline. It's damn shitty, Boys." Then he turned to Bob. "Listen, m' friend. That was real dang nice to hear. Nice of you to play f' me. I 'preciate that. You really should be a' talking with Jack. I think you two might get along all right. Do ya write any of yer own stuff yet?"

"Well, yes. I've been doing some writing, sir." Bob glanced sideways at me. I surmised he was lying.

Woody said, "Good. I thought so. You've got okay interpretations of my stuff, but I was thinkin' that I'd like to hear if you had some a' yer own. Nex' time. Nex' time f' sure, Bob. I'll be wantin' to hear some of 'em."

"Yes sir. OK then! I'll do my own Woody song then, like yours only mine. Thanks for today. Lettin' me play and all. Thanks."

"You're more'n welcome. And, Mahlon. Gosh darn it, I don' know how or where this fantastic stuff o' yers comes from. I swear! Wh'rever it is, it's an education to visit, but I wouldn' want t' live there, that's fer damn sure. Thanks fer the trip, a slip, a flip to lose my grip."

I told him, "Sure, any time. I'll come back soon, but not, I think, on Sundays." I finally had the nerve to touch on our sensitive subject. It just didn't seem entirely right, avoiding it completely.

Woody's eyes shifted back and forth, locking finally on my good one. A spike of his old spitfire self had surfaced in his scowl. A growly, familiar "Stay the hell away from my wife. She's my *wife*, dammit." fell from his barely moving lips. I heard Bob's quick inhale, then he held his breath.

Probably only a minute passed – or two or four. Woody shifted his gaze to Bob and his jaw muscles relaxed as he looked Bob over, up and down, and finally stared at that well-traveled guitar case dangling at the end of his skinny arm.

I wasn't sure which one of us that Woody addressed with "but don't leave me alone too long either. Damn, an hour seems so short and the day so long. Maybe another time, and sooner rather than? Bye, fer now."

"Goodbye, Woody." I doubted I'd be back though. I felt guilty about how I'd made him upset. Funny how 'So long ago' can still be fresh.

"Goodbye." Bob echoed. "See you soon again, Mister Guthrie."

We hefted our stuff and left Ward Forty, shuffling scuffily down those hard hallways.

Outside was already dark – a February gloom that holds no promise for better times. Just cold, and colder still, coming to your town soon. We stood silently at the bus stop, shivering, and it was about twenty-five minutes until the right bus came and we got on board. There weren't many riders so we took separate seats, a couple rows apart. I guess we each had a little sorting-out to do, to put the afternoon in perspective. I didn't mind the time alone. In fact, I surprised myself and even got in a tiny snooze. A little dream echoed words and faces from the Washington dining room boil-up with me and Woody, and Steinbeck, and the lovely, shapely Mary…

I AWOKE AT the last few sharp turns into the bus terminal. Bob had moved himself to the seat across the aisle and had been watching me as I slept, near as I could tell.

"Hey, Mister Blaine. Having a nice private nap?" he drawled in his annoying Midwest accent.

My tongue was half-stuck to the roof of my mouth. I fished out my handkerchief to wipe a little drool from my chin and wetness from my irritated eye, set my glasses back square on my nose, sniffed and replied, "Yes. Now hungry. Let's catch a bite before we head home, shall we?" He was really getting under my skin, but I also figured he should have had some of that twenty left.

"Sure 'nuff."

We found a small Greek cafe, Savinal's (I think), just a few doors down from the depot, and grabbed a table in the back. The place was crowded with tipping customers, down-and-outers, starving Armenians, and riffraff from the bus terminal. We fit right in. I ordered a gyros with no tahini, and Bob had a hamburger, fries, coke. Real cosmopolitan fare.

"Thanks again, Mister Blaine. I consider myself fortunate to have met you. Who knew? Woody Guthrie is a friend of yours! But there's more to that tale…" He had a sly little grin at the side of his mouth and gave me a look like we shared a new secret.

"Oh yes. I could share our dirty laundry. Washington. Steinbeck. That's just a start. We go way back. But let's keep this between us, huh Kid?" I grimaced him a 'secret grin' back. I had no intentions of explaining the delicate dangers of nude wife-drawing. He frowned, and lit a cigarette, and blew smoke my way. He picked a bit of stray tobacco off his lip and flicked it to the floor.

"What about the drawings from today? Any chance that I could get a look at those? Woody sure seemed amused, or bemused." Bob was eyeing my portfolio, one eyebrow arched extravagantly.

"No chance tonight, Junior. Maybe sometime, down the road," I lied, and he probably knew it.

Our plates got plopped onto the loud tabletop and I attacked my sandwich, he his. We chomped. I changed the subject. "You know, we were lucky to see him in a good mood today. And I think he was enjoying your... renditions... of his songs. Maybe, anyway. You going to go back? If you can, look up this Jack Elliott fella before you do, because, sure as hell, Woody'll ask you about that. That kind of intent means a lot to him, especially nowadays."

Bob stared off somewhere else. "I will. Thanks for the advice. It means a lot to me too, what he thinks. Of me. And ...songs. I'd like to meet his family, too. You say they come on Sundays?"

"Yup." Of course, that's why I *didn't*. Come on Sundays. Different wife and all, but still...

"I think I'll go back this Sunday. Or as soon as I track down this Jack Elliott fella. I'll bet he's playing in the Village this weekend. If I'm lucky, that is. And, you know... I've certainly been lucky, uh, lately." He smirked... again. Part of me wanted to punch him.

"Yes. Yes, you have, Junior."

But one could argue, so had I. Luck comes in an array of colors and vibrations.

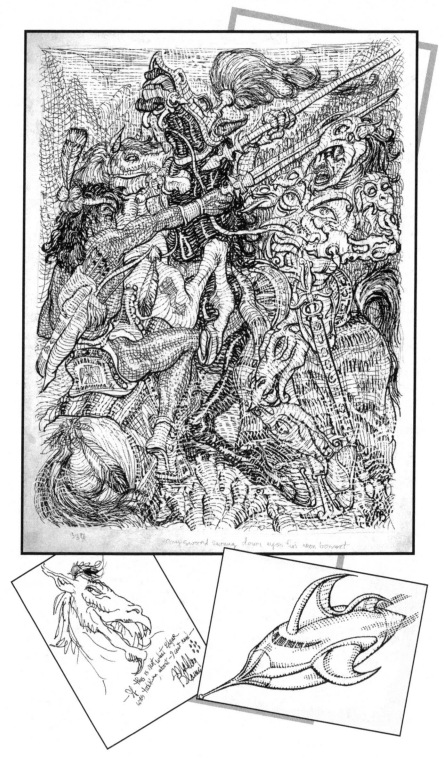

my sword swung down upon his iron bonnet

Burroughs Books

1962

"ARE YOU INTERESTED in Burroughs?" they asked.

I was thumbtacking an "Adventure" sign to the end of a bookcase. It had been calligraphed by yours truly to match my couple dozen other subject signs, all residing at eye level.

"Burroughs, eh? Edgar Rice Burroughs and Tarzan and love between savages? What makes you think I'd be interested?" I responded politely, I thought. Before answering, Jack One (Biblo) smiled at Jack Two (Tannen), who was his typical grim-faced self. Both were in their standard garb for a workday of the printed word: edge-worn wool jackets, drab sweater vests, dimly pleated slacks, and achingly polished shoes. Two owls, peering through horn-rimmed pop-bottle bottoms, talking to a third such creature.

"We've recently realized that several of his books never had their copyrights renewed so... public domain now. Not any Tarzan because that's a trademark. But Mars and Venus and other adventures are fair game. Quite a variety of stories, really. We just thought we might return... you, rather, might want a chance to return to your Days of Glory. You certainly must remember back that far."

"Hmmmm…." My stomach growled too, harmonizing with my contemplative hum.

He added icing to the cake. "Illustrated books! Mahlon, my friend, think about it: a Vandercook, or a Clifford-style thing. Nothing quite as grand as your John Day books, of course. We're thinking five to seven drawings for each title. And dust jackets, of course, in color. Whaddaya think? We've got to jump on it though."

These two gentlemen had been treating me pretty well lately. I mean, we'd known each other since about day one of their bookstore. Over thirty years. Even though they'd never gone the route of Brussel or Gurney by publishing the kind of questionable material to which my talents were certainly more attuned, they definitely had experience reprinting old stuff for new audiences. Usually non-illustrated though.

Here they had a good idea, I guess, to leap ahead of the crowd and issue the Burroughs stuff that was up for grabs. The old collectable editions kept climbing in value. Most of the quaint paintings that had been their illustrations weren't bad. But this – this might be a renewal for Burroughs and a spark for me. I played cool, as is my nature.

"I really don't think you can afford a draughtsman as qualified as myself, Gentlemen. Although the offer intrigues me a tad, that tad is merely a tadpole. Let me sleep on it a day or two and see if the little tadpole grows into either a frog, or a goddamn prince. How's that sound?" I said.

"Sure. Suuurrree," drawled Jack One.

Jack Two had already left to answer a paying customer's question about the sale-books out on the sidewalk table. Plus, he didn't get my humor unless he was in the mood. I could tell he hadn't been in the mood, as usual.

"Of course, Your Majesty," One continued, with a little bow. "Why don't you just sleep on it? Dream away of little amphibians swimming clouded waters of musty swamps while growing arms and legs. And when the crowned one spits its tongue to nab some innocent, defenseless gnat, let's talk again. No hurry. Just climb up to your luxurious penthouse in the sky. Our sky. We'll chat in the morning."

"Oh yes," he added, before turning to go price some older tomes, "and I'm certain that you'll be quite happy to know that there will be enough remuneration to pay your current rent, your back rent, and then some."

Now... he didn't have to bring rent up! I couldn't see if there was a glint in his eye or not. I decided to assume there wasn't.

I said, "So! Gimme one of those damn Burroughs books, and let me see what I might be getting into. I can still read, you know!"

He reached around from behind with a handsome red-bound copy of *The Moon Maid* in his hand. It was probably from the '30s – a Grosset & Dunlap sporting a dull grey frontis painting by old man St. John, who had been a purveyor of adventure scenes with bizarre creatures and half-naked characters. He was also the gold standard as far as Burroughs illustrators.

"This is one of the titles, I take it?" I asked.

"One of three we're launching Canaveral Press with. But a bunch more, and soon. I think there might well be something in there to... well, just read the dang thing and tell me what you think!" he said, turning and walking away.

Let's see, little tadpole. Let's see what a few hours, and the scent of sweet pipe tobacco, does for your life cycle.

"What's that?"

"Beg pardon?"

"That. Those numbers." Jack One seemed genuinely mystified, pointing to the back of one of my first Burroughs sketches. "Weird. Arithmetic?"

"It eases my mind, focuses and eases. Good for headaches."

"It kind of gives me a headache. Division, of some kind, must be."

"You almost have it. Square root."

"What do you use it for?" he said.

"Did I mention focus? Headaches?"

"So you just take a number and puzzle it out, for fun, to find the square root?"

"Yep."

"Amazing. Ever hear of crossword puzzles? Or maybe anagrams?"

'This works for me. Those don't, for whatever reason. Don't think I haven't tried everything."

"Guess I can't argue with that. How's it going, anyhow, with those *Moon Maid* drawings?" He started fidgeting with a stack of papers on the table next to the window. "These them?"

"Yes. The most preliminary of preliminaries. It's going all right. But let me get a couple done before you go messing them up, will you Jack? I mean... cripes!"

"Yes sir. No problem there. I'll give you a few more days, but then I'd like to see something. The Public, Mahlon; The Public demands Burroughs, and we're gonna give it to them! Yessiree."

"Good-bye Jack. See you tomorrow. Good-bye. Bye-bye." I think he got the hint.

I was alone. Just a four-story building with mice and roaches and a quarter of a million volumes of dead words. Time to get some drawing done.

And I did.

HERE'S HOW I proceeded with the whole Burroughs project. Eight books, eight projects.

First, I'd read each book cover to cover, beginning with *The Moon Maid* – a science fictional epic. As I began I realized that it's just old-fashioned adventure and quite well written. I'd never read Burroughs' stuff back when, although I'd seen the books around since forever. Big kids like them, but they seem to have an appeal beyond nostalgia and the used-bookstore guys are continually buying and selling them to collectors.

I tracked the action as it developed and stuck notes into the book where there was a potential spot for a drawing. I'd got about a dozen into *The Moon Maid* by the time I was through. Returning to the first note, I did the roughest of sketches of that scene in pencil, on an 8.5 by 11 piece of plain old typing paper. I always reread the section a few times, to make sure there's nothing amiss, because anyone reading later can very easily spot mistakes when the finished work confronts them at the turn of the page.

The second draft of the drawing was also on small scale, and I laid the blank paper right over the first drawing. I could see through the paper, so I traced the basic elements that I liked and changed or refined a bit as I went. It's quick and I like it better than erasing. Drafts one and two together took about 10 minutes. But I did a first rough of all the book's chosen scenes, then ran through the second drafts all in a row too. That's it for this size.

The finished size was based on the Bristol board, in this case 18 by 24 inches. Whatever the art store had. As well as vellum sheets the same size.

The next step was another rough sketch, but I focused on blowing up the size to fit the final dimensions. All the steps from here to the end – except the finished drawing – were on the vellum. OK, call it tracing paper, if you must. I don't shiv a git.

Thus step by step I'd refined the composition. At each stage I let it sit for a bit. I laid out all the drawings for the book's separate illustrations next to each other when I'd completed a phase, to get a sense of consistency in approach and composition. Consistency sometimes means meaningful change, too. I didn't want them all looking too much the same. But they're really like siblings and should share enough traits to be recognized as related within each book.

Two to three of these vellum drawings, and I was ready to tackle the final. Since the Bristol is completely opaque, I needed to transfer the last sketch – I couldn't trace it. I took a thin sheet of paper and, using the side of the pencil point, I covered one side with a thin layer of graphite. This was physically the hardest on my arm, the sweeping-scribbling while holding the pencil horizontal to the paper, and it always wearied me out. That's the transfer sheet. I laid it graphite-down on the Bristol with the final preliminary vellum drawing on top of that, pinned all three to the drawing board, and traced all my main lines with a firm hand. This transfered a faint graphite line drawing onto the Bristol.

Then it was the pen and the ink final version.

BUT... THAT WAS just the technical side.

I aimed to create the actors and actresses, heroes and villains, sets and scenes as the author had presented them in the text – as well as the emotions, thoughts, causes and effects, actions and reactions. Then, for Burroughs especially, there are the creatures! I personally have no time for incorrect anatomy. True, he didn't always exactly spell out every detail, but to ignore what is spelled out is, I think, criminal. As good as the other Burroughs illustrators were as painters or draughtsmen, I had seen far too many instances where the written fictional reality was overlooked or ignored. And usually for no good reason. Perhaps the poor fellows had too wee an imagination to be able to visualize the written word. I don't know why, but it irks the bejesus out of me, that much I can tell you.

There is one general thing, too, with Burroughs. Seems like he had been stuck in some virginalized Victorian dungeon of romance. Although it works for him (and his avid readers) of course, it's a bit out of my comfort zone. Obviously. So I approached it from a more juvenile and innocent viewpoint, sex-wise. The non-villainous men would be a bit boyish, and the heroines would be "unawakened" adolescents in the drawings. These stories have love - not lust. So too for the illustrations.

So there.

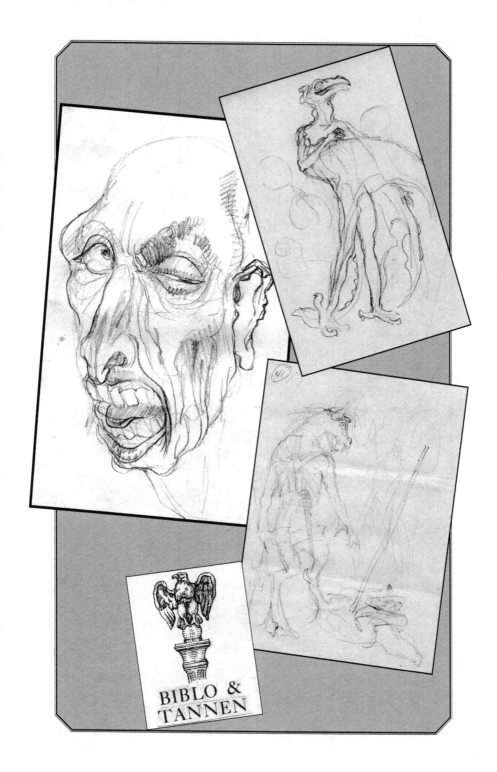

Carradine the Thespian
1932

THAT FELLOW REALLY gives me a chuckle.

Myself, Paul Muni and John Carradine sat chatting on the darkened movie set.

"John," I asked sweetly, "why do you always play such sneaky, salacious, sinister, slimy characters? Is it the inner you, coming out?"

He grimaced a grin, then scowled, then slyly grinned again. "You could make that accusation of almost any one of us in the acting business, Mahlon. We are paid to fool the public. And you? Why do you paint such wanton, worrisome paintings? For yourself? You have no 'public.' What are we to make of *you*, in this regard? Hmmmm?" he mellifluated sourly.

"Perhaps neither of us should give away any strictly personal secrets. Yes, my audience is so very small, whereas yours? Well, certainly not large. No, not large... but..."

The kindling was lit.

"Damn you, Blaine! Now you've spoiled my mood! I'm thinking of getting one of Flynn's cutlasses, super-sharpening its fine curved edge, and using it to take the skin off your bones while you watch. Would that satisfy you? Shit! Shit. Go read a book or something." With that outburst he spun back to Muni, who had been wrestling a toothpick around his front teeth and patiently awaiting the outcome of our repartee.

"Paul," said Carradine to Muni, "can you use your pull on this drama and get mister shit-head fired or something? He's beginning to get on my nerves in a decidedly unpleasant way."

It was almost too easy. John was nothing, if not predictable.

Muni, however, was not about to be helpful for he was as amused as I at the outburst by Carradine. "Hey, John, simmer down. I don't want to get in the middle of one of your family squabbles," Paul said with a chuckle.

"Family! What the hell? What are you talking about?" rumbled John.

"I seem to recall," said Paul, "maybe a year or so ago, a conversation at the Trocadero, over drinks. I had come up to you and Mahlon chin-wagging conspiratorially and sat myself down at your table – after your well-lubricated invitation. You said to me, and I quote, 'Paul, my friend, let me introduce you to my long lost cousin Mahlon Blaine.' I said, 'Cousin? How do you mean?' Whereupon you insisted that your maternal grandparents had been cousins, or some vaguer relationship more or less removed, and here you were, now reuniting the family."

"Really? I don't recall," said John, with a little snooty sniff, his forehead losing its crimson tinge. Then he sneezed, probably from the dusty old velour curtains hanging right behind us onset.

Paul went on, "Gesundheit. Anyway, you fellows had had a few drinks already. The three of us extended the party until about four o'clock in the morning, as best as I remember. 'Family! That's what's most important!' you kept booming in your magnificent stage whisper. I think they heard you all the way to the Santa Monica Pier."

John studiedly shook his head, staring at the floor. "Damn. I did? I said that? Well..." and he turned back to me, cooling off slowly, no longer smoldering. In an uncharacteristicly quiet tone he asked me, "We are cousins?"

"Mahlon Carradine Blaine. At least it says on my birth certificate which was unfortunately lost years ago in a fire, as happens sometimes. But I swear it's true. What do you make of that?"

Paul and I watched him stand up. "Family," he slowly said, "the least important thing in the world. And you can quote me on *that*!" He stomped off, stage right. If he'd had a cape, he would have flung it over his shoulder like a Musketeer.

Somewhere he's probably still steaming. And I'm still chuckling. And for all I know we may still, indeed, be actual cousins.

If Betty Were Here Tonight

1916

SAN FRANCISCO IN 1916, and me somewhat out of my element.

I closed the heavy door behind me too forcefully, which made the large glass panel rattle shrilly. No one looked up, so maybe it was a perfectly normal amount of force and cacophony. This establishment, *Bonini's Manger,* had been recommended to me as a more-than-reasonably priced boite where one could fill up the inner furnace for the day – on a dollar. This now being noonish, I was anxious to try the "Bohemian Lunch" for only fifty cents, as noted on the simple posterboard sign facing outside. If the food were as good as touted, I thought I just might offer to paint them a much better placard with some eye-catching colors and an amusing figure or two interacting with the lettering – in return for a few free lunches. But only if the food were good.

One indication: the place was busy, and as I cast about for a spot to sit I spied Betty De Jong who spied me back, and we rendezvoused where she had already homesteaded a small battered basic basswood table near a front window.

"Mahlon Blaine. *Bon jour*. I am happy to see you! Please join me here," invited Betty.

"Indeed, I shall. You know, I was over across the street, at 608, and obviously got the number wrong as the dry goods merchant did not offer to quell my hunger. Luckily, reconnoitering, I noticed that my remembered recommendation did not match reality, by that smallest of digits: 1."

"And, who might have told you only an address, no name?"

"I admit, it was merely overheard late last night. Wine then, and wind now, may also have conspired to lead me off-course. But here I finally am, and certainly hungry."

"*Oui*. Chilly today, but warm yourself with 'Bohemian'," she recommended. "That's what I've ordered, *cherie*."

"Thank you, kind lady, for that thought. This being my first time here, I suppose it wisest to follow your lead."

"How long have you been in this city, *Monsieur* Mahlon Blaine?"

"Just a few months, three or four. And you?"

"Oh, I came over from Paris last year. With the European War, it has been horrible, horrible. So many dead. Sometimes, though, I think it may be worse for the young men to be only wounded. To 'only' suffer. The dead do not suffer, do you think?"

Her abrupt seriousness caught me off guard and I paused before responding. "Well, that's one way of looking at it. I'm glad that our country has not entered into the fray... yet. But I fear we will, if the Kaiser keeps at his craziness."

She was silent for a while, looking at me with great sadness in her eyes. Now she merely poked at her plate of hearty food. Meanwhile, the waiter had set my own plate in front of me.

"*Pardon, Mademoiselle*, as I begin my meal. My stomach will not wait."

"Oh, go ahead. I myself am no longer hungry, just thinking about what is going on as we speak, back there. I was tired of it and had heard so much of the wonderful atmosphere here, free of war. Where the Art could still flourish! But, I must admit, after these last two years I am not sure of the power of the Art. I continue, as I have commissioned work. It is work, but where has my heart gone?" She paused, to look me in the eye. "Where is your heart, Mahlon Blaine? Where is it, right now?"

She was not in a mood to hear any of my usual poor humor, obviously. And as I looked back, into her eyes and perhaps into her soul, I felt sorrow seeping there. Permeating. The sorrow that was born of the war, or of Art, or of being outwardly successful, yet still incapable of happiness and peacefulness. That was how she appeared to me.

"I wish that I could help. Is there some way?" I asked. It was a feeble offer. What could I do?

"I don't know... *je ne sais pas*." She pushed aside her plate and buried her face in her arms folded on the small table.

I had eaten but half my plateful and suddenly it was plenty. I waved the waiter over, paid both our bills with a silver dollar, and, standing up, leaned over Betty and spoke quietly, "I can walk you back to... I don't know where you live. I myself live a trolley ride away, if that's any help. But..."

She looked up quickly, almost hitting my nose with the back of her head, then rose to her feet and turned to look at me again. Her left cheek was flush and so near to my chin. I was surprised. I thought she had been crying. She had no tears. She had a defiant, steely color flooding her eyes. She pinned her hat on her head and gathered her small bag.

"Come with me, please, Mahlon Blaine. Yes. Come with me." Together we left *Bonini's* for the first and last time.

She started slowly, but soon increased her purposeful pace. I was striding beside her and to keep up I wove my arm between her arm and body and pressed myself close. Shoulder-to-shoulder our steps became one as she led the way, turning corners seemingly at random. I got a little lost and we came upon a stoop where we climbed ten steps to a sturdy front door and entered.

"My studio," she said as she unlocked the door on the second floor, towards the back of the building. I entered first, and she swung the door closed behind us and bolted it. She reached up to my shoulder and, with a surprisingly firm grip, turned me to face her squarely and simply stated, "I need you to draw me, please, and it must be now."

I started to ask, "Is this a..." but she quickly put her lilac-scented fingers to my lips for silence.

"Please. I am no artist today. You must be the artist. I will be the subject. No questions. Please," she pleaded quietly, desperately.

"Of course. Whatever you need, Betty."

I watched her countenance assume the same strange combination of steeliness and sorrow I had witnessed at the lunch table. She asked me to help her move a chair. It was a large, stuffed, high-backed monster, and she wanted it against the wall and on a large rug that was already situated there. Then we placed another, simpler chair - wooden, no arms - near the door. She pulled three sheets of drawing paper and a lap-sized drawing board from a tabletop and gave them to me along with a half-box of hard vine charcoal, and sat me down in the wooden chair. This was all done hurriedly yet somehow sadly. "Please, while the afternoon light still favors us," she said.

I quickly pinned one of the blank sheets on the board while Betty scooted to the far end of the room and through a narrow doorway. Bathroom? Closet? I didn't know. After a minute she burst from that place, ran the length of the room, stopped in front of the big chair and faced me.

Standing erect, draped to the floor in a white sheet, eyes closed, she released the shroud from her shoulders. She had taken her clothes off in the other room and now stood, feet planted firmly together on the rug, and looking me in the eye.

She nodded once. "Now you may begin. Draw what you see."

I was slightly startled but she was indeed beautiful. I have sketched beautiful nude women many times – today my eye was first drawn to her face, her eyes. She kept that gaze anchored on me as I began. The light was still quite good, coming through the frosted age-etched glass of the side windows. And the dark chair and deep red rug richly contrasted her pure white skin. Her gentle contours were easy to distinguish, even to a half-blind woodchuck like me. I finished a detailed sketch of her face, wild hair (which she had unpinned when she had shed her clothing) and well defined shoulders.

"Done," I said. "*Portrait of a Lady Painter.*"

"Continue, please. Mahlon, I want you to make a record of me as you see me now – as I am at this moment. The whole of me. *C'est tres importante a mois.*"

"Yes. I can do that… for you," was all I could think of to say.

She slowly lowered herself into the immense gulf of that chair seat. Her eyes never left mine. "Begin again." She sat very still, bolt upright, and watched me. This time I drew her whole figure, the rug edge, the chair back. A few marks scattered on the page to hint at the wallpaper design behind her. I was careful with the sharp lines as well as the smudges, to capture her slim roundness against the dark upholstery. Under these circumstances I found myself disinclined to alter what I perceived to be an almost perfect form and countenance. The mood in the room guided my hand, the charcoal responded splendidly on the paper's surface.

"Done. Our light is still good and… you hold a pose well," I said.

"Another." She spoke the one word so very quietly, yet I was compelled to follow instruction.

She leaned into the chair back and inched her hips forward a bit. Her arms went up and her hands went over the chair back and held on, tightly. And she slowly relaxed her legs and let her feet slide forward on the rug until they had found their equilibrium there, about one foot apart, and her un-tightened thighs let her knees spread slightly, slowly. All movement ceased.

"Begin." She said, closing her eyes.

I drew. There was a completely resigned quality to this. A vulnerability. A weariness. I hesitate to even call it a pose. I drew her unashamedly giving herself permission to… I don't know… give up? Had her defiance left her? No. It was still there under the skin but buried a little deeper. As I refined and filled in detail, I sensed calmness permeate her. It would normally be difficult to catch in a drawing, but I believed I was quite successful. Her overwhelming need for me to succeed was compelling, spreading through the room, infusing my sensibility.

"Done," I said, quietly. I was surprisingly drained having done merely these three drawings.

She pulled her body back into itself, into its everyday, meet-the-world composure, and used her hands and arms to cover her sudden modesty, turning her head away. She'd never opened her eyes to look at me since we'd begun the last pose. She just said, "Take the drawings and leave, please."

I sat immobile. I wasn't clear that it would be prudent to just leave, with Betty acting so, well, sad and disconnected.

I'll admit that I had had certain thoughts on our close walk over. Thoughts about making love to this strong, successful French woman, this artist perhaps somewhat like myself. Perhaps she'd been a kindred spirit who desired companionship at a moment in time. It was a passing thought.

Clearly her decision had been made. This was not about lust, or sex. The connection had meant far more to her and, I had to admit, myself. "Go, now. Please. Just go. And just... remember. For me." She wouldn't look up.

"All right, Betty. I understand," I lied. How could I know what was behind this afternoon encounter? I mean, really? As enormously touched by her actions and her beauty as I had been, my heart and soul were mine alone, as were hers. I couldn't penetrate. No one could.

I carefully rolled the three pages together, hoping their charcoal lines would not smudge until I could get them home to apply a fixative. I was already thinking about studying them in tomorrow's light, to see if I had actually captured what I thought I had seen of her soul or whatever she had allowed me to see. I was already beginning to look ahead to our next strange encounter. Perhaps I was a bit in love.

Yet I knew I could not really expect anything. Maybe I might just hope, though. "And... thank you." I was painfully polite.

I left, silently closing the door. What an afternoon it had been! The early winter dusk gathered as I pulled my collar up against the inevitable San Francisco breeze and headed for the trolley stop to catch a ride home.

I ENDED UP sleeping past my usual arousal the next morning. Truthfully, I slept well into the afternoon. I groggily rolled over on my belly and heard my stomach sing its usual low-throated serenade, only more urgently. Once awake and headed out to find a bit of late lunch at the corner café, my head was filled with anticipation at the thought of, hunger having been sated, coming back to my room and studying my three strange-encounter drawings of Betty. Her "love letters" to me, I thought.

Entering the coffee shop, I grabbed an afternoon paper that someone had already read and left near the door. Front page, the third column, the story:

> SAN FRANCISCO, Jan. 21 - Miss Betty De Jong, a painter of wide reputation, died early today from a self-inflicted bullet wound in the head. The police said they had virtually completed their investigation of the case, including examination of Dr. William S. Porter, a well-known physician of Oakland, who was in Miss De Jong's studio when she shot herself.

I slumped onto the nearest empty chair. My legs were wobbling, hands shaking. I forced myself to read on:

> After several hours of questioning, he was permitted to go to his home. An inquest will be held tomorrow.
>
> Dr. Porter met Miss De Jong, he said, last year during the Panama-Pacific Exposition, at which she had several exhibits. Dr. Porter said

he was to sit for his portrait yesterday, but was unable to keep the engagement, and called at the studio to so inform the artist. Soon after his arrival, the physician declares, Miss De Jong began discussing suicide, all the while holding a small revolver. For three hours, the physician said, he tried to persuade the young woman not to think of such a thing. Finally, when he was about to leave, he said, Miss De Jong shot herself in the temple.

The police said tonight that they found in the studio not only complete corroboration of Dr. Porter's story, but evidence that Miss De Jong had carefully set the stage for her death. When Dr. Porter went to the studio at 6 P. M. he found that the furniture had been re-arranged. He said he was conducted to a chair that had been placed by itself near the innermost wall of the studio. Under this chair was a rug about eight feet square. Miss De Jong seated herself on a big chair near the door, produced the pistol, and informed him that she was going to kill herself before he left.

"I started toward her," said the doctor. "She pointed the gun at me and said, 'Don't leave that rug, or I'll kill you first.'"

Finding serious argument unavailing, he said he tried treating the matter lightly.

"You seem to have everything very nicely planned," he said. "When are you going to do this dreadful thing?"

"The second you step off that rug," the doctor said she replied. It was shortly after that, he told the police, that Miss De Jong, in a conversational tone, said, "You may go now."

"I thought I had succeeded in making her change her mind," he said, "or I would have been there yet. As I stepped off the rug she fired. You know the rest."

"I thought," said Deputy Coroner Michael Brown, "that Dr. Porter ought to have been able to take the pistol away from the woman, but when I saw the room and the chair I knew that he could not. I sat in the chair. It was one of those deep-seated affairs that you can't get out of without effort. They were twenty feet apart, and he had no chance."

A cablegram to Miss De Jong's sister, Dr. De Jong of the Hospital Hotel Dieu in Paris, was sent today by Mlle. Marguerite Saligne, with whom the artist had been working in the raising of funds for the French wounded. Miss De Jong was a native of Paris. According to her friends, none of them had heard her talk of suicide.

At the Golden Gate Park Memorial Museum today crowds gathered before two pictures of Betty De Jong that had been draped in black velvet. The pictures were 'The Pancake Vendor,' a young Dutch girl in costume, which had been purchased by the museum, and 'The Black Hat,' a portrait of a woman. In the same gallery is a bust of Dr. William S. Porter, by the sculptor, William S.Mannatt.

I KNEW THAT if I were to make my way to the memorial at the gallery, my new San Francisco friends would be crying, reminiscing and trying to figure everything out. Incapable of moving, unable to feel, leaden to my core, I could only sit, drained.

The coffee shop folks left me alone, thankfully, as I had no idea what I would have said to them. I didn't have any words in my head, only grey. It must have taken an hour for numbness to take hold to the point where I could finally stand and shuffle to the exit and stumble home in a fog. I welcomed a shroud of sea mist that descended between the buildings.

I eventually found myself on my bed on my back staring at the ceiling, watching shadows and reflections pin-hole-camera'd on the cracked plaster. I lay there straight through until daybreak, dozing off a few times. I would return to Betty sitting in that dark chair, staring at me, and I'd wake up.

It was several days before I could go out to face my friends. They enquired where I'd been, asked if I had heard about Betty. All that sorrowful wondering, non-understanding oozing from their throats. I obfuscated and deflected and never told them about my hours with her just before the suicide. I hadn't a clue of what it had meant, and I knew that they would not know either, and I didn't want to hear them discuss it, her, and me.

MY BETTY DRAWINGS? I had never planned to show them to another living soul. But every once in a while I would take them out and ask Betty, "Why?"

I look into her eyes as she had looked into mine.

If she has an answer there, I have never discerned it. Was that my shortcoming as an artist, or was it ultimately hers? Are artists judged more by their work, or their suicides? At least I never took that particular step, so for me it'll be the art alone.

C'est la vie.

Goodbye Washington Square
1966

WHAT A WAY to spend a warm sunny day.

Sunday afternoon is my 'meet the public' project. It's a chance for me and a bunch of other yay-hoos to size each other up, form an opinion and then continue to go our separate ways none the wiser. A mutual aphorism society, you might call it.

I have an old alarm clock that I use on rare occasions nowadays, and this was one of them-thar occasions. Sunday morning I needed to rise early to get done what needed to get done, then hustle over to the Square to get my spot. Since a body just can't do such a thing on an empty stomach, first up was breakfast.

I've got my trusty fry pan, spatula, and a little bottle of olive oil, and luckily I can still buy eggs three at a time from the bodega on Eleventh. Plug in the hot-plate, a couple slices of day-old, toasted in the dry pan, then add the oil and crack an egg. Today I used all three eggs: long day ahead. Toast dipped in yoke, and whites cooked through. No runny whites for this fella! And leave a tidbit for my mouse. A man without a mouse is like a day without sunshine - dark and dreary.

Full up, I decided a shave would be nice. Too bad I didn't have enough time. I quickly looked through a pile of drawings that I'd accumulated through the week, then stuffed the whole lot into the folder, and put the folder next to the half-dozen gouache paintings on illustration board and another half-dozen watercolors on nice Arches paper. Nothing was matted or framed. It all went into the larger portfolio with the cracked handles.

After tying up the sides as best I could (seeing as the ties were broken and retied so many times they were barely knots on knots), I grabbed my jacket – the one with suede lapels and leather patches on the elbows. Actually, it was my only jacket. I jammed the old brown fedora on my head and started down the three flights to the ground floor of the bookstore. I parked the folio against the hall wall to detour to the facilities on the second floor. One thing to remember on these Sundays - an empty bladder is a good thing to have with you on the streets of New York City.

Alice was already at the front desk. "Morning, Mahlon! Heading out for Washington Square this fine sunny morning?" She seemed in a good mood, but I thought it was a pity that you had to have a bookstore open on a Sunday, just to earn a living nowadays.

"Alice, my dear, I am on my way to find the one honest man out there, and sell him a priceless work of art. Wait. If it were priceless... Never mind. I shall put a reasonable remunerative value on the work, and we shall hope for a reasonable outcome to the negotiations."

"Well, you have a fine day, and don't get sunburnt. Will I see you later?"

"Don't know, don't know. We'll see how the crowds are. Maybe I'll be back before you leave." And I was out the door, onto the sidewalk. I bumped a passerby with the folio. "Sorry." I muttered to no one in particular as I hustled away. "Mustn't be late. Very important date."

Two streets and three avenues over to the Square, and I ain't as young as I used to be. But then, who is? There was a trickle of sweat running down the small of my back by the time I got to my spot. Now, no one has a spot, really, in this section of the park. But I had been regular for maybe ten years and it was understood: don't mess with the glass-eyed old guy.

I laid five of the landscape paintings up against the bottom of the fence, leaning so people walking by could see them behind the drawings that were spread on the edge of the sidewalk. The corners were held down against the wind with small rocks, bits of broken pavement, whatever could be found nearby because nobody liked to haul that paperweight stuff around. Hauling the art around was bad enough. I clothes-pinned another ten or so drawings up on the fence above, emptying the portfolio – including a couple old drawings I'd had tucked away too long, perhaps.

I had chosen this spot way-back-when ten years ago because, across the sidewalk from it, there was a particularly comfortable bench. An actual, well-designed park bench. The kind with the sturdy slats that formed a curve for both your butt and your back. I sat there, sketchbook in my lap most of the time, sketching, and keeping an eye on the 'buying' public. Although, mostly, it was the 'browsing' public mixed in with the majority of the 'I don't give a shit' public.

You could tell about people, just by watching. That's what I was sketching for, even here: to catch that essence of where their minds were at, as revealed by their body language. Not easy. A challenge, even for me, but worth the effort. Always was and will be.

A very round young man stopped as he came to my display. He stood right in the center of my display array and looked carefully from drawing to drawing on the sidewalk, then painting to painting leaning against the fence bottom, and lastly at the clothes-pinned gallery. His eyes retraced their path. He leaned in, focusing on a particular one on the fence, then leaned back and looked left and right. Seemed as though he wanted a word with the artist, so I started to stand up from my bench.

He had swung around now in his search, spied me straitening up and stepped over, saying, "Don't get up. You the artist?"

"I have been called far worse," I said, sitting back down. "And by better men than you." I winked at him and motioned him to come over and sit down next to me. "The shade is nice. So. You like art?"

He sat down with a cat-like movement of ease and rubbed his hands together, as if warming them. He occupied a houndstooth sport coat plus an argyle sweater-vest. "I like your stuff. This is your stuff, right? It's pretty good." He was also nodding his noggin.

"Gorsch! Tanks mister!"

"Sorry." He stopped rubbing his hands. "I don't know you and you don't know me. But, damn! Your stuff is pretty damn good, in my opinion." He looked from me back across to the fence. "Pretty... damn... good." And again back at me.

"I've been at it a long time. I'm ancient. These, however," I said as I swung my arm like a pretty girl at a car show would to draw attention, "are brand new merchandise. Mostly. And for sale!"

"Of course." He didn't look as if he had any money to spend, but then, neither did I. Yet you never can tell. "Say, do you mind? Can I ask you about one of them?" he asked.

"Sure." We both stood up and took the five steps across the sidewalk. "Which one?"

"That one."

"That one? *Unknown Nude*."

"Yes, but..."

"But?"

"It's... perfect! I mean, she's perfect!"

"It's a drawing, young man. Of the tried-and-true genre of the masters: the human form."

"But she's, I guess, I dunno, uh... lovely? More than lovely! Is she real?"

"This is art, my friend. I am not here to provide matchmaking," and I added "tsk, tsk, tsk."

"Oh, man, you know what I mean! Nobody - no *body* - is that perfect, sitting there like that. Right? That's what makes it art and not a photograph, right? It's what you did! That's what gets me!"

I knew what he meant, of course, because that's what gets me, too. That's why I do it. "I made her perfect, because she is an ideal. I deal only in perfection, nowadays. I'm too long in the tooth to do otherwise."

He looked me over. Then looked back at the figure on the paper. "But she's so real. So alive. That's really something. I wish I could do that, draw like that."

"Maybe you merely need the right model. So, you're an art student?"

"No. Law. NYU. And broke: b-r-o-k-e."

"Starving artist and starving lawyer? A swell pair we are."

Oops. I interrupted our conversation. "Say, would you mind? I've gotta attend to a call from another perfect creature - Mother Nature. Could you watch my stuff for about five minutes?"

"OK. What if someone wants to buy something?"

"Sell it to 'em! Make up a price. I gotta run." I hustled gingerly toward the street.

The coffee shop across the way usually doesn't let non-customers use the facilities, but the artists had special permission because they added to general clientele numbers and I was one of the regulars. I was back in the time I had allowed myself.

"Sell many?" I asked.

He grinned a little sheepishly. "Some skittish fella asked me, 'Where's the old guy, the 'dirty pictures' guy?' But he wouldn't stick around."

"Oh yeah, little checkered cap, white mustache? He'll be back. Nothing else?"

"Nope. But, say... I've got to get back to studying. Thanks for letting me enjoy your work. Maybe I'll see you back here some Sunday, if this is your weekly gig?"

"Anything is possible. But listen, I can't cart all this art back with me at the end of the afternoon. There's too much. Could you do me another favor? Why don't you take the Unknown Nude with you."

He glanced at me, at the drawing, "I don't think so, Sir."

"Thanks for the 'sir' Sonny, but I insist. I pay a fair wage to my workers whether Wobblies or not. And you can just owe me the difference. Maybe some legal advice sometime? Never know when a man needs to see a lawyer about a horse of a different color, or some-such."

"Well, sure. I can't believe... thanks, Sir. Thanks." Now he was grinning as I was un-clothespinning the sheet from the fencing.

"You are generous Mister..."

"The name is Mahlon Blaine. m a h l o n b l a i n e." I stretched my arm and pointed. "One more thing: don't show that drawing to just anybody, now. And never let me see your name on the police blotters. Or my name either, for that matter."

He thought it was a joke. I was only half-kidding.

"Ha! Thanks, Mister Blaine. Thanks again."

He headed for the west side of the Square with the drawing of Betty De Jong rolled up and tucked under his arm. I was happy to make him happy. And he liked my work, so he must have had a good eye.

I, too, had had a good eye. Also a not-so-good eye and suddenly unexpected tears running down my cheeks as I waved good-bye to my ever-un-answering mystery woman. I had certainly given her plenty of time and now my time was short.

Review View
1963

"MAHLON. SOMEBODY LIKES you. Look." Jack Two was holding out a digest sized science fiction magazine.

"Beg pardon?

"The editor. We've gotten a review of our Burroughs books. He likes you."

"What the forget-me-not are you getting at? That I'm not likable? Tosch!"

"Well, suit yourself." Jack Two dropped the volume on the wooden chair by the door, and turned. As he headed down the stair I heard him mumble: "You always do."

I kept working on the painting at hand. The large devil-lady had built herself a house of cards. All the little bastard face-cards were threatening to tumble. Who was I to stop them? They, too, had a mind of their own, it would seem. And also, you can't stop a watercolor once it's started. The medium does not allow. I am nothing, if not a slave to my medium. Always.

So I finished up on the lady – hooves just so, horns just so, two-fingered hands just so. Just so I would be able to give this lady the aura of fun she deserved. I whisked my brushes in the cleanest of the several glasses of water on the table, patted them with a dry cloth between my fingers and placed them carefully, bristles shaped to points and pointing up, in the tin can to the left.

I stood slowly, as befits a man of my age, and took the sideways shuffle between the stacks of books on the floor, over to the chair by the door, and picked up the magazine. Something to do with fantasy, or maybe science fiction. I took it down the hall to my bedroom, sat in the shabby but real-leather club chair I had rescued from someone's trash and wrestled upstairs here a week earlier, opened and read.

I no longer have the magazine. I shall not attempt to recreate the wording of his observation and opinion. But I remember smiling, reassured.

Thank you. Somebody has finally got it right.

A Child Asleep

1925

I REMEMBER A scene.

Of course, it originated ages ago. It has probably altered in my grey matter, shelved away all those years, and I hadn't even thought about it since I couldn't tell you when. But it has haunted me since I arose this morning to discover it smack-dab across the front of my brain. So perhaps I dreamt something like it again last night, or perchance a part of a crumb of a tiny morsel of last night's supper set it off, woke it up, from when I was eight, nine maybe. I had stopped wetting the bedclothes a year prior to that. I can't tell you how I know that, and why I am so sure, but I am. It probably doesn't make any difference anyway. Just thought I'd throw it in. Too much information? Awwww... too bad.

I SEE MYSELF, in a dream, sleeping. That's right, I'm sleeping within the dream itself. Tucked into a little wooden bunk, the kind you don't see too much in real life nowadays, like from Shakespeare's day. It's a relatively tight fit, with my head, hands and feet touching all four sides of the carpentered box. Not very comfortably, but it would seem that it's something I'm used to. It may be in the winter months, as the comforter I am sleeping under is very thick and heavy, constricting my movement. Just my head and my arm are sticking out of the covers. I'm confident it's me, just look at that head of hair! My hand is in a little fist, poking or swinging (I'm not sure which) through the air.

I'm looking at people walking by, like on a busy sidewalk in town. But the buildings are either not there at all, or they are so vague that I can't remember them being there, so it might not be in a town or city. And yet I do have some inkling of a sign, hanging as though from a shop front. Can't quite read it though.

The people aren't actually moving. They've stopped, in mid-motion like snapshots, or statues. Maybe they actually are statues. All adults, and a good-looking bunch they are! Muscular, smooth, trim. Blazingly white. Well, that makes sense, as behold: they're marble statues, from antiquity, maybe Greece or Rome or maybe from Da Vinci's time. Definitely of a classical stance.

The main characters, the pair centered, are a male and a female. They might be a couple as they are quite close and heading the same direction. She has a demure tilt of the head and he is tipping his bowler hat politely (as they've come up on another stone lady).

They are a bit the worse for wear: her sculpted arms are broken off just below the shoulder while the gentleman's entire head is missing, broken away at the base of his neck. Her only bodily coverings are a length of fabric slung to barely hang on her hips and draping all the way to the ground, and her stylish felt hat sports a large brim. His stylish outfit consists of a short white glove on his bowler-tipping hand and matching spat-encased footwear. Her figure is quite lovely, breasts not large, hips well rounded, waist slim; he is fit, abdomen and legs rippling with muscles, and his private parts covered with a large fig leaf. Tasteful.

The stone lady whom he is hat-tipping to is very sleek and slim, stopping for a moment on the sidewalk to powder her nose. Draped over her arm is a fur. Her hand is holding a dangling beaded handbag that, were it not so long, would fail to discretely conceal her private parts. Her legs? One is broken off at the knee, the other follows fine shapeliness to a slippered foot. Her bobbed hair is encased in a futuristic-looking helmet resembling a mask of some sort. Nonetheless, she is a lovely creature indeed.

Dominating the rest of this scene, a policeman. At least I think he is a policeman for his headgear is a militaristic cap with some sort of half-moon insignia at the front and he has a simple badge pinned to his left nipple. He is exceedingly muscled – one hand toys with a huge billy club the size of a baseball bat. With a small bearskin slung over his left shoulder and a belt holding a large fig leaf over his manhood, his outfit is complete. But, oh, there seems to be a devil's head behind one of his shoulders and a soldier's head behind the other shoulder. He's turning his head to listen to the devil, I fear. Or is he glancing down at the phallic fire hydrant that is perched on the sidewalk? I can't decide which, maybe both.

Also, now I can read some words inscribed on an advertising sign in the background: "Joe Blitz Co. / Fig Leaves." Ah, an entrepenuer.

I am in bed, dreaming that I am in bed, dreaming, I think.

SO. THAT IS what I remember. I'm really no Freudian, Jungian, or charlatan. I'm only a guy with a kid's old dream. You can take it or leave it but I'm stuck with it. One can't wish dreams away, dream dreams away, nor evict them like unruly tenants.

But there is one thing that works, at least for me: I can draw them.

To Bernita

1951

DEAR BERNITA,

I am incredulous! I have not seen you for nine (eleven?) years, so I hope you don't mind me still calling you Bernita. It's a familial name, and, although I've long not been a member of the family, I'd like to think that we still have at least our brief history together as a positive memory. For both of us. If my addition is correct you are twenty-eight, right? I hear you are married! My how time has flew.

I remember the very first time I met you. You were seven. Your mother and I had worked together at the motion picture studio for a few months, and had liked each other for quite a while. On one of her days off she brought you down there. I'm not sure if she knew I'd be working that day or not, she never told me either way. But my suspicion was that she *did* know I would be there, and she wanted to get your (and my) first reaction to each other, in a neutral setting.

We got along splendidly! I pretended that you were your mother's sister and you played along with that scenario. We were very much like grown-ups, who were really children at heart. What fun! Probably an important clue for your mother. I hope she remembers that first meeting with happiness in her heart. I hope you will too, as the years creep along one by one.

It wasn't too long, it seems, before your mother and I were pretty sure we wanted to get married. She told me that we must have your approval. I said, "Of course" and I meant it. One sunny Sunday afternoon, out in your back yard under the huge Catalpa tree with the old wooden bench, you were playing with the Kachina 'Dolly' I had painted so brightly and brought from Arizona.

"'Nita," your mother said. "Can we ask you and Dolly something rather important?"

"Of course, Mother. What is it?" (You always called your mother Mother. Do you still?)

"Well, you know Mahlon and I like each other immensely? You know that, I'm sure. Am I correct?"

"Yes, Mother. You are correct. But that's a silly question. Why is that 'rather important?'"

"Well...." she winked at me. "Mahlon and I have decided that we'd... like to... get married! We are excited! And we want to know what you think."

You were quiet, raising one eyebrow then the other and consulting with Dolly (the Buffalo Dancer – do you still have her?). "Yes! I think yes! Yes, yes, yes get married, married, married, marriiiiiiieeeeeeeddddd!" you squealed. (So my suspicion was, that you were in favor of it.) You jumped up and gave us a hug – a kind of all-around hug that we all gave each other simultaneously.

An entirely new life thus began for me. I had never been married before, did you know? Not even once. And children? I had never had children of my own, nor spent much time around other people's children either. Now, with you and your mother, I had a whole family – all at once. It was warm and wonderful, I must say. At least at first.

I know you were sad that the wedding didn't happen in a

church, with people and flowers and music. But, if you think about it, look how important you were in the ceremony! You were flower girl and bridesmaid and practically best man. I am sorry that they didn't let you sign anywhere on the marriage certificate. And I agree that it doesn't seem fair that Uncle Walter however got to sign. If I had it to do over again, I would surely have insisted that your name also be on the official document. But, no one else was an "official confetti thrower" nor an "official taxi-cab hailer" either. Maybe it all evens out, in the long haul and maybe you've forgiven me by now?

Once the marriage was official, you were so good to stay with Grandma and not raise too much of a fuss. Your mother and I needed those days away, to get to know each other a little bit better. By now, of course, you yourself know why they call it a "honeymoon," and you will perfectly well understand. Anyway, I thank you for your patience back then.

We returned and we all moved in together, one big fam damnly, with Grandma and Grandpa... I hope you don't think I teased you too much. I am reasonably sure I teased your mother more. Maybe she and you remember differently.

These days I think about our trips to visit Na-Na in Oregon. Do you think about those? Na-Na was so happy the first time I brought you to see her. She never thought I would get married. I kept telling her, "Na-Na, you know me – I have to have the absolute right person, and I am willing to wait. Please, be kind enough to wait *with* me." And then, I arrived with TWO of the absolute right people! She could hardly believe her eyes!

Know that she loved you and your mother too. She surely did.

Oh! Remember the time we were going to the picnic grounds in the county park? Na-Na's donkey harnessed to her decrepit buggy holding us, our basket of chicken, rolls, all the best fixings, and headed the five miles through the forest to the park, only to have that huge spruce decide to fall, all of its own accord, and almost hit us? We all peed our pants that day!

Those were some good times, all right.

Alas there were sad times as well. But we survived them – together. It's a good thing we had each other, for without that...

It certainly wasn't your fault for anything bad that happened. That stuff just happens. No-body, or no gods or devils, make the world either a good or bad place. It is what it is, and people just cope. This is a hard lesson to learn, and no fun to learn it, but I have always believed it to be true.

One of our hardest things was losing your Grandpa Fred. We all knew he was ailing. Even he knew it. But that stubborn fool said that his duty called, and he could not shirk it. Worst of all, since that legal business was all the way back East, we probably will never know the dirty dealing, and, him being the lawyer under the gun.... I would not be surprised if there wasn't some serious high-monied funny-business too. He shouldn't have gone. Too dangerous, we all said and we didn't know even the half of it. Fifteen years past, and we still don't, damn it!

He'd collapsed at the train station here, but even ailing, his gift of persuasion... I could not talk sense into him. Weak as he was, off he went and two days later was dead. A horrible loss, and I am sorry that the adult-you did not get to know him.

And now, Na-Na. It is an unspeakable thing to lose your own mother, I've discovered. Don't much recall my dad, but my step-dad, C.D., was a good guy. He was good to Na-Na, right up to the day he died. And she was good to everyone. Especially me, her only son. Na-Na has left us – I mean me – and it's all gone to hell, pardon my *Frenchoise*.

I've died inside. So strange – like losing your own soul, yet there you are left with a greyness of mind, of heart. Perhaps now I understand better what your mother went through in 1936. But too late to help, of course.

I don't have to tell you failure is not pretty. Back then I failed her, we failed you and ourselves, even though we tried not to. It's a *God Damn Shame* how life gets sometimes.

I apologize to you, right here and now, period.

If I were a praying man, it would be for your wonderful life ahead. When you look back at that part of your old life where the

'Mahlon fella' was, I hope it doesn't look too terrible. Please don't blame me for everything that went wrong. I certainly hope you don't blame your mother either.

By the way, between only you and me, I still love your mother. How could I not? I would give, well, anything, to get back our life the way it was. But, that is not to be. Not to be.

So. This letter. I know, I know... usually my letters are full of drawings and diagrams and fun asides. Little characters jump about among the letters and sentences and make amusing comments, and funny faces. Maybe, someday, I will send you another letter like that. This isn't it.

Say 'Hello' to your mother for me. Or... maybe you'd better not. It's probably better for everyone if she thinks I've moved on. We'll just leave it at that.

Take care, Little 'Nita. You shall always be the daughter I never had, but had anyway, and was proud of it.

Perhaps you will write me back? Will you??

Very truly yours,
Mahlon Blaine, Artist, Stepfather

NOW I WISH I'd mailed this letter. Why didn't I? Why?
Yes, it's seventeen years too late.

*My eyes wandered around the
room as if to seek something I
had lost.*

A Dangling Conversation

1967

IT'S BEEN SEVERAL weeks, at least. I don't even recall her
name right now.

"Tell me, if you can," I said quietly, breaking the warm silence. She had been lying motionless on the wood floor, cush-
ioned slightly by a small faded oriental rug.

"Tell what?" she sleepily muttered.

Cracked, dusty windows let in a diluted flood of sunshine
in a loping angle across her breasts. My two dollars were laying
on the plain wood chair that held her neatly folded clothes. She
stared at the ceiling, but let one eyebrow raise a smidgeon. I answered her.

"I want to know your thoughts about me drawing you."

"Right now?" shifting her weight ever so minutely to the left,
but not enough to matter to me, the artist.

We were well into a late afternoon session. I was dimly distracted and a tad forlorn, for no specific, discernible reason, sitting ten feet away on my other wood chair. "Yes. Go ahead and
talk, and I'll keep drawing. I'm just curious, I guess."

"Why? What are *you* thinking about *me*?"

"Tut-tut and tut again. Let's not change the subject, shall we? And anyway, I'm not thinking at all, really. You're there, the drawing is here, I'm looking two places at the same time with only one eye. Do you imagine I can cogitate while I'm doing that?"

"Don't know anything about any codger bait."

"Yes, well… I *can't* cogitate and also draw. I *just* draw. So… now you. Your thoughts, if you would."

She paused. Her right hand casually began tapping deep red nails upon a sinewy inner thigh, silently dimpling the flesh a tiny bit, temporarily. "I've only done a little posing for students and maybe even a little more for artistes like yourself. But I know that I prefer the students."

"Why?"

"That's an easy answer, mister. They ain't weary." She stopped the finger movement.

"I see. Maybe. Weary?"

"Everyone stares at the pose, at me, but… now that I've been modeling for a little while, I kinda notice postures in people. Standing, sitting, how they hold their heads when they don't think anyone ain't really watching. I see them kinda from the side of my eye as I gaze past them at the walls. How they'll sometimes breathe and sigh and sigh again. It's become real easy to tell the weary ones. And they ain't the students. The students are excited or something, and focused."

"That's probably because they *think* they don't know what they're doing. That takes a lot of extra concentration. Professionals don't have time for that nonsense."

"'That nonsense'…" Her voice trailed off. A rather long pause, then, "Alright, what are you doing now?"

"Left hip, contour shading, following the light reflecting off arm onto belly, bones arranged beneath are providing almost unseen structure, hard, holding flesh taut, edge curving back, then around, and so forth."

I half-imagined that I could see her mulling over my words, maybe trying to put herself in my place to guess how I noticed

her shapes. She took a full couple minutes. The sunlight continued to flow across her bareness, its edges rising and slumping as
it hugged her various and sundry lithe and lovely curves.

"Okay mister. Do you think that I'm going to screw you just
because I'm naked here? Is that what you're up to?" Her gaze
continued to bore into the cracked paint on the ceiling tiles.

"For goodness sake, lady. Where's *that* coming from?" I let
my drawing arm slump to my side and with my left hand took
my unlit pipe out of my mouth and tap-tapped the stem on the
paper in front of me. "I don't think anything of the sort. Of. The.
Sort."

"Well, you asked. You wanted to know, and those are my
thoughts, fella."

"That there's going to be some screwing going on?"

"No, no. Just the opposite."

"Of course, of course. And the opposite of screwing is…?" I
was genuinely interested in her answer. I certainly didn't have a
suitable answer to that one. Not today.

She smiled a little. "Unscrewing, I guess. But… how do you
unscrew?" She smiled a bit more, still staring straight up, but
tried to hide her amusement. Her belly jiggled, then her breasts.

"My dear, what I am doing way, way over here is 'unscrewing,'
if anything is. Maybe it's my specialty, come to think about it. Yes,
that's it. I shall call this masterpiece: 'Unscrewing the Model.' "

I put my pipe back in its secure corner, firm in my mouth,
and resumed the work at hand, the drawing. I was merely trying
to get to the finish of what I felt I needed to, here, to be unfrus-
trated. It was an *artiste* thing. I was not in the mood for *sketchus
interruptus.*

"I will be done with your services in a mere few-and-half
minutes, if you care to be still that much longer, sweetheart. And,
additionally, I sincerely hope your no doubt handsome boyfriend
greets you tonight with a big hug. You deserve at least one hug.
And maybe he does too, for all I know. Me? I'll probably have visions of Botticelli around midnight, and I am not complaining."

But I *was* complaining. I realized that I couldn't remember the last real hug I had gotten from anyone. Anywhere. Certainly not from my ex-wife, my ex-stepdaughter, Tina, Chrystal, Betty, that receptionist at John Day Company, Botticelli, nor Venus on the half shell.

AND THE PLAIN fact is, I still don't remember – neither hug nor hard-on.

Like I said, it's all been a while.

The whole series of my life appeared to me as a dream; I sometimes doubted if indeed it were all true, for it never presented itself to my mind with the force of reality.

Epilogue

1969

I AM, AND was, Mahlon Blaine. Indeed.

Along the way I've occasionally asked myself, why are you writing down all this stuff? Pretty good question.

Who is likely to ever read the perambulatory non-adventures of a bum like me? I always used to be busted, and of course I'm still broke. Ready for the rubbish pile. I'm surprised I got this far, really. Seventy-four years and change, and some of what that all was, now writ down here in my own words. Big deal.

The eye is shot. Really shot to hell these last few weeks. Maybe it's this damn writing that's put the nail in that coffin, but it finally got to where it was eventually going to anyway. Although a half-sighted artist may benefit by seeing the world minus the distraction of stereoscopy, a fully blind artist is like a wheelbarrow full of rocks: the sooner dumped, the better.

I make no claims about my place in the past, present or future world of art. I did what I did until I couldn't. "They" will no doubt pass judgement, should "they" ever run across my obscure work. I know with certainty, now, that I won't be around to bask in praise or understanding, or to defend against attack or ignorance. Fine.

Maybe I am a lucky son-of-a-gun after all. Time will t

[END OF MANUSCRIPT]

Mahlon Blaine died in a rented room at the Mills Hotel in New York City.

His body was discovered January 18, 1969. The Deputy Chief Medical Examiner determined that case number 612's death was from natural causes, specifically occlusive coronary arteriosclerosis. No autopsy was performed. No funeral was held. Interment was probably at Potter's Field, but... they don't keep records.

An artist must leave this world, but art remains behind. It may be either forgotten, or seen with eyes that might sympathize, and reply.

GRATEFULNESS

Thanks to all my contacts and helpers, readers, writing group chums, sharers of MB art, especially photographic portraiture from Nathan Goldstein. And Steinbeck, Oxen, and MB bookplate images from Bonhams & Butterfields.

Great appreciation to the following friendly folks who spent hours with both MB and (often with intervening decades) myself: Nat and Flo Goldstein, Lilyan and Morty Berger, Minna and Jake Brussel, Gershon Legman, Billie Dunninger, Bob Richmond, Maxine Dunninger Hohneker, Jack and Frances Biblo, Jack Tannen, Alice Ryter, Nathan Melniker, Gertrude Briggs, Herbert Oxer, R. and L. Wilbur, Eva Mason, Bernice Butell, Susan Flego, Richard A. Lupoff, Jake Zeitlin, Celie Marvin, as well as Dr. Harry A. Royson.

Also I am indebted to Katherine Ballard, Deborah Nelson, Joanne Sonstein, Terri Gallahue, Dr. C.J. Scheiner, W. Hallam Webber, Cliff Roberts, Scott Daniels and the Oregon Historical Society; and Amy Kirkpatrick for her designer's eye.

And, of course, special thanks to my lovely wife Norma J. Talbot.

– Roland Trenary

Recent books from Grounded Outlet:

Mahlon Blaine ~ One-Eyed Visionary
From 1917 to 1967, illustrator Mahlon Blaine *revealed* his subjects – from Demons to Deities, Maylasians to Martians, Biology to Biography, Lasciviousness to Literature. He painted, but is best known for his pen-and-ink. He was an uncanny artistic master of the mundane and exotic who lived for decades in cheap hotels and borrowed rooms, acutely observing humanity while wielding pens and brushes dipped in wit and wry.
Paperback, 148 pages, 450 b&w ill. A biography, an art book, a bibliography. 2013.

Mahlon Blaine's SINDBAD
Rescued from 1936: the fabulous illustrations which Mahlon Blaine created for *The Adventures of Sindbad the Sailor.* Enlarged and enhanced in appreciation of the original black and white drawings, but also suitable for your personal coloring enjoyment. Additionally, lyrics of seven new Sindbad songs offer a fun perspective on the Sailor and his 7-verse mission.
Paperback, 60 pages, 33 b&w illustrations. A read-aloud book, an art book, a coloring book. 2013.

Other Mahlon Blaine publications:

The Art of Mahlon Blaine
Edited by Robert Arrington, from Peregrine, with a lengthy reminiscence by G. Legman and bibliography by Roland Trenary. The first book about Mahlon Blaine.
Paperback, 100+ pages, 90 b&w and 8 color illustrations. 1982.

The Outlandish Art of Mahlon Blaine
Edited by Brian J. Hunt, from GB Graphics. An enormous compilation of Mahlon Blaine's best illustrations.
Paperback, 450 pages, 600+ b&w illustrations (only 9% also appear in *Mahlon Blaine ~ One-Eyed Visionary*). 2009.

Made in the USA
Charleston, SC
29 March 2015